Praise for the novels of Sarah McCarty
Jared

"Rural romantic fantasy fans will fully relish Jared's tale."
—*Midwest Book Review*

"A sexy cowboy with bite." —*TwoLips Reviews*

"*Jared* shows that Sarah McCarty is an author you want to read . . . [She] definitely pushes the imagination with the deviousness of the vampires from Sanctuary. *Jared* will suck you in with its captivating characters, dramatic plot, and tempting love scenes!" —*The Romance Studio*

"The lead couple is a super pairing and the support cast is extremely well drawn. The story line is fun to follow as the lead couple fall in love while dodging the enemy and each other." —*Alternative Worlds*

Promises Reveal

"Few writers can match the skill of Sarah McCarty when it comes to providing her audience with an intelligent, exhilarating Western romance starring two likable protagonists. The fast-paced story line hooks the audience." —*Midwest Book Review*

"Entertaining . . . Kept this reader turning the pages. I've got a soft spot for Western historicals, with their hard times and smooth-talking cowboys. Ms. McCarty delivers on both of those fronts."
—*Romance Reader at Heart*

"I absolutely adored the chemistry and witty banter between these two spicy characters, and the sex, as always, was titillating, sizzling, and realistic . . . I don't know how she does it, but I want more and more and more. You will too once you read this fantastic tale."
—*Night Owl Romance*

"A must-read . . . Enticing and erotic . . . I am already craving more!"
—*Romance Junkies*

"Highly entertaining . . . Plenty steamy . . . and a great complement to the series." —*A Romance Review*

continued . . .

THE SHADOW WRANGLERS

SLADE

Sarah McCarty

WITHDRAWN

BERKLEY SENSATION, NEW YORK

THE BERKLEY PUBLISHING GROUP
Published by the Penguin Group
Penguin Group (USA) Inc.
375 Hudson Street, New York, New York 10014, USA
Penguin Group (Canada), 90 Eglinton Avenue East, Suite 700, Toronto, Ontario M4P 2Y3, Canada
(a division of Pearson Penguin Canada Inc.)
Penguin Books Ltd., 80 Strand, London WC2R 0RL, England
Penguin Group Ireland, 25 St. Stephen's Green, Dublin 2, Ireland (a division of Penguin Books Ltd.)
Penguin Group (Australia), 250 Camberwell Road, Camberwell, Victoria 3124, Australia
(a division of Pearson Australia Group Pty. Ltd.)
Penguin Books India Pvt. Ltd., 11 Community Centre, Panchsheel Park, New Delhi—110 017, India
Penguin Group (NZ), 67 Apollo Drive, Rosedale, Auckland 0632, New Zealand
(a division of Pearson New Zealand Ltd.)
Penguin Books (South Africa) (Pty.) Ltd., 24 Sturdee Avenue, Rosebank, Johannesburg 2196,
South Africa

Penguin Books Ltd., Registered Offices: 80 Strand, London WC2R 0RL, England

This book is an original publication of The Berkley Publishing Group.

This is a work of fiction. Names, characters, places, and incidents either are the product of the author's imagination or are used fictitiously, and any resemblance to actual persons, living or dead, business establishments, events, or locales is entirely coincidental. The publisher does not have any control over and does not assume any responsibility for author or third-party websites or their content.

PRINTING HISTORY
Berkley Sensation trade paperback edition / December 2011

Library of Congress Cataloging-in-Publication Data

McCarty, Sarah.
  Slade / Sarah McCarty.—Berkley Sensation trade paperback ed.
    p. cm.
  ISBN 978-0-425-24139-4
  1. Vampires—Fiction. I. Title.
PS3613.C3568S53 2011
813'.6—dc23

                                    2011036961

PRINTED IN THE UNITED STATES OF AMERICA

10 9 8 7 6 5 4 3 2 1

For all of you who convinced me
that cowboys would make good vampires . . .

Thanks!

❧ 1 ❧

SHE wasn't alone.

The inner prompting nudged at Jane again. She turned around and looked over her shoulder for the third time. Arrays of test tubes and carafes, a stainless steel refrigerator, and open-space units greeted her gaze. Every one of her five senses told her it was just her haunting the lab at the midnight hour, but the sixth sense, the one whose existence she could never justify through analytical methods, was clamoring for attention. Strong enough that if it wasn't for the fact she was living it, she'd think this was a scene from a slasher movie and the bad guy was about to rise up, knife in hand, and strike the blow that would set the tone for the rest of the movie.

She shuddered, too easily imagining the spray of fake blood. It might be time for her to cut back on her movie watching, because for sure, her imagination was going into overdrive. Actually, it had been revving up since she'd gone home tonight and found someone had very carefully gone through her apartment. Ever since, she finally admitted to herself, last year when Trancor had started responding to her, suddenly requiring monthly reports with discreet yet thorough questioning. Now, it was either do or die with the research on which she'd worked so hard.

A bling from her personal laptop snapped her head around. A little fanged smiley face sat on the screen. She frowned more at the leap of excitement than at the interruption. She was entirely too attached to the amorphous man known only to her as Vamp Man.

She didn't need her mind anywhere but where it was right now, and Vamp Man was definitely a distraction. Had been since the day he'd circumvented the security system on her laptop. A mind capable of that was naturally fascinating. The fact that he had a very dry sense of humor had kept her from cutting him off completely. She had a fondness for hackers. The way their minds worked just naturally meshed with hers. Her job involved hacking parts of the human gene code, so she could appreciate the skill it took to crack computer code.

Vamp Man was a particularly charming hacker. There was something addictive about their interaction, a certain verve to which she looked forward every day. She shook her head as the trickle of unease increased. There was just no shaking the feeling that someone was watching. She checked the lab again. Still nothing untoward, but the hairs on the back of her neck didn't stop crawling.

The bling came again.

You there, sweetness?

After another glance over her shoulder, she typed an answer.

I'm here.

Where's here?

Perhaps she was feeling a false sense of connection, but chatting helped with her nervousness as she waited for the wipe program to load.

The lab.

It took longer than it should for him to answer, and with each pulse of the curser, her inner sense of panic grew.

You alone?

She typed what she feared. *I'm not sure.*

There was no delay on this response. *Get out of there.*

The abrupt order fed into her terror. Did he know what she could only sense? How?

The tap of the keys seemed to echo louder as she rapped out the short retort. *I can't.*

Now.

Why?

The question generated another of those pauses. *You're not safe.*

She glanced around again. *How could you know that?*

I do. Now move!

The bar at the bottom of the desktop screen reached the end of the box. The wipe program was loaded.

Thank you.

While Jane appreciated Vamp Man's concern, there was no way she could leave. The bits and pieces of information on this lab computer were too sensitive, and the risk that anyone who found the research could put the pieces together and use her work as a deadly weapon wasn't one she was willing to take. She wasn't about killing people, but sometimes discoveries were a double-edged sword.

The laptop beeped for her attention. *Damn it, you're still there, aren't you?*

She ignored the question. The wipe process would have been so much easier if she could have had the program installed and waiting, but the company's periodic sweep of the lab computers had made that impossible. She hit the run button. The whole procedure would take about two hours. She needed at least the first pass completed before she left. She had to be sure her research was gone. She'd started out hoping to find a way to ease world hunger by maximizing the body's ability to obtain nutrition from not so traditional sources, but along the way she'd discovered the combination of amino acids, proteins and DNA that optimized the nutrition of any food for any specific group of people. But applied in reverse? Those amino acids and proteins attached to specific invasive DNA could easily be a biological weapon that could cause nations to waste away. Specific nations. Specific races Specific families. She shuddered. Trancor's interested had peaked right about the time she'd realized what she was looking at. The laptop blinged two times in rapid succession.

Jane!

Answer me!

Vamp Man was getting antsy. So was she, and there still wasn't any discernible reason for it. Reaching under the desk to the keyboard tray, she turned off the safety on her revolver.

She picked up her soda and then reconsidered. Maybe her problem was that she was drinking too much caffeine. The can settled back on the utilitarian desk with a soft click.

Another bling from her personal laptop. She looked up. Vamp Man had signed off. She felt strangely abandoned. Of all the men she'd known—and there had been quite a few during that punish-herself phase she'd gone through before realizing that as an adult, she was in control—for some reason she'd expected him to have more staying power.

"Just goes to show there's no telling with men."

The sound of her voice blending with the hum of the climate control system only added to the spooky atmosphere. The lab might be her home away from home, but at midnight it did not provide a stay-with-me hug of security, which was utterly ridiculous considering the state-of-the-art security system and the heavily armed guards who roamed the halls. She should feel completely safe.

"There's no telling with women, either."

She spun her chair around at the sound of the low drawl, tinged with a hint of the West. Stopping its rapid spin with her foot, she fumbled behind her for the gun, unable to take her eyes off the man in front of her. One second she'd been alone and now, well now she was staring at the epitome of every woman's dream. The man had the requisite broad shoulders and lean hips of an athlete, but he packed something more compelling than a great physique. Something she couldn't quite put her finger on, but it stole the breath from her lungs and raised the hairs on her forearms in an agony of awareness. Maybe it was the uncompromising masculinity of his harshly squared features. Maybe it was the utter sensuality of the mouth set in that rawly handsome face. Or maybe it was just the way he stared at her with those hazel eyes that wavered between bright green and calm. Damn, he had strange eyes. Beautiful, but different. She cocked her head to the side as the scientist inside her took over. They almost seemed to glow, and within them was an expectation she couldn't quite make out, but maybe if she just looked a little longer . . .

He took a step forward. Panic flared as he leaned down, but she couldn't move, couldn't do anything but stare into those fascinating eyes. Metal scraped across metal, and then the heavy weight of the gun pressed into her hand. "Next time, grab the gun before you turn around."

She blinked as he straightened. The logic of his statement sank through the haze clouding her mind, like a rock hitting the still waters of a pond. The ripples of alarm spread outward as she looked down and saw the gun was in her hand. When she looked back up, he was leaning against the opposite table, arms folded across his broad chest, muscles straining the white, heavy cotton of his shirt. The lock of thick brown hair that fell over his forehead just completed the image of total bad boy. She hefted the gun and pointed it toward him. "Thank you."

He didn't even blink as the muzzle centered on his torso. "Why didn't you leave when I told you to?"

It took her a second to process that. "You're Vamp Man?"

He arched his brow at her. "Who else would I be?"

Even in her wildest fantasies about him, she hadn't imagined him looking like this. "Any one of the other billions of people who inhabit the planet."

"But you couldn't logically expect any decent percentage of them to know where you were. I would even go so far as to say not any of them know what you're doing right now."

"You would?"

He motioned to the desktop screen behind her. "Wiping out the corporate hard drive isn't something that's generally smiled upon. Even for the eminently talented and courted researcher Jane Frederickson."

She followed his gaze. The progress was just beginning to register. She pushed the chair until her body blocked his view. A pointless gesture, but it still made her feel better. "And you'd know about this because . . ."

"I'm an intelligent being who knows that your work has progressed far beyond what you've let on."

"So?"

"So now it can have a whole different purpose than what was intended."

For a split second the worry she'd been battling for the last year suffocated her in a flood of panic. Had he gotten past her firewalls and false trails? Did he have the information? Quickly behind that came the next thought. *What in hell will I do if he has?* Her finger tightened on the trigger as everything inside her rebelled at the thought of taking a life.

"I also know the possible mutations of your work put you in danger."

"And you've come to save me." As if white knights existed outside fairy tales.

Again that eyebrow winged up. For a simple gesture he seemed to be able to imbue it with several meanings. This time, patient amusement. "You're in over your head."

"In an hour I'm not going to be."

"You're not going to get that hour you're counting on."

"Confirming my worst fears is not endearing you to me."

"I'll work on it."

She motioned with the gun. "While you're working on that, why don't you tell me how you got in here without sounding the alarms?"

"I'm a scientist."

"Not an explanation."

His head canted to the side. "I'm good with electronics."

"No one's that good."

"The fact that I'm standing here would argue otherwise."

Yes, it would, which just gnawed the edges of her temper more. She'd insisted on tweaks to some of the security elements herself. Elements she thought plugged the only holes. Yet proof that they hadn't was standing right in front of her. "You're not as interesting in person as you are online."

He actually smiled, revealing even, white teeth. "You're just irked that I got past the security system."

"Not entirely." She was also irked that he was so good-looking.

Good-looking men were a faithless lot, and she would have far more preferred he'd had the stereotypical geek look she'd imagined. Someone to whom her own geeky looks might be of interest.

His head lifted and a sudden stillness wrapped around him, as if he were a predator scenting danger. When he glanced down, the green in his eyes was more pronounced and the illusion of light in his eyes was stronger. "Pack up your laptop and let's go."

"Let's go? Since when did I give the impression that I'm going anywhere with you?"

"Since Sanctuary just showed up."

She slapped his hand as he reached for her laptop. "Who the hell is Sanctuary?"

He kept leaning in. "Men whose acquaintance you do not want to make."

"The guards will stop them."

"Humans are no match for Sanctuary."

He said "human" as if he were speaking of another species. "Humans? You're not delusional are you?"

It would be a shame if he were delusional.

"Not anymore."

Now there was a comfort. "Then I think we can leave security to handle whatever you're worried about."

This close, she couldn't ignore his scent. Crisp, like nightfall tinged with a subtle male musk that wrapped around her senses in a comforting hug. She could breathe in his scent forever. She should push him away. She knew that, but the scent just tempted her so. As did the sense of strength and protection Vamp Man produced. She'd never been protected. Never known the illusion of being safe since her mother had remarried when she was eight. It was as seductive as she'd always dreamed it would be. Vamp Man's hand brushed her hair as her laptop clicked softly closed. "We've got to go, sweetness."

The intimacy lingered after he straightened. "That nickname is more annoying spoken than when typed."

His fingers brushed down her arm with the lightness of amusement in his voice. Unplugging the cord from the socket, he said, "I'll keep that in mind."

Only to annoy her more, she was sure. "I'm not leaving."

His arm came around her waist as he straightened. "Yes, you are."

He lifted. She twisted, straining to see the screen on the desktop. The program wasn't fully implemented. Kicking back she grunted, "I need more time."

"For what?"

What did she have to lose with honesty at this point? "For the wipe program to finish. I can't risk them stopping it."

He looked at the computer with the barely there completion bar and let her go, his eyes narrowed and energy focused toward the screen with such intensity she swore she could almost see it.

"What's your sub password?" he asked.

"What makes you think I have a sub password?"

Not even a blink disturbed his composure. "You're too smart not to."

At least he saw her as smart. "What do you want it for?"

"To fix the program so they can't stop it."

"You can do that?" She heard the sound of something crashing outside in the hall. She jumped. He didn't.

"Yes."

It should be easier to imagine pigs flying. But it wasn't. Vamp Man had a way about him that inspired confidence. "What's your name?"

"I need to give you that for the password?"

She put the gun on the table and her hands on her hips. "I'm not giving the password to someone I know only as Vamp Man."

His lips twitched. "You don't see me as a superhero?"

The name *was* kind of superheroish. She couldn't hear anyone approaching, but she could feel them—dark, malevolent shadows on her consciousness. She took a shaky breath and hugged her laptop to her chest. "No, but I'm beginning to wish you had some hidden powers."

She had generalized feeling that superpowers were going to be called for to get her out of the mess. Vamp Man touched her cheek. No one had ever been so careful with her, but she kind of liked the way he did it. "Then today's your lucky day. My name's Slade. Now give me the password before I have to take it."

A shiver of dread ran down her spine. In that second she gave him what he wanted, feeling as if she was saving her own life even while giving it into his care.

"Kitty poo."

The keyboard tapped, the computer revved and revved until she thought it would explode. She shoved her laptop and cord into her backpack. Suddenly, Vamp Man grabbed her arm and shoved her toward the back of the office as another crash came from the hall. This one was followed by a soft thud. It sounded distinctly like a body hitting the floor. "Run."

There was only one exit. A small door without a window. She reached it, hesitated. What if there were more on the other side?

The door swung open all on its own at the same time that Vamp Man's hand hit the small of her back, propelling her through. "Go."

Since she didn't have any choice, she ran awkwardly, carrying the laptop. It would have been so much easier if Slade had grabbed that, too. The door slammed shut behind them. She glanced back at the door, then at Slade. Her gut said he had something to do with the door slamming shut when no one was near it. The arch of his brow acknowledged the question on her lips. She didn't ask it. If he was telekinetic, she didn't want to know. She much preferred to think of him as Vamp Man—computer geek extraordinaire.

The wall behind them vibrated as something slammed into it. She spun around. Slade's arm snaked around her waist and lifted her off her feet. "Keep going."

She didn't have any choice but to clutch the laptop and let him sweep her through the huge room with incredible speed. When the next door swung open and he put her down, he didn't need to say a word. She ran as though her feet had wings. Whatever was banging against the wall was coming through. And no way in hell did she want to see what it was.

"Where am I going?" she called over her shoulder, catching a glimpse of him standing in the middle of the corridor. His shoulders squared, feet braced shoulder-width apart and two vaguely human hairless hulking pointed ear creatures rushing at him with mind boggling speed.

"To the garage. Hurry."

He didn't have to tell her twice. She ran as if her life depended on it. Which it probably did. Her footsteps echoed—a hollow, pounding sound that slid under the pounding of her heart, amplifying it. Snarls chased her down the hall. No human made noises like that. Creatures in horror movies made noises like that. The snarls grew louder. The memory of what she'd seen grew stronger. Clearer. The pointed ears. The misshapen skull. The bloodred lips in the ghastly white face. The fangs . . .

Monsters. The word whispered through her mind. The edge of the laptop cut into her arms through the pack as she drove herself forward. There was another crash followed quickly by an inhuman howl. The hair along her arms rose and a cold chill slithered down her spine.

"What is that?"

It was five more steps before she realized Slade wasn't with her to answer. Slowing, she looked over her shoulder. She couldn't see him. She stopped at a doorway, pressing her back against the smooth surface of the door, doing her best to disappear into the shallow indentation. Leaning forward, she peered down the eerily lit hall. Why did emergency lights have to throw off that putrid color that made everything look so abnormal? And where was Slade? What could be keeping him?

More snarls ripped down the hallway from behind the closed door. *Oh heck, not that.* She remembered how he'd stood braced for a fight. Of course that. What else would someone called Vamp Man, who'd come into her lab at a time when she needed saving, do when monsters appeared? He'd fight to buy her time. Whether she wanted him to or not. Good grief, she was living in the middle of a comic book! Complete with her own superhero named Vamp Man. Could her night get any weirder?

The door that had closed behind her when he'd set her down burst open. A man came running down the corridor, little more than a blur in the weird lighting. It was Slade, but not a Slade she recognized. His face was distorted and his eyes were glowing, adding a whole new level of freak to an already freaky night.

She watched him, clutching her computer so tightly the case was in danger of breaking. "I just wanted to stop world hunger."

The discovery of a new humanoid species, she would leave to other scientists, those trained for it. The ones who didn't find it shocking. The closer Slade got—the more she was able to see the morphed state of his face, the thrust of his brow and cheekbones, the enhanced fullness of his mouth—the more she pressed back into the door. It wasn't natural, right, or absorbable.

He slowed.

Keep running. Keep running.

He stopped in front of her.

Nothing could prevent her from flinching as he reached out. "You're afraid."

It took all her courage to pretend she wasn't about to expire from terror on the spot. She pushed off the door. "What makes you say that?"

"I can hear your heart racing."

"I'm out of shape." It wasn't a huge lie.

His words were strangely distorted. "Will it make you feel better or worse if I believe that?"

"I guess that would depend on which answer will keep me safer."

It took her a moment to figure out that the baring of his teeth was a smile. The fangs it exposed commanded all of her attention. It took another moment to find a coherent thought. Those were dang big fangs. "Take your pick."

He held out his hand. "I think you're out of shape."

Did that mean he didn't want her to be afraid of him? She wasn't certain enough to put her hand in his.

"I'll force you if I have to."

She didn't doubt he meant it. Didn't doubt he could, but still she couldn't take his hand. Not with the memory of those fangs lingering in her mind.

Something flashed behind the glow in his eyes. "Don't make me force you."

"Turn your head."

"What?"

"Turn your head."

After a look, he did. Without the strangeness of his features, she could pretend he was just a man like any other. She took his hand. The brush of his thumb across the backs of her fingers was a surprisingly soft gesture for the fierceness of his appearance.

He glanced down at her, a question in his strange eyes.

"I'm very good at make-believe."

"Why?"

Inside, everything slammed down. She forced a small smile to her lips. It probably wasn't too convincing, but that could be attributed to the direness of their circumstances. "It's something every child indulges in. Didn't you?"

"No."

She found that hard to believe. "Try again."

He glanced back the way they had come. "Maybe later."

"Don't tell me there are more of those *things*."

With one tug he had her out of the shallow haven of the doorway and into the openness of the corridor. "Yes."

Her heart pounded with such force that she couldn't breathe evenly. She pulled in a tattered breath, afraid to look, unable not to. The corridor was empty, but the sense that at any second it would be full of frothing-at-the mouth creatures didn't abate. "What part of 'don't tell me' did you not understand?"

If he smiled she was going to slap him, superhero or not.

He started off down the corridor, dragging her faster than she could run. "Apparently the part that said you were serious."

When she stumbled, he just lifted her. It happened so fast that she didn't have time to realize her feet weren't touching the ground, that they peddled pointlessly.

"I'm always serious," she gasped. "I'm a scientist. We have no sense of humor. Ask anyone."

She chose to interpret the grimace on his face as a smile.

"I'll keep it in mind." He set her down in front of the heavy-duty door that led to the garage.

She'd breathe a lot easier if he had just opened it. Instead he steadied her with a hand on her upper arm.

"Once you go through that door, I want you to run like hell to the left."

"Why left?"

"Because to the left is my SUV."

Of course it led to his SUV. Superheroes always had some sort of macho car. "I have my own car."

He nodded. His hair fell over his brow. Her fingers itched to push it back. "Twenty spaces up and to the right. You'll never make it."

She didn't ask how he knew either fact, but she believed him. Which was maybe the scariest thing of all.

"You're saying there are creepy crawlers on the other side of this door."

His shrug was a flex of his massive shoulders. "It's likely."

"You don't know?"

"I can't be sure as they're probably masking their presence the same way I'm masking ours, but it would be a logical conclusion."

A logical conclusion. *Good grief!* She glared at him. "You're pretty much winging this, aren't you?"

He didn't deny it. "No one expected you to come here tonight. It was very out of character."

He said that as if it were a crime. She put her hand on the door as if the cold metal could transmit the threat of danger on the other side. "I'm working on spontaneity."

"You could have picked a better night for it."

"It appears to me that this was the perfect night, because if I were sitting at home, I'd probably be a monster snack."

"They don't want to eat you."

"I'm so relieved."

As if he'd known she'd been stalling while she worked up her courage, his hand slid off her arm and rested beside hers on the door. It was a very big hand, twice the size of hers and lean with inherent strength. "Are you ready now?"

She nodded and took another breath. "Where's your car, again?"

"Six spaces up and to the left."

"How will I recognize it?"

"It'll be the one you can't see."

His hand shifted to the wide bar. As he pressed it and the mechanism clicked she asked, "Anything else?"

His hand in the middle of her back pushed her toward the expanding opening.

"Yeah. Run like hell and don't look back."

❧ 2 ❧

JANE made it a few steps into the garage before the lights went out. In an instant there was nothing around her but inky darkness and the certainty that monsters lurked, claws curved, fangs bared, ready to tear her apart.

They don't want to eat you.

Faint comfort there. She bumped into something hard, bruising her shoulder. A column. She wrapped one arm around it, hugging it as tightly as she held her laptop. She desperately needed something solid to hold on to. Her nerves crawled under her skin, and she dreaded the moment she'd be grabbed by the unseen ... things. She braced against the fear. The emergency lighting came on, a flicker at first and then full strength, bathing everything with its eerie green glow. The sense of being in a horror movie increased as the alarms went off, screeching their warning. Behind her was Slade and the monsters. Ahead of her, she didn't know what waited.

How will I know which car is yours?

It'll be the one you can't see.

Dear God, what had she gotten herself into?

The things that had come after them were not human, yet Slade had faced them down without blinking an eye. That meant, in all likelihood, that he wasn't human. *Oh damn.* And he had fangs. She rested her head against the column, resisting the conclusion that wanted to be drawn. Her day was not improving.

Jane inched past the column. No sound came from beyond it. Then again, the creatures that had stormed into the lab hadn't made any noise. They'd just been there between one blink and the next. Grotesque mutations invading her private space as if they had the right. Slade had known they were coming, and if she got to see him again, she would ask how. But whatever sixth sense had alerted him to the presence of the bad guys, she didn't have it. And she had no way of knowing what was ahead, and what was behind. Sweat dampened her armpits. The laptop felt like a brick in her arms.

It was awkward to hold. She wished she could risk hiding it, but the only reason the creatures would be in this part of the lab would be for her research. Of their own volition or because someone sent them. If they had any kind of brains whatsoever, they would assume she carried important information on her computer. In fact she did. Just not the kind of information that would matter to them. But one never knew when a red herring would be useful, so Jane wasn't putting the computer down. She reached the third parking space without incident. Looking around, she still didn't see any sign of bad guys, but the hairs on the back of her neck were standing on end. The fact that she was in the parking garage only added to her fear. She hated parking garages. They were dark and scary, and way too many horror movies featured them as the places where the heroine met her death. She did not particularly want to meet her death today.

Gunfire snapped out of the recesses of the building, staccato punctuations to her slowly settling understanding. This was real. There was danger. And Slade had told her to run.

But she wasn't running. She was crouched beside a stranger's car, hugging the shadows as if monsters couldn't see in the dark. That was stupid, and she did try very hard never to be stupid. Leaning around the fender of the compact car, she first checked right and then left and then, feeling ludicrous, even up. But this was a night of weirdness. And she'd seen *Blade* about fifty times. And those things looked close enough to the vampires in that movie to make her believe that maybe that movie wasn't so far-fetched. She recalled that the *Blade* vampires scaled the walls. Maybe these things could, too. Pressing her head to her forearm, she shook it.

Whatever they were, she needed to get out of here, back to some normalcy so she could think. Casting a glance to the other side of the garage, the pink, rounded fender of her Volkswagen tempted her. There was nothing more normal than her little pink Bug with its bright yellow seat covers and fuzzy dice. Where it sat was the brightest spot in the garage. Almost like a sign.

Run and don't stop.

She shook off Slade's order. She'd already broken one caveat, what was one more? Especially since she didn't know whose side Slade was on. Just because he was against the monsters didn't make him *for* her. Another volley of gunfire inspired her. She didn't even know where Slade's car was, but she knew where hers was. What's more—she patted her pocket—she had the keys. Escape was a matter of simply arriving at its side. Staying low, adrenaline pumping through her veins and driving her breath in rapid bursts, she rushed to her car. She reached its side without incident. So far, so good. A little of her confidence returned. Too active an imagination had always been her curse.

Pushing the button on her key fob, she reached for the handle. The door didn't open. She pushed it again. The lights flashed, the lock made a clicking sound, but the door wouldn't open. It took her a moment to realize she was pushing the lock button rather than the unlock button.

Calm, she needed calm. Shifting her thumb to the correct button, she pushed again, ignoring the shaking in her hands and the lingering sense of dread. She just needed to focus on one thing at a time. Just one thing. The door opened.

The reassuring scent of the leather interior and the hamburger she'd had for dinner greeted her. Normal. Very normal. After sliding her laptop behind the seat, she grabbed the wheel and pulled herself up. Her back touched the seat, and the cushioned surface cradled her in familiar comfort. The air left her lungs in a long sigh. She'd made it. She reached for the door to pull it closed.

The hiss of her name was the only warning she had. There was a sense of evil so strong that it sank deeper than the claws into her shoulder. Before she could scream, she was yanked out of the car. Fetid breath hit her face. She had the impression of red eyes boring to her soul, and then she was ripped free and thrown backward. Pain exploded from her shoulder. There was an unearthly growl overwhelmed by a deadly snarl. Two shadows collided on the far wall, twisting and turning in a grotesque dance. Loud thumps and then . . . She hit the cement wall. More pain and then no more breath.

Another hand on her arm, this one much gentler.

"Damn it, Jane, I told you not to go to your car."

"Safer." Was that her voice, so weak?

"Not with Sanctuary waiting for you."

Sanctuary? She tried to open her eyes. Something sticky blocked her vision. Pain lanced outward from her shoulder. She reached out. "What happened?"

Her hand was caught in a larger, rougher one. A tingle went down her arm, spreading outward in a sense of connection.

"You didn't do as you were told."

"Says you."

"Yeah."

A cloth wiped gently at her eyes. Connection became comfort, and along with that comfort came the urge to lean into him. Weakness. She couldn't afford to be weak. Pushing back against the wall, Jane braced so she could stand. It hurt. So much at first that she couldn't place the source. Clutching her stomach against the nausea, she gasped as the realization kicked in. "You implied they wouldn't kill me."

"I'm positive that wasn't their orders."

How did he know that? More than that, where was the thing? "Where is it?"

"Dead."

She pushed her hair out of her eyes. She hated having her hair in her eyes. "Are you sure?"

Slade's fingers grazed her temple. A barely there touch that sent heat deep into the cold knot of fear in her gut, loosening its grip.

"Deader than a doorknob."

"They can die?"

"Of course." His hand slid under her arm and steered her around something. "Just not easily."

Her vision blurred and her head pounded. Did she have a concussion? Should she be moving? "I can't see."

"You don't need to."

The hell she didn't. "I need to rest."

"We don't have time. Sanctuary travel in packs."

"Like wolves?"

"Something like that."

Green lights flashed with sickening flickers in the periphery of her vision as he dragged her along. Packs were good. She used one for her laptop rather than a briefcase. *Oh damn. My laptop.* Planting her feet she turned back. "My laptop!"

He popped her forward. "We don't have time to get it."

She planted her feet again, shaking her head to clear it, wincing as pain stabbed deep. The room spun again as he raced her forward, rushing her along so fast it felt as if her feet didn't touch the floor. Clawing at his grip she snapped, "It has information in it."

He cursed and spun them around. She went flying outward like the lash at the end of a whip. He hauled her back in, anchoring her to his side with a grip that felt like a vise. She gasped.

"Sorry." With a glance down he loosened his grip. "Where is it?"

"In the backseat of the car."

"Figures." He said that is if she were a never-ending inconvenience. If her head didn't hurt so much and her stomach wasn't rolling so hard, she'd snap at him for the attitude. After all, she hadn't asked him to come along and ruin her night. She hadn't asked for the monsters to raid her lab. She hadn't asked her company to turn on her. She hadn't asked her mother to look the other way all those years ago when her stepfather had knocked on her door. And the very last thing she'd ask for right now was the burn of tears behind her lids. But that wasn't stopping it from happening.

Slade propped her against the wall. Her knees trembled. "Don't move."

She missed the warmth of his body immediately. More so, the illusion of safety he provided. She locked her knees. "Don't dawdle then."

She was proud of the quip if for no other reason than for the mockery it made of the tears. She wasn't a helpless little girl. She was a woman, more than capable of handling whatever life threw at her. Even if it was spooky, ugly, monster men. *Oh God, the monsters.* They were still around, still a threat. She straightened, searching for a weapon. Unless she popped the underwire from her bra, she was defenseless.

In the blink of an eye, Slade was back at her side, her pack slung over his shoulder, adding shock to her spook. She jerked away from his hand. "What do you do? Fly?"

"Something like that."

Something like that. She took a breath, her heart lodging in her throat. He'd said that about the monsters, too. There were questions a woman who played it safe should never ask her savior. Not when there was danger all around and she didn't know who to trust, but there were times when sensibility failed her. This was apparently going to be one of those times. Looking Slade in his beautiful-yet-strange eyes, remembering his speed, his strength, feeling as if invisible doors she never wanted opened were cracking, she asked, "What are you?"

Without even a blink, he answered, "I'm a vampire."

SLADE had to be joking. Or insane. Now there was a comforting thought to have as she was dragged through the garage alongside Slade. A vampire. *Oh God.* Her head still spun, her vision was still blurred. Maybe she'd imagined the whole conversation. Slade came to an abrupt halt. Nausea roiled as her head snapped forward and then back into the solid muscle of his shoulder. She closed her eyes. More pain. More stars shooting across the black screen of her lids.

"You still with me?"

She'd puke if she nodded. "Unfortunately."

Good grief, how could he chuckle at a time like this?

"Can you stand on your own?"

"Of course."

"I'd believe that more if you opened your eyes."

So would she. Cracking her lids, she saw they were at the far side of the garage, standing in front of an empty space.

"Happy?"

"Not really. You look a little shell-shocked."

"Must be all the excitement."

Another smile. Her heart, which should have been too exhausted from all the jolts she'd given it this evening to respond, skipped a beat. Damn, why couldn't he have more of a bookish look about him?

"Must be."

He let go of her elbow. She hadn't realized how much she'd been leaning on him until he took his hand away. She stumbled.

"Hell." His reflexes were all that kept her from pitching to the floor.

"I think I have a concussion." It was a remarkably coherent statement, considering the circumstances, and she was proud of it.

"Great."

"You're the one who tossed me like a rag doll."

"I figured it beat being disemboweled."

The image that conjured did nothing to soothe her nausea. "Oh God."

She clutched her stomach.

His grip on her arm tightened. "We don't have time for you to puke."

Did he think it was something she could control? "Then don't paint disgusting images."

"Fair enough." Taking her hand, he placed it against cool concrete. Leaving his hand covering hers, he slid his other under her hair, against the nape of her neck. It was surprisingly cool. Soothing. "You need to stand up straight."

"Okay."

A slight tingle spread out from beneath his hand. The pain diminished and the nausea lessened. His palm felt so good against her skin that she just wanted to lean into it and linger in the comfort and strength he offered. Alarm bells went off again. Weak. This was weak, and she could never afford to be weak. Pushing back, she stood. His hand fell away. Licking her lips, keeping her eyes closed against the continued need to vomit, she asked, "Am I upright?"

His fingertips grazed her shoulder blades. "Close enough."

She sensed more than heard him move away. A disturbance in the energy that connected them. *Good grief, just let it be the concussion that made me think we were connected.* "I thought we didn't have a minute."

"Not one to spare, but this I planned on."

He was definitely farther away. Maybe ten feet? She heard something scrape and then a short curse. She opened her eyes just in time for the inch-by-inch revelation of an SUV that couldn't be in that empty parking space, but was. The silky material slid off the roof of the car and into Slade's arms with a momentum that belied its gossamer appearance. And amazingly, Slade went down under it.

Though it was a ludicrous question, she asked anyway. "Need any help?

The seemingly lightweight material barely moved when Slade braced his shoulder under it. "I just need a minute."

"A minute for what?"

"For this damn energy cloth to lighten up."

Energy cloth? There was no such thing as energy cloth. Inching closer, she tried to slip her finger under the edge draped on the ground behind Slade. It was like trying to slip a finger under a concrete wall. "This is heavy."

"No shit." His voice was strained with effort. "I can't seem to separate the amount of energy it absorbs from the weight it takes on."

The cloth absorbed energy. For a moment fascination outweighed fear. "You created this?"

"Yes."

Something banged in the far end of the garage. Fear returned in a rush as Slade's nostrils flared and his head lifted. She jumped and stumbled back, looking in the direction of the sound, seeing nothing. "They're coming, aren't they?"

"Yeah. Damn it." With a grunt he hefted the material, folding it multiple times until it was small enough to pick up. He paused for a moment, balancing the weight in his hand, before tossing it to her.

"Take that and get in the car."

Instinctively, she caught the now normal-weight material. Terror made her scream as blurred shadows rushed them. Slade dived for the attacking shadows as she dived for the passenger door. As she yanked the car door closed, something hit it. The car rocked. The window shattered. She threw her hands over her head as glass rained down around her. The material protected her from the worst. More thuds against the car. More of those horrific snarls. Curling in the seat, Jane bit her knuckles through the cloth, keeping the screams trapped within, waiting for the gouge of claws in her skin, waiting for the end. She didn't want to die like this.

The sudden silence was more shocking than the clamor of battle. Over the hum of the emergency lights she could hear the rasp of breathing. Someone—something—was alive. Slade. Was it Slade? Or was it something else and Slade lay on the concrete needing help while she cowered like a chicken? Pushing her hair out of her eyes, Jane scrambled out of the car. Glass crunched as her feet hit the pavement. One look and she breathed a sigh of relief.

Slade stood in front of her, the back of his white shirt torn and wet with blood. Through the gaping tear, she could see the tan of his skin and the darker color of torn flesh. Damaged, but alive. Slade was alive. Her heart started hammering. She wanted to smack him. "Damn you, how dare you scare me like that?" He made a noise that sounded distinctly like a . . . growl? "Did you just growl at me?"

Slade turned. He was as ugly as any of the monsters—forehead predominate, fangs sticking out, eyes glowing. Frighteningly different, yet somehow, blessedly familiar.

I'm a vampire.

Even now, looking at some pretty convincing evidence, she couldn't believe. But she did take a step back.

"Yes."

It came out as another deep rumble that should have terrified her, but didn't. Forcing herself to take a step forward, she put her hands on her hips. "Well, stop it."

This time he didn't growl. He cursed as he squatted by the nearest . . . body. He was surrounded by twisted, bloody, unnaturally still bodies. One, two, three. She stopped at three, because it was either three or four, but if it was four, a head was rolling around somewhere unattached. "My God, what did you get me into?"

"I didn't get you into anything." Slade pulled something from one of the bodies before moving to the next. "I'm trying to get you out of it."

His voice was as distorted as his face.

"I was doing fine on my own."

The look he shot her said it all, and he was right. She had gotten herself into this, by taking a high-paying, do-what-you-want research job funded by shadow companies. Jobs like that didn't come without strings and she knew it, but the lure of the research had drawn her. The temptation to wipe out hunger for the world's children had been too potent to resist. She knew too well what it was like to be desperate and hungry with nowhere to turn.

Monster Slade took her arm. "Get in the car. Now."

She didn't want to get in the car. She didn't want any part of this. What she did want was an explanation that made this all plausible. Putting her hand over his, she demanded, "Who are you?"

"Vamp Man, remember?"

How could she forget? She'd thought it was a joke, a cute little play on words, but he was serious. Believed it. Maybe even was it. Dear God, was she going to have to believe in vampires now? "You really meant it when you said you were a vampire, didn't you?"

Another push and another step backward brought her up against the car. "You were the one who thought I was joking."

"Who in their right mind would take you seriously?"

"You." More pressure.

She resisted. "Look, I may be a lot of things, but I'm not stupid enough to get in the car with a vampire."

He jerked his thumb toward the bodies behind them. "You want to stay with them?"

Hell no. "Not really."

Grabbing her pack off the floor he thrust it at her. "It's either me or them."

She took it. *Great.*

"If they're called Sanctuary, what do you call your group?"

"Renegades."

"Perfect."

He glanced over his shoulders. His nostrils flared. She knew what that meant.

"Don't tell me more are coming."

"Yes."

"I told you not to tell me that." She fumbled for the door handle. "Good God, do they breed like rabbits, or what?"

Slade's hands covered hers. Warm, hard, rough with calluses, redolent with an energy that sank through her skin and seeped into her nerve ends, soothing the frayed edges. "I won't let them hurt you, Jane."

"Great."

The door opened. "You don't believe me?"

He arched that brow at her. She'd always been a sucker for a man who could do that. The angles in his face seemed softer, more normal. Was he changing back?

"There's only one of you and heaven knows how many of them."

"But I'm making you a promise."

He closed the door. She watched as he walked around the front of the car, every move graceful—the way a predator was graceful—the flex of muscle a smooth transition to power. He turned and caught her looking at him. She blushed. He winked and slid into the driver's seat. With a flip of the key, the engine roared to life with an incredible pulse of power. "Is the engine altered?"

"I'm good with mechanical things."

She glanced in the rearview mirror, the hairs on the back of her neck rising as shadows flickered. "Are you as good with mechanical things as you are with energy?"

"Fair enough."

"Do you think you could step on the gas pedal before the rest of those things get here?"

He cut her a glance that could have meant anything. "No problem."

The car rumbled out of the garage and into the night. No moon broke the blackness around them. Just empty spaces in which any number of things could hide. Leaning over, she glanced in the rearview mirror again.

"Can't they hear the engine?"

Slade shook his head. "I've got a shield on the energy and an illusion over the car."

"An illusion?" The only thing standing between them and those monsters was an illusion? "Our safety net is an illusion?"

His smile was a quirk of the corner of his mouth that made her wonder how it would feel to touch her tongue to the slight dimple. Dear God, was she losing her mind?

"Sometimes an illusion beats the heck out of reality."

"Like when?"

He cut her a glance. "Like when you thought I was human."

He had her there. Unzipping the pack, she ran her fingers over her laptop. There were no dents in it, no broken edges on the first two corners, but the third hadn't fared so well. "Damn."

"What?"

"I think those bastards killed my laptop."

"Their boss won't be too happy to hear that."

"What do you mean?"

"They want you, and they want the information, sweetness. Can't interpret one without the other."

"Well, they can't have either."

"On that we agree."

He was a very strange man. "What are you going to do about it?"

Reaching forward, he turned on the radio. "Kidnap you myself."

The sound of soft blues music filled the car. Her heart skipped a beat.

"Kidnap?" This was a kidnap?

"Best way I know to keep you safe."

As if she should believe the man with those fangs and that still slightly morphed face. She put her laptop back in the case and zipped it. "What makes you so qualified for the job?"

He smiled, the man superseding the monster in the blink of an eye. With a jerk of his chin, he indicated the lab rapidly being left behind. "Because I'm the badass vampire who can kick Sanctuary's butt."

❋ 3 ❋

"**A**RE we going anywhere specific, or are we just going to prowl the night in this gas hog?"

Slade glanced over at Jane. She sat in the passenger seat, clutching that laptop like a security blanket, staring out the window as if the scenery beyond was particularly enthralling rather than just deserted streets with a touch of winter lingering upon them. The edge to her question was echoed in the set of her mouth. She had a pretty mouth. Wide, neither thin nor full, but made for smiling. Right now it was set in a straight line.

He wished he had an answer for her. Something concrete. Something to soothe her nerves, but in reality, it wasn't up to him where they went.

"I guess that depends on you."

She didn't look at him. Somewhere between the concussion and now, she'd developed an attitude. "You mean I have a say in all this?"

He swerved to avoid a pothole and bit back a smile. "Since you are the only one who knows where you've hidden your research, I'd say that makes you queen of the day."

He had to give her credit. Not by a twitch did she betray surprise at the statement.

"What research?"

He glanced in the rearview mirror. He couldn't see Sanctuary following, but the hairs on the back of his neck were tickling. They were out there.

"The research those goons back there were looking for."

"You mean those goons you hired to make you look good, and to foster a false sense of security in me?" she asked.

He was right, her mind didn't stop, it just went off on some weird tangents. "Damn, I wish I'd thought of that a couple months ago. It would have made things so much simpler."

Now she did glance at him. The black and white of his night vision caressed the planes of her profile. She wasn't a beautiful woman, but she was sexy, with an earthy, girl-next-door kind of cute tossed on top. With a snort that did nothing to diminish her appeal, she muttered, "And I'm supposed to believe you're some sort of genius."

Despite the danger, he couldn't help being amused. "I never said I was some sort of genius. You're the one who gave me that appellation."

"I think I was overly impressed with your ability to crack my security code."

He cocked an eyebrow at her. "I think the proper statement would be that you were thrilled that I cracked your security code."

Another glance, this one as autocratic as any queen had ever tossed. "That doesn't even make sense."

"It does if you were bored and looking for a little mental challenge."

"I'm a top research scientist in a lab that will give me whatever I want. How on Earth would I be bored?"

A shadow in the side-view mirror caught his eye. The faintest flicker of light. Not a solid image, but something more dangerous. Sanctuary. Rubber squealed against pavement as he made a sudden left turn. "You lack social challenge."

Grabbing the armrest, she asked, "Are you saying I'm awkward?"

He checked the rearview again. "No. I'm just saying it's been awhile since you had someone to match wits with."

Her eyes narrowed and she glanced at the passenger-side mirror. There was no way she could see Sanctuary. Though she had to be terrified, she didn't betray an ounce of fear. His admiration for her, which had been building over the past few months, increased that much more. "And you appointed yourself my court jester?"

The arrogance of the tone made him smile. "I may have been toying with taking on the role."

That might just have been a huff that preceded her mandate. "Well, if I'm going to have an opening for a court jester, then I'm not taking the first applicant that comes along. There will be an application process. I assure you, my prime requirement will not be a determination to win the position by subterfuge."

Shit. They were coming up fast on the crossroads at the edge of town. East circled back. West headed into the country. He headed west. The rows of houses got farther in between. The yards larger. "I haven't tricked you."

She looked behind again. "So you say."

"Yes, I do." He couldn't see the flicker in the mirror anymore, but the hairs on the back of his neck were practically dancing. "Hold on."

He hit the gas. The powerful engine roared to life, accelerating with the bit of his energy he poured into the engine, giving it that extra boost just as a Sanctuary vampire appeared in the rearview.

This time there was nothing fake about her gasp. "What was that?"

"Just one of those trumped-up goons you think I conjured."

"Seriously, what was *that*?"

He couldn't blame her for the shock. Sanctuary didn't improve in looks when they were up close and personal. "I already told you—Sanctuary."

"And what the hell is Sanctuary?"

"An arrogant bunch of vampires . . ." He took the next corner too fast, levitating the car as it tilted up on two wheels, holding it on the road until gravity took over again. The wheels hit the road with a thump. "Who seem to think your research on how genes and amino acids interplay in nutrition is damn interesting."

Jane's grip on the handle above the door was white-knuckled, but her voice didn't lose a bit of its arrogance as she retorted, "Of course it's interesting. I wouldn't be studying it otherwise."

"It's not your study they're interested in. It's what you discovered that's captured their attention."

"I haven't discovered anything."

It would be nice if they all could believe that. "You haven't announced anything, but you've discovered something."

She narrowed her eyes again, this time at him. "And that's why you're here."

No sense in prevaricating. "Yes."

Her start reverberated through the seat, going from her to him, connecting them as the pulse of her fear shot through the crystal clarity of their connection, souring the purity. Reaching back along the same path, he sent a wave of calm. He didn't want her to be afraid of him.

"Would it be easier for you to believe if I told you I was part of a supersecret government organization hired to protect you from Sanctuary spies?"

"No."

Well that was short and to the point. "Then, yeah, I'm interested in the same thing they are for totally different reasons."

"What are their reasons?"

"World dominion."

She didn't look shocked, which confirmed his suspicion that she already knew that her discovery could be used as a weapon.

Her brows rose. "And your reason?"

"Personal."

"How personal?"

"Very personal."

"You know that's not good enough."

There was that flicker of energy to his left. *Shit.*

Slade yanked the wheel to the right, cutting across a lawn to the alley between two small strip malls.

There was barely room for the car. Jane screamed. Her fear poured over him in waves, calling to him. She needed him. Slade slammed the connection closed, the distraction too much. Instantly, everything inside him howled in outrage at leaving her alone with her fear, repeating the only truth his vampire cared about—she needed him.

Images raced by. A trash can crumpled under the wheels. The lid flew over the hood. Throwing her hands over her face, Jane screamed again as the plastic hit the windshield before tumbling over the roof. Gritting his teeth, Slade swore as the urge to take her in his arms threatened to override the need to escape.

"Get control of yourself."

The order came out more growl than words.

"Me?" she squeaked, clearly outraged. "I'm not the one driving like a maniac on steroids."

Shit. How could she crack jokes, as terrified as she was?

"Just do it."

Beyond the alley was a ditch. The physical toll on his energy was huge as he levitated the SUV over it. It slammed down on the other side, grass and dirt spraying as the wheels found purchase.

Jane gasped but didn't scream. Instead, she clutched that laptop as if it were a lifeline while he accelerated to a hundred and thirty miles per hour.

In a perfectly reasonable tone, Jane pointed out, "There is no fuel that will take an internal combustion engine to that speed, that fast."

"Nope, you're right about that."

Her frustration reached out and snapped at the edges of his nerve endings.

"Are you just physically incapable of delivering a straight answer?"

"My brothers seem to think so."

"You have brothers?"

"You sound surprised."

"I am. I thought supersecret special-agent types were loners."

"You watch too much TV."

"My friends say 'not enough.'"

The car hit a bump, bounced high. There was no stopping the flip, so he rotated into it, levitating the SUV to keep it off the ground, the strain on his energy telling in the shaking of his hands as the car righted. Too many more moves like that and they'd be helpless as newborn babes against Sanctuary.

Jane didn't say a word through the maneuver, but her scream

echoed in his head. Though he couldn't afford to spare the energy, Slade smoothed calm over her fear.

I've got you. You're safe.

The shocks groaned as the wheels dug into the ground. The car shot forward, toward the cornfield ahead and to the right.

As if nothing amazing had just happened, Jane said, "That's simply not possible."

"Not for humans."

Her calm broke on a sharp, "Stop harping on the fact you're not human."

Sanctuary was nipping at their heels, his energy was running out, and dawn was coming. He didn't have time for her games of self-denial. "Stop harping on the fact that I am not, and get with the program."

The car plunged blindly into the tall corn, the stalks snapping under the wheels and whipping at the sides.

"Oh my God." This time she grabbed his thigh. Her first voluntary touch, and he couldn't appreciate it. *Shit.*

"I won't let anything happen to you, Jane."

The noise of the stalks beating against the vehicle almost drowned out her voice. "Just shut up and concentrate on not crashing."

"I'm multitasking."

Her grip tightened. "I'm not impressed."

The hell she wasn't. "Really? I thought that last maneuver was pretty slick."

"You would."

"Hey, it kept us from being caught."

"Who can catch this? We're doing one hundred thirty miles per hour across a cornfield!"

Her words came out choppy, her voice distorted by the car's bumpy course through the rutted rows. Slade couldn't afford to smooth the ride. Levitating the car, scanning and cloaking, was draining his energy fast. If he could keep them running until dawn they'd be okay. The tinted windows of the SUV would offer him some protection from the sun that their pursuers wouldn't have. "Sanctuary."

"Sanctuary. Again with Sanctuary. There's nobody out here but us."

She wanted so much to believe that she was trying to convince herself of it. Maybe a bit of fear wasn't a bad thing. Slade fed a little of his awareness into Jane's senses. "Can't you feel them? Even if you can't see them, your instincts have got to be telling you that 'something this way cometh.'"

She licked her lips. "Of course I have a sense of danger. We're driving at an alarming speed!"

"They are moving just as fast."

She glared at him. "It doesn't make sense that anything can keep up with us."

"You haven't met anyone from Sanctuary."

She cut him another glare, one that said she clearly didn't appreciate his response. One that sneaked past his guard and caught the edge of sexual tension, bringing it into play.

"Are they stronger than you?"

"No, but they outnumber me, and you are a definite weak point."

She frowned, tapped her finger on the armrest, and glanced into the side mirror.

"Yeah, but an enhanced machine should outlast Sanctuary."

"I notice you don't say 'outrun.'"

There was a loud thump on the top of the car. A sizzle snapped across the roof, followed immediately by an unearthly scream as a man tumbled to the ground behind the vehicle.

Jane gasped. "Sanctuary?"

"Yeah. For the short term, it might help you to think of them as jaguars and us as impalas, outmaneuvering the attack."

Jane let go of his thigh. "We're the bottom of the food chain?"

He glanced over. "At the moment."

There was another thump. Another scream as the defenses he'd put in the vehicle and enforced with his own energy shattered the nervous systems of the Sanctuary vampires who were attacking.

The draw on his strength was incredible—more than he'd anticipated. He'd have to revisit his calculations.

"For heaven's sake then, keep your eyes on the road and drive faster!"

Slade didn't have the heart to tell Jane they'd maxed out on fast. And time. Between the edge of the cornfield and the road there was a three-foot ditch. At full strength he could levitate the SUV over the ditch, but now he didn't know if he had the reserves to get the car safely to the other side. He glanced up at the lightening sky. Jane's gaze followed his.

"If they're vampires, isn't sunlight deadly to them?"

"Yeah."

"So we just have to stay ahead another few minutes."

"Yeah." If they were especially lucky. If Sanctuary hadn't developed shields. If, if, if.

Jane dug her nails into the seat. His thigh muscles flexed with envy. *Shit.* How could he miss her touch now?

"What aren't you telling me?"

The tinted windows would give him some protection, but not enough. And they wouldn't do anything to protect them against the werewolf allies of Sanctuary. Without a doubt, the vampires would

mentally telegraph to the weres their last sighting, and those weres
would, with that tenacity they were known for, hunt their prey.

"I'm vampire, too."

"Are you telling me that in a few minutes, while we're driving
one hundred thirty miles per hour down this field, you're going to
go out in a puff of smoke?"

"Your concern is touching." He angled the SUV so it ran paral-
lel to the ditch.

Ignoring his sarcasm, she demanded, "Is that what you're telling me?"

"Nothing so dramatic. The windshield will protect us some-
what."

"Us? I don't have any problem with the sun. Since you do, it's
the fact that you're still driving this car that has me concerned."

"I won't crash the car."

"Like hell." She looked behind them. "Are they still following us?"

He shook his head. "The vampires have dropped back."

"So why are you saying that like Sanctuary is now the least of
our problems?"

"There are werewolves, too, in league with Sanctuary."

"Of course there are. What's a good horror flick without a werewolf or two?" She paused, took a breath, and then said in a perfectly
level voice, "I assume it's only a few and you're not talking thousands?"

"We don't know."

"Oh for heaven's sake!" She threw up her left hand, the other
staying firmly clenched around the laptop. "How can you possibly
have enemies and not know who and how many they are?"

"We're working on it."

The first rays of the sun peeked over the horizon. Even the
dense shading on the window couldn't prevent the blinding burn.

Slade blinked and sucked in a breath. *Son of a bitch.* Jane fumbled in her backpack. Leaning over, she pushed something on his face.

The relief was immediate.

"Sunglasses," she explained.

There was more rustling as he blinked the tears out of his eyes.

In a voice as cool as a cucumber, she informed him, "There's a tree in front of us at two o'clock."

He adjusted the wheel to the left, blinking rapidly as his vision cleared. The glasses were dark, the rays of the sun still weak. As a temporary fix, it worked. He could see.

"Thank you."

The backpack rustled as Jane rummaged through it again. There was the sound of plastic being rotated on plastic, then the squish of something being squeezed out of a tube. It was all very clear to his acute vampire senses. The scent of coconut filled the car. The distinct sound of a seat belt being unbuckled snapped into the silence.

His "Put that back on" collided with the belt buckle hitting the side of the door.

"In a minute."

The end of the field was coming up. Another ditch. Reaching over, Slade tried to push her back. Tucking herself beneath his arm, Jane avoided his attempt and slathered something cold and slimy on his face.

"What the hell are you doing?"

"Just in case your windows aren't as perfect as you implied, I thought a layer of sunblock might help."

"You carry sunblock in your laptop bag?"

"I believe in being prepared."

Of course she did. He could feel her stare. Could see the ditch getting closer. *Shit.*

"I'm assuming it's the UVA rays that get to you?"

"The UVB pack quite the punch, too."

The stuff was gross, damned near intolerable, but nowhere near as intolerable as the thought of what could happen to her body if the truck bounced out of control. She was human and, he glanced down at her arm as she brushed the cream over his forehead, not built sturdily, even for a human.

"That's enough. Now get back in that seat and put your seat belt on."

"In a minute."

More cream glopped into her palm. He could feel the stuff sticking to his hair.

"Now, before you get hurt."

"At this speed, the statistics of me surviving a crash, seat belt or not, are between zilch and none."

That was not a fact he wanted to hear. For the first time in his vampire life, he hesitated, his foot hovering between the gas and the brakes.

The glasses bounced on his nose as she worked the cream under the lenses. The next rut cost her her balance. Gasping, she clutched at his shoulder.

Her nails cut into his skin through his shirt. Her scent wrapped around him, slipping beneath the stench of coconut—apples scented with spring and a hint of fear.

"Get that damn seat belt on now."

"When I'm done." She rubbed the cream down his neck and onto his chest, her fine-boned fingers skating over his skin with an efficiency that had nothing to do with passion, but caught his interest anyway. Another distraction. The next bump sent her fingers over his chin. The tips rested against his mouth for a heartbeat, and in that heartbeat, he nipped them, letting his reaction to her touch roll over her, smiling grimly when she sat back in her seat on a gasp and those big eyes watched him in shock.

"That was uncalled for."

She really did have a bossy side.

"Then do as you're told." The ditch was coming up fast. He switched his foot from the brake to the gas. "Put your seat belt on."

She grabbed the belt. "Why? Are we going to crash?"

"Why don't you work out the statistical probability of that in your head while I figure how to get us over that ditch."

She hauled the belt over her shoulder and fumbled with the snap. "You're not very soothing to be around."

"Thank you."

"That wasn't a compliment."

It was now or never. He punched the gas.

She looked up. "Oh my God!"

The last syllable ended on a high-pitched scream as Slade threw a wall of energy in front of the tires, creating an invisible ramp to catapult the SUV up to the necessary elevation to clear the ditch. His strength wavered. He gritted his teeth, reaching deep. He wouldn't fail. Not her. Not in this.

His strength snapped. The car landed hard, bottoming out. Metal ground against metal. The SUV swerved, rocked up on two wheels, teetering as it raced on.

A hand squeezed his. Energy, soft and feminine, touched his. Blended. He grabbed it. And in the next second did what he thought he couldn't. He levitated the huge vehicle into a straight line. The wheels gently reconnected with the road.

When he looked over, Jane was staring at him, the shock and fear in her big green eyes mixing with fascination as he released his hold on her energy. She'd saved their lives. "Thank you."

She didn't answer, just kept staring at him.

Shit.

There wasn't anything he could do about it now. Between the agony of the sun, the demand of day sleep, and the drain of getting Jane out of that lab, he was about done in.

It must have been damn obvious, too, because, with a shake of her head and absolute expectation of being obeyed, Jane snapped, "Pull over."

"Not yet."

He could hold on for a little longer. Long enough to get her to safety.

"Prioritizing our risks right now, you passing out at the wheel tops the list. That being the case . . ." Her hand closed over his on the wheel. "Pull over."

She was right. He pulled over. Slade unsnapped his seat belt and tilted up the wheel. Hooking an arm around her waist, he pulled her onto his lap as he slid over. The laptop caught on the wheel. She landed half on his lap, with her soft butt cradling his cock.

"Wait a minute."

He did while she set down the laptop, letting her scent sink deep, letting that sense of recognition reverberate hard on that sense of right he'd felt from their first email exchange. Her energy had always been very pleasing, and it had only gotten better as time passed. She wiggled around. His cock hardened.

"This would be a lot easier," she grumbled, bending to put the laptop on the floor, "if you weren't so big."

His cock surged hard and strong, uncaring that this wasn't the time, just liking the way she felt, so different yet so familiar. This close, he could see the perspiration on her temple. Smell the acrid taint of fear under her bravado. She was terrified, but covering well. He pressed up.

"But you like me big," he said, just to get her mind off the fear consuming her.

She stiffened but didn't counter. Too bad. He could use some distraction, especially as she dragged that soft ass across his groin. Gritting his teeth, he flopped to the opposite side of the seat. She adjusted the steering wheel and the seat.

He only had a few minutes before he blacked out, which made the perk in his cock pretty close to a miracle. A totally unappreciated one if Jane's glare and "harrumph" was anything to go by.

"Ignore him, he has no manners."

"So I noticed."

Go figure, she was a good sport on top of everything else. He reached for the seat belt. She shook her head. "You need to be in the back."

"No."

"From the look of you, you're going to pass out any second, and the backseat offers the best protection from the sun."

"I can't protect you back there."

This time she didn't bother to hide the roll of her eyes. "Not to upset the day with logic again, but I think the number-one priority is for you to get in the back and stay out of the sun so you can live to fight another day or whatever it is you men say during a testosterone high."

It galled the hell out of him that she was right.

He squeezed over the seat, landing on his ass with one booted foot stuck on the back of the seat. "You, woman, are bossy."

"So are you. I'm just holding my own."

The darkness was coming fast. He had only moments. "Do you really think you're equipped to handle this?"

She put the car in gear. "I have no idea, but I think we're both about to find out."

Shit.

❧ 4 ❧

SHE had so not signed on for this, Jane thought as she drove the SUV down the road. She was a researcher. She worked from the safety of her lab on theories that grew from solid fact. She'd never had any desire to be a hero, so what in hell was she doing driving at dawn in some sort of souped-up magic tank that was masquerading as an SUV? She was not adventurous and certainly not GI Jane against the world.

The morning broke with a peaceful beauty—pale pinks blending with the gray. Pretty. And deceptive, because she could feel the danger still lurking in the prickle of hairs along her forearms and the churning in her gut. Behind her, she could hear Slade breathing. Even that wasn't right. His breathing was too shallow, the rhythm of it too uneven. Instinct demanded she pull the car over and check on him, but that feeling of danger said "Put the pedal to the metal and drive like a maniac despite common sense," though common sense told her to keep the speed to sensible. She swore. She hated conflict. Order was more her style.

Taking a deep breath, she focused on the here and now. She didn't know these roads. She was in the back of beyond, but if she remembered correctly from the maps she'd checked when moving to the area four years ago, this road had a lot of sudden turns. Which meant she'd better slow down. The last thing either of them needed was for her to crash the car. Whatever magic Slade had that enabled him to clear three tons of metal over a ditch in a single bound wasn't in her repertoire.

Slade made a strange noise. Risking a quick glance over her shoulder, she asked, "You okay back there?"

The sound that came back to her could have been a grunt or a snore. More light flooded the horizon. Normally, she would have greeted it with a smile and a big virtual hug—she loved mornings—but if she was gonna buy into all this vampire crap, and she really didn't see how she couldn't, the sun was her enemy. It had the power to do the one thing the fang-bearing Sanctuary monsters couldn't. It could kill the man who was her protector. Not a good thing.

Not that maybe she couldn't find somebody else to help her, but it had always been her philosophy that a bird in hand beat the heck out of two in the bush. And Slade was one heck of a bird.

The comparison immediately struck her as wrong. Birds were lively, gentle, fragile creatures. Slade was passionate intensity simmering between layers of fake calm and poised anger. Pure sexy bad boy, and in any other environment she might just have succumbed to the temptation he posed. The last time she'd had a red-hot affair with a man like Slade, had been, well, never. She sighed. Might as well face it: men like Slade didn't come along too often, and when they did, they were usually candidates for scumbag of the year, not the heroes of fairy tales.

She glanced toward the backseat again. But Slade had hero written all over him. He'd risked his life for her. Bled because of her. As recommendations for trustworthiness went, that was the best she'd had so far. He might even make relationship material. Not that she'd had too many of those, either. As always, when she got to the end of a research project the thrill of an approaching solution consumed her mind and left little time for dating. Heck, half the time, she forgot to eat. Men weren't even on the agenda. Now, before she could even turn the hormones back on, here was Slade. She'd been interested in him when he'd been a blip on her computer screen, a rare enough occurrence in itself. Any red-blooded woman would be interested in him after meeting him in person, but what unsettled her was the feeling that there was more than hormones at work here. Why or what, she didn't know, but there was chemistry between them. Even, maybe a . . . connection. Good God, she was running for her life in a race against time to protect research she never should have pursued. She didn't have time for a connection!

The pavement came to an abrupt end. She hit the brakes as the car bumped down off the pavement into a series of ruts that threatened to vibrate the powerful vehicle right off the side of the road.

"What's wrong?"

Sure, now he woke up. "Tell me, if the sun touches you what does it do?"

"Beyond hurting like hell?" His voice had a shadow of its normal timbre.

"Yeah. Beyond that."

"It's probably the equivalent of pouring a bucket of acid on human skin."

Acid burned through tissue in seconds. "Do you keep a blanket in here?"

"No."

"What about that energy blanket thing? If you get that over you, will it block the sun?"

A pause. "Probably."

"Then put it on."

There was a rustle of leather and material. "You like to give orders, don't you?"

"I find it's easier than arguing."

"That really works for you?"

Up to the left was a clearing. A house sat back from the road, listing to one side, so she assumed it was abandoned and might just do as a place to get Slade out of the sun. "With sensible people, yes."

"Are you implying I'm not sensible?"

"Maybe just a little. Remember, I saw you throw yourself in front of Fang and company."

"That, sweetness, was the smartest thing I ever did."

She turned into the drive of the deserted house. "Then I guess that makes you either stupid or a genius."

"Genius." The word reverberated strangely, sounding louder in her head than to her ear.

"You just go right ahead and keep believing that." There was an even more dilapidated barn to the right of the house. She pulled up in front of the double doors. "I think we can hide you here."

"Hide?"

"That tightness in your voice tells me you're in pain. You need medical help."

"Nothing I can't bear. It's certainly not enough to send me running with my tail tucked between my legs."

No one would feel compelled to obey that rasp of sound. But she did. On a level she couldn't explain. Pushing the urge aside, Jane put the car in park. "I'm calling the shots right now."

"Says who?"

"Says me."

"What gives you the authority to be barking orders?"

She looked around, seeing nothing but weeds, trash, and woods. "The fact that I can walk in the sun."

The next grunt *was* weaker. Jane looked over her shoulder. Slade was lying on his back on the seat, hands over his face. Blisters populated the red, angry flesh of his skin. All that from the few weak rays of the sun that permeated the tinted interior? Damn!

He slid his hands away from his face. "Caleb is going love you."

"Who is Caleb?"

"My brother." His voice was barely audible.

Opening the glove compartment, she saw a flashlight, but no gun. She really would have preferred the gun. Unfortunately, her survival instincts weren't what they should be. She'd left it at the lab when Slade had grabbed her. Damn it. She snatched up the flashlight and eased the front door open, using her body to block the light, doing her best to shield him from the insidious rays of the sun. It spilled around her as if she were no barrier to anything at all. Damn, she hated feeling helpless.

"Good to know, in the unlikely event we ever meet."

"You'll meet. I'm insisting on it."

"Is he also a vampire?"

"Yes."

"Then don't count on it."

She closed the front door. He said something she couldn't make out. She stopped, just in time, from opening the back door and asking, "What?" Placing her hand against the window, wishing she could see through the dark glass, she asked, "Just how hurt are you?"

"I'll be fine if I get some rest."

He needed rest. Protection from the sun. Jane couldn't take her hand from the window. Couldn't break the fragile connection. Another bit of vampire lore that had an anchor in reality. That no woman could resist them. "Playing the hero takes a lot out of you, huh?"

"It can be hard work."

She bet. "Do you do it often?"

No response.

"Slade?"

Damn. Had he passed out? Another glance around showed no sign of movement in the early morning light. Hopefully, it would take forever for the werewolves to find them, and hopefully, she'd be long dead from old age by the time that particular bit of folklore became part of her reality.

She headed for the barn doors. The chain was not a good sign. Though heavily rusted, it still looked strong enough to fend off her efforts. Her only hope was that the lock wasn't very strong. A tug proved it was stronger than the muscles in her hands and arms. Which was not saying much. When she went to the gym, she pretty much did the treadmill and ignored everything else. She yanked the lock again. Maybe she should have worked more with the weight machines. Then again, muscle wasn't everything. She grabbed a piece of metal pipe from the pile of brush and trash at the side of the building. Innovation could often make up the difference.

Swinging the pipe, she banged on the lock. Once. Twice. The force resonated around her. So loud. She looked down the road. There were no other houses in sight, but who knew what was beyond the trees. Or for that matter, in the trees. This was not a situation to give a body a warm fuzzy. She needed to get them hidden, and fast. Taking a firmer grip on the pipe, she stabbed downward. Metal clanked. And there might have been just a bit of give in the mechanism. Give would be good about now. She'd had enough problems in the last few hours.

Four more tries, each blow ringing like a warning shot through the early dawn, and the lock gave. Hallelujah! She dropped the pipe on the ground, grabbed the lock, and untangled it from the rusty chain, staining her hands and clothes orange. Great. She'd just bought this shirt.

No matter how quietly she tried to slide the chain through the door handles, it made an ungodly racket. As it clanked its way to the ground, she bit her lip and froze. The hairs on her arms prickled. Her breath stilled. Who had heard the raucous sound? Seconds passed like hours as she waited for the attack. Her lungs ached for air and it still didn't come. Maybe they'd truly escaped.

There are werewolves, too . . .

Releasing her breath, Jane reached for the handle. Her hands shook like leaves, making the simple move almost impossible. They weren't safe. They had fricking werewolves to worry about. Of course, because everyone knew vampires weren't enough.

"I hate you," she muttered in Slade's direction. Kicking clods of dirt out of the way, she hauled the doors across the uneven ground. She hid behind the door for a second, just in case any four-legged inhabitants decided to take a shot at freedom. The one thing she didn't need was to end up in the emergency room, getting rabies shots. She checked the top of the doorjamb. She also didn't need a heart attack from a spider dropping on her head. The wisps of web floating about looked old and flimsy. No self-respecting spider would take up residence in them. She pulled open the second door without incident. Maybe her luck was turning.

It was dark inside the structure. Dark enough to make her uneasy. Dark enough to make Slade happy. At least she hoped that was all it would take to make him happy. Grabbing the flashlight from her waistband, she shone it into the interior. It was a big hollow place made even bigger by the dark corners. Too dark corners. A flick of the flashlight revealed why. The two side windows were painted black. Probably to discourage burglars, but it suited her purposes.

"Perfect." The place was about perfect.

Against the far back wall there were two stalls with a large, built-in metal and wooden box between them. The box could be her salvation. She hurried over, that sense of urgency still pushing at her. It didn't look as big close up, but—she glanced back at the car—if Slade could tuck his knees to his chin, he might fit. A sunbeam slipped through the cracks of the old structure and tickled the corner of the box. As the sun rose, there would be more stray beams. That box would be Slade's sanctuary. All she had to do was get him there.

Hurrying back to the car, the sense of danger looming right along with her panic, Jane made her mental list. First and foremost she had to get Slade in the box. Then she had to hide the car. Lastly, she had to hide any sign they'd been there. No problem.

Maybe not joining the Girl Scouts in her youth had been a mistake. Her outdoor skills were at an abysmal low. With another quick glance around—she was beginning to feel like the need was a tic—she eased open the driver door.

"We're in luck."

"That would be a nice change."

Yes it would. Sunbeams battled to invade the car. Jane imagined she could smell flesh burning. "Are you okay back there."

"Just toasty."

"Now is not the time for jokes."

"You tell me when there is a better one."

She shook her head and smiled despite herself. "After I get you in the box."

"A box?"

She turned the key in the ignition. The engine purred to life. "Don't sound so freaked. Don't vampires sleep in coffins?"

"Only in the movies."

The car eased forward. "So what do you sleep in?"

There was a pause before he answered, and when he did, his voice rose and fell in an uneven cadence. "A nice big bed."

Jane inched the vehicle forward. It was going to be a tight fit through the doorway. "A vampire who loves his creature comforts, eh?"

"Damn straight."

The right mirror caught on the jamb and snapped against the car frame as it was designed to do. She jumped anyway. "Well, since the sun isn't having any trouble coming through the space between the wood, you need to be somewhere safer than this SUV."

Material scraped against leather. Warm breath stroked her neck. "You're not damaging my truck are you?"

She gripped the steering wheel, irritation flashing through her at her reaction to that incidental caress. Being turned on in this situation would make her the cliché she simply refused to be—the sex-starved researcher.

Air woofed past her ear in a grunt of pain, or a chuckle. Again, as with everything about this man, it was hard to tell. "The one thing I don't need right now is a backseat driver."

"You're doing fine."

She glanced over her shoulder, took in the impression of Slade's profile, absorbed that ever so pleasing scent that surrounded him, and flexed her fingers. "If that's the case, you should be more focused on your preference for comfort than on my driving."

Several small breaths puffed past her ear. Definitely a chuckle. Even under pain and pressure, the man could find humor. Was there anything about him that wasn't pleasing? "Just how small is this box."

She pulled up as close as she could to the stall and to the right of the box before killing the lights. "Let's just say that I hope you're very limber."

He groaned.

"I'm taking that as a yes."

"Take it as whatever you want." Leather creaked as he sat back. She hopped out of the car. "It isn't safe for you here."

She went around to the back door. "I'm getting the impression that it isn't safe for me anywhere."

She opened the door. His hand caught hers, the hard calluses on the palm rough against her skin. A shiver went through her as his gaze met hers.

"You need to get in that car and drive like hell out of here."

"Because the wolves are coming."

"Yes."

She stood back, giving him room to come out. "I don't believe you."

"The hell you don't."

She'd always been a lousy liar. "Do you realize that you swear a lot when you're upset?"

The only thing to come out of the back of the SUV was his growl. "Do you realize that you change the subject when you don't like the way a conversation is going?"

"Yes. It's called 'being tactful.'"

"I'd call it 'running away.'"

He would. The man seemed to love conflict.

"I beg to differ. May I ask you a question?"

"Shoot."

"Do vampires feel pain?"

"All vampire senses are heightened."

She glanced down at his fingers, which were wrapped around her wrist. The ravaged flesh split to the bone. "Then how come you're not screaming?"

"I'm trying to impress you."

As if any man oozing that much testosterone needed to worry about impressing a mousy little scientist with zero man-killer skills.

Leaning forward, he cocked his brow and asked, "Is it working?"

Rolling her eyes, she said, "Consider me impressed."

"Good." He tugged her forward, into the darkness of the car interior. The hairs on the back of her neck rose in warning. She braced her feet.

"What?" he asked.

"I'll wait out here."

"Afraid?"

Even though she couldn't see it, she bet the arch of his brow was higher. "Not at all. I've just got a weak stomach."

The length of the next pause made her feel guilty. She heard the pass of his hand over the scruff of his beard.

"Guess I do look like something the cat dragged in."

"You look like you need to be in a hospital," she countered.

And that was her fault.

"I'll improve."

She glanced at the box again. A beam of sunlight from the open doors had reached it. "Wait here."

"Yes, ma'am."

Amazing how much sarcasm could be put into two syllables. Mr. Slade, whoever he was, did not like taking orders, but that was just tough. Right now she was in charge, and while she didn't know how long she could maintain that control, it was something she wasn't giving up. Especially since she gave orders much better than she took them.

Heading back outside, she grabbed the chain and lock from the ground and dragged them back into the barn. Next, she pulled the doors closed, yanking hard when the right one caught on a stone. That intruding beam of sunlight winked out, but others were springing up as the sun rose in the sky. She eyed the chain. It wasn't much in the way of security, and certainly not against creatures that could catch an SUV traveling at full speed, but it couldn't hurt to chain the door. The thick, heavy links kept kinking up as she threaded the chain through the handles, but at last she was done and slid the lock through several of the metal loops. Though it wouldn't latch, the lock would help keep the chain in place. The right door handle sagged as she let the chain go. Hopefully it wouldn't rip out under the weight. The chain that had looked so substantial before now appeared woefully inadequate as it dangled lopsidedly between the rusted handles. Wiping her hands down her jeans, she sighed. It was going to have to do. She headed for the box.

Slade slung his long legs out of the car. "Hey."

Stepping over his scuffed boots, she avoided his hand and ordered, "Just stay there a minute."

Before she dragged him through the trail of sunbeams, she needed to check to see if he was going to fit. The metal lid of the box opened with a groan worthy of a horror movie. Perfect. Just perfect. Now she had ambiance to go with the terror wending through her bones.

Inside there were a couple of dead spiders and a few leftover oats. And rust. All in all, if she was looking for a positive sign, this could be it. That was a plus. She'd been dreading a *Willard* moment, with rats pouring out as she opened the lid. Dead spiders she could handle. Rats, not so much. She left the lid open and went back to the car.

Slade was waiting, but she didn't flash the light on this face. She didn't want to. One, she hadn't been lying about the weak stomach, and two, the horror-movie analogy wouldn't leave her brain. Slade hadn't shown any blood-sucking tendencies, but if this were a horror movie, now would be the moment where it all went bad. He had her trust; she was trying to help him. In any decent horror movie, it was time for the kill shot.

"C'mon."

There was a long pause, then the rustle of clothing against the seat back, and a groan. She slipped her shoulder under his arm.

"News flash—now is the wrong time to faint."

"I never faint."

"Pardon me. Get weak at the knees."

"I don't do that, either."

Lord, he was heavy. "What do you consider the proper terminology for a man about to pass out?"

"Men don't pass out."

"Then we'll go with mine. Don't pick now to faint. We need to get twenty feet, to the box, before you can pass out." He grunted. "Can you make it?"

He stood, swayed, his height taking him past her ability to support. "I'll make it."

If sheer determination was a guarantee, she'd bet he would. Unfortunately, she had a bird's-eye view of his face. Ghosts had more color.

She took an involuntary step backward as he leaned forward. He placed his palm on the SUV. "Don't worry. I'm not lusting for your blood."

"I didn't think you were." The shiver that went down her spine made a liar out of her. She took another step backward.

"Sure you were. That's why you keep stepping away."

"Maybe I'm just afraid you'll fall on top of me and squash me flat."

"I wouldn't squish you, sweetness."

Sweetness. Why did he keep calling her that? She flashed the light in his face. His eyes burned back at her—an icy gray. Funny, she'd thought they were more green than gray before. Light played unmercifully across his horribly burned face. Her stomach turned. The left half was worse than the rest. His eyes closed as he took slow, even breaths. *Oh God*, he looked near death. "I can't catch you if you faint."

"Already told you, men don't faint."

"Good." She flashed the light toward the box. "You need to get over there."

He straightened. "No problem."

Looking at how he weaved, she had her doubts. More beams propagated in the dark interior.

He straightened and swayed. "I'll be better by nightfall."

"You're delusional."

"No, I regenerate."

She paused, excitement flaring. That was intriguing. "Really?"

He cracked an eyelid. "I should have known that would get your blood pumping."

"It's not—"

"I can hear it, Jane."

How was she supposed to respond to that? "Sorry."

Tiny white lines fanned out from the edges of his lips. He took a step forward. "Don't be sorry. I'm probably one of the few people able to understand your reaction."

Using the side of the SUV to steady himself, Slade took another step. Jane couldn't stand it as he wavered. Whatever was wrong, he was definitely on his last legs. She wrapped her arm around his rock-hard waist.

"That's not necessary."

"If you knew me as well as you think you do, you'd get that it's totally necessary."

His arm came down across her shoulders. A heavy, surprisingly comforting weight. "I guess you're right."

Jane had been humored enough in her professional life to recognize when it was happening. Slade was definitely humoring her as he gave her just enough of his weight to make her feel useful, but not enough to strain her back. It was a surprisingly sweet thing to do. They reached the end of the hood. The last fifteen feet, they were going to have to do on their own. She bit her lip.

"Slade?"

His finger brushed her cheek, almost as if he knew her worry. "What?"

"If you make it to the box, I'll let you kiss me."

"Deal."

She wondered if he was smiling. She wondered how much he was hurting. She wondered if they were both going to see the night. "Ready for the last few steps?"

"Not really."

"Let's pretend."

"You do an awful lot of pretending."

"I learned young."

"Learned how to pretend?"

"No, learned that it helps."

"With what?"

"Dealing."

He let go of the hood. The first step was solid, the second shaky. The third sent them tumbling. Slade spun them around, taking the brunt of the impact. The flashlight beam sliced through the murk and dust motes, revealing the rusted tin roof. Her breath woofed out as she landed on top of him. She was vividly aware of every plane, every hard muscle of his lean form. She looked down at his hand, pressed over her stomach. The skin on the back was split and oozing. Her stomach rose. *Oh God.* "I'm going to be sick."

He didn't let her go, didn't move, just breathed slowly and steadily as his fingers spread across her abdomen. Her stomach roiled some more.

"Let me go."

"No."

Something touched the edges of her mind. A soothing warmth that fanned inward along her bloodstream. His fingers splayed further, his cuts oozed more.

"Look away."

"It's not going to help."

"Humor me."

She did. The warmth spread, drawing her attention inward, toward the comfort of that heat. The nausea abated. She let out a breath.

"Better?" he asked.

"Yes."

Leaning back against him, she gave him her weight, letting him hold her for a second. Just one second. He didn't even flinch, just took it as if it were his right. "I've got you, sweetness."

That "sweetness" ruined everything. Jane slid to the side, which was as far as he would let her go. Sunlight touched her toe. She turned and grabbed his hand. "You need to stand up, now."

"I'm working on it."

She tugged. He didn't move. "Why are you so weak?"

"I used a lot of energy levitating the car and feeding power to the engine while masking our presence."

She blinked. He'd done all that? He *could do* all that?

"Add to that the fact that I'm naturally sluggish during daytime, and my body's efforts to heal the burns . . ." He stood. "And it pretty much adds up to shutdown."

"You can't control it?"

Again, the touch on her cheek. "Even vampires have survival instincts."

She supposed they did. Twisting out of his embrace, she motioned to the box. "You need to get in before you fry."

He didn't move, just stared at her with those strange eyes that contained those strange, mesmerizing fires. "I freak you out."

She rubbed her hands up and down her arms. "On many levels."

"Any of them good?"

She wasn't touching that with a ten-foot pole. Standing, she ordered, "Get in the box."

He held out his hand. She did her best not to look at the torn skin as she braced her feet. "On three, okay?"

He nodded. "On three."

"One, two, three." She hauled back. He pushed off. The momentum was enough to send him forward. She stumbled backward. Her knees collided with the back of the box. His hand slammed into the wall above her. His arm wrapped around her, keeping her from falling into the box. She quickly twisted, catching her weight on her hand, taking the burden off him. His touch didn't leave her. It lingered in tingles of warmth that were deceptively calming. She closed her eyes and breathed out a sigh of relief. "We made it."

"So I see."

When she opened her eyes, he was looking down into the box. "You weren't kidding about it being a tight fit."

He was right. It didn't look possible. "It's the only place here that the sun can't reach you."

"True enough."

She couldn't say Slade's descent into the box was graceful, and he didn't look comfortable once he was in there, seeing as his knees were nearly up around his chin.

"Are you going to be okay?"

A band of sunlight sneaked across her forearm and flirted with his shirt.

"I'll be fine. Close the lid."

She didn't have any choice. Before she could close it all the way, he caught the edge. "A soon as you close this lid, I want you to get in that car and drive due north."

"Drive to where?"

"As far as you can get. I don't want you to stop. Just keep driving. Don't use your credit cards, don't use anything. Don't trust anyone."

"Why?"

"I want you to disappear."

She could only stare at him. "I can't do that. I have a life."

"If you don't do that, the life you're going to have left isn't one you're going to like."

"How will I know if you're okay?"

"I wrote down an email address and password. It's in the glove compartment. Memorize it and then destroy it. A week from now, log in. I'll have directions for you."

There were so many holes in that plan. "And what if you don't?"

His eyes met hers. The flames were more apparent now, blending with the gray and green, weaving in and out of the darker flecks. "Then don't stop running."

"You're a little ray of sunshine, aren't you?"

"Yeah. That's me." He grunted. "There's also cash in the false bottom of the glove compartment, along with a gun and instructions on how to use it."

"I won't need that." It was a knee-jerk response that sounded stupid as soon as it left her lips.

His gaze met hers. "You need to be prepared."

Yes, she did.

From his unfocused gaze, she figured it wouldn't be long before he passed out. Still, she couldn't bring the lid down. Slade wanted her to abandon him to whatever came. She bit her lip. "You make it."

"Never had any plan otherwise. Close the lid, sweetness."

"You remember, you owe me a kiss." She had no idea where she got the nerve to demand that. It had to be the stress.

Slade didn't miss a beat. "That's a given."

He tugged and the lid came down with a thump, shutting her off from the warmth of his gaze, the force of his personality. The barn suddenly felt very big. Very empty. And the box was a very obvious hiding place. Goose bumps crept up along her arms.

"Go, Jane."

She shook her head and took a step back. Slade was right. She needed to get out of there.

To stay was pure idiocy. And geniuses didn't do idiocy. They only dealt in logic.

❧ 5 ❧

TURNING on her heel, Jane tucked the flashlight into the back of her waistband and headed to the SUV. Not because Slade had given her an order, but because she didn't know what in hell else to do. She wasn't Wonder Woman. She was a human female of above-average intelligence. She didn't have superpowers. She couldn't run at a hundred thirty miles an hour, and she was reasonably sure her three-times-a-week yoga class didn't equip her to deal with werewolves, even if they were only half as fierce as lore provided. She ran her hand through her hair. Her fingers snagged in a knot. She yanked, but it held against her fingers. The keys jangled accusingly in her pocket.

"Damn it!"

Despite how pointless she knew looking back was, she still couldn't help it. The box sat in dappled sunlight, innocuous and . . . vulnerable. Everything in her rebelled at each step that took her away from it. It was wrong to leave Slade there.

She opened the car door. The warning bells chimed as she put the keys in the ignition. In the rearview, the barn door loomed.

Freedom. Escape. So why couldn't she take it? *Damn.* Maybe because she'd forgotten to unchain the stupid thing? Instead of getting out of the car and handling the last barrier to her escape, she sat there, indecision gnawing at her. What if the werewolves came while Slade was helpless? What if he couldn't heal as fast as he claimed?

Jane licked her lips. Slade had a huge hero complex. Big enough that it might prompt him to lie rather than tell the truth. If she took the car, and the vampires who had chased them last night found him in a weakened state, he wouldn't have any way to get away even if he was in perfect health. If injured, he'd be a sitting duck.

But she'd be safe.

Her survival instinct wasn't as developed as it should be, because being safe at the cost of Slade's life didn't sound as enticing as it should.

"I'm not a hero."

The words landed harmlessly in the car's interior.

She turned the ignition. The car hummed to life. She checked the gas gauge. Three-quarters full.

Drive due north . . . I don't want you to stop . . . There's cash in the false bottom of the glove compartment, along with a gun and instructions on how to use it.

Slade had made sure there'd be enough of everything for her. Even in the event that he wouldn't be there to help. She squeezed the leather-wrapped steering wheel. He'd known he might not get out of this alive. And he'd come for her anyway. Her own hero. Twenty-five years too late to be the answer to her childhood prayer, but he'd finally shown up.

She cut a glance heavenward. "You've got a weird sense of humor."

A lightning bolt didn't strike her dead. A sign she was going in the right direction?

She told herself she'd started the engine to keep herself warm against the chill of the dawn and the depth of her own terror, but no amount of artificially generated heat could warm the cold inside her. For God's sake, she was contemplating leaving a man to die. One who'd saved her life.

She turned off the engine. She'd learned to live with a lot of things in her life, but that guilt wouldn't be one of them. For better or worse, it would be her and Slade against whatever the day brought. She took the keys out of the ignition, bumped her elbow on the gear shift, and dropped the keys. Something on the floor under the seat bumped her hand. It was small and oblong. Not the keys. Switching on the light, she studied it. A transceiver was hidden under the front passenger seat. A cautious hope bloomed inside. A transceiver meant Slade had someone to talk to. Help.

Unless he hadn't known it was there.

He had to know. A man who could manipulate energy had to be able to detect it. Why hadn't he used it? Maybe because there hadn't been time? Sanctuary had had all night to make their move at the lab while she'd been destroying files and shredding paper. The fact that they'd waited until just before dawn would make sense if they wanted to make it tough for other vampires to pursue them. Especially if they'd planned on passing her off to werewolves. But Slade hadn't known that. He hadn't expected her to break her routine and go to the lab. He'd thought he had more time.

Reaching down again she scooped up the keys and the transceiver. Nothing like the option of communication to brighten a woman's day. Leaning over, she popped open the glove compartment. The false bottom took a minute to figure out, but when she did, the money and gun, plus instructions, were there. She grabbed her bag and shoved the money in. Before she grabbed the gun, she checked the instructions. Slade's handwriting was bold and concise, like the man himself. The instructions stated that the gun had a safety and it was loaded. Good. After reviewing the how-tos, she dropped it in the bag and gave it a pat. Nothing like being armed to boost a woman's confidence.

She headed over to the box. "Slade?"

There was no response, but she hadn't really expected one. Placing her hand on the lid, she searched for that sense of connection. Needing it. All she found was an empty echo of nothingness. *Damn it.* She'd put Slade in the box to save him from the sun, but what if he was dying from his injuries? There was no way to know, and with the sunbeams bursting through every crack in the dilapidated building, no way to find out.

"Why isn't anything ever easy?"

She looked at the device in her hand. There was no obvious on/ off switch. It was possible that Slade's ability to manipulate energy was what activated it, but it was also possible that the easiest solution was the most logical and that would mean a pressure-sensitive, or photo-sensitive, switch. She put the oblong device in her ear. Beyond a slight buzzing sound, like crickets in the distance, which could just be an echo of the air between her ear and the device, she heard nothing. Maybe it was sound activated.

"Hello?" Nothing. "Hello? Is anybody there?"

It might be her imagination, but the crickets seemed livelier.

All vampire senses are heightened.

Maybe even their sense of hearing? "You're going to have to speak up. I can't hear you."

Excitement flared. The crickets were definitely jumping around in there, and it was in response to her speech, which meant there was someone else at the other end.

"Where the hell are you?" blasted from the earpiece. Yelping, she batted the device out of her ear. It flipped to the dirt beside the box.

"Oh shit." Dust billowed as she dropped to her knees and fumbled for it. "Where the hell are you?" roared out of the device again, followed quickly by a very disgruntled, "How in hell does Slade calibrate this thing. I can't hear a thing."

Another voice came through, just as male. Just as arrogant, but with a touch more patience.

"What do you need to calibrate?"

"There's a woman on Slade's transceiver."

"About time the man got out."

She finally found the stupid transceiver. Naturally, amidst a pile of cobwebs. Shuddering, she brushed them off.

"You're too loud now," she yelled into it.

"Who are you?"

"Stop yelling." She needed her eardrums.

"Don't tell me what to do, woman. Just tell me what you did with Slade?"

Woman? "I put him in a box."

Static crackled over the connection. "Damn it, Derek, fix this thing. I think she said she put him in a box."

The other voice came again, calm but faint, over the connection. "It's calibrated for Slade's voice. Just keep her talking, and I'll have it in a minute."

"Why in hell doesn't it just fix itself?"

"It's a machine," Derek retorted.

"Good to know I'm not dealing with total idiots," she muttered as more static crackled.

"Hurry up, Derek. I think we're being insulted."

There was no "think" about it. "What do you need me to do?" she asked.

"Keep talking."

"What do you want me to say?"

"Whatever you want."

She launched into a rendition of "Mary Had a Little Lamb." A male chuckle, rich and warm, filled her ear. Good to know she was capable of entertaining. When she got to "its fleece was white as snow," Derek said, "I have it."

"Put the transceiver in your ear," blasted out of the device.

"As soon as you stop yelling. I need my eardrums."

The man dropped his voice. She put the device to her ear.

"I'm here."

"Good. Now, lady, who are you?"

"Who are you?"

There was a pause. "Caleb. Slade's brother."

Thank God. Family. "How do I know you're Slade's brother?"

"I look just like him."

Fat lot of help that was. "I can't see you." Which he knew.

"Where are you?"

He kept asking her that. How hard would it be for someone to hack a frequency? Triangulate a position?

Keep talking.

Unease pushed aside her relief.

"I'm not going to tell you that. I just need to know when night comes, which way to drive."

This time there was no mistaking the sound that came over the transceiver. A growl, like a dog. Or a wolf. Slade had warned her six ways to Sunday, and she hadn't listened. "Oh my God, you're one of them!"

"Wait!"

She wasn't waiting for anything. Snatching the earpiece out of her ear, she threw it on the ground and stomped it hard. She kept stomping until there was nothing left but smashed fragments. Tiny fragments that most definitely could no longer function as a tracking device.

God, she hoped he hadn't kept her talking long enough that he could trace her. Grabbing her bag off the floor, Jane dug around inside until she found the gun. Pulling it out, she stared at the fragile, rusted barrier on the door, backing up until her butt hit the box, her nerves jangling with images of fanged demons drooling blood, breaking through at any second.

Don't trust anyone.

Oh God, what had she done?

Bracing herself with one hand, she sat on the wooden box and shoved the bag behind her. The muzzle of the gun followed the trajectory of her gaze as it bounced between the windows and the door.

"Slade?" No answer yet. Just hoping. Stupidly, pointlessly hoping.

"I screwed up," she confessed, sliding back until her shoulders hit the wall, keeping the gun trained on the door, knowing in her gut that they were coming. Knowing it was her fault. Weariness and despair waged for supremacy.

"But don't worry. I'll fix it."

She didn't have any choice.

"WATCH the gun."

The order snapped Jane's eyes open. Oh God, she'd fallen asleep. It was almost dark in the barn, but she knew *they* were here. She recognized that voice. Picking up the gun, she pulled the trigger. There was a flash of light and an explosion. The recoil slammed her back. The gun jumped in her grip. Her hands hit the wall above her head. Clamping down, she held on to the weapon. *They* were here. The voices from the device. Scrambling back, she listened for any sound that would give away their location, their number.

A hand on her arm yanked her sideways. "Settle down!"

And go willingly to her death? Not hardly. The fingertips of her right hand brushed the edge of the box. She grabbed it, taking aim in the second before the monster's strength overwhelmed her. "No."

Frantically, she squeezed the trigger. The report filled the interior with a howl of violence. Vicious swearing preceded the yank that hauled her off the box and up against a very big, very solid male body. With disgusting ease, the man turned her and pressed her so close she could feel every ridge of his six-pack abdomen against her spine.

Son of a bitch. In her whole life, she'd never seen a real-life man packed with muscle, yet in the last twenty-four hours she hadn't met anything but. It wasn't fair.

"Slade, haul your ass out here."

The order boomed above her head. The same voice she'd heard over the transceiver. Holding on to calm with the same frantic need with which she'd fired the gun, Jane kicked back, aiming for the knee. Something thudded against the wooden wall. Another hand grabbed hers. The same man, or someone else? Gouging down with the heel of her fancy boot, digging for the kneecap, she grabbed the hand, yanked it to her mouth, and bit down. The coppery taste of blood filled her mouth.

"Here now, you don't want to do that."

She pulled back, letting the blood spill, shuddering as her stomach revolted, repulsed. He was right. She didn't want any of this, but Slade needed her. He was helpless. More swearing, a snarl, and then, "Damn it, woman, stop fighting."

Slade's voice, yet not Slade's. A trick? It had to be a trick. She fought harder. The man behind her squeezed his arm around her chest, stealing her breath until her threats were just broken gasps. There was another snarl. The hand left her mouth. Turning her wrist, she angled the muzzle at her attacker's leg. Was Slade awake? Capable? "Run, Slade!"

Before she could squeeze the trigger, the gun was torn from her hand.

"Sorry, cutie," the other man, little more than a deep shadow, said.

Cutie? "Let me go!"

"In a minute. When I'm sure you're not going to unman me with that knee."

She was going to do more than unman him. She saw a shadow move toward the box lid. She watched helplessly as that shadow bent and an arm extended into the box. Oh God, they had him. "Leave him be."

There was a groan from the box. Something metal gleamed to the right. The gun? *Dear God!* They were turning the gun on Slade.

"Look out." In desperation, Jane twisted out of her captor's grasp and leapt for the gun. An arm snaked around her waist. The gun exploded as she was yanked back.

"Goddamnit, Jane!"

Slade.

The arm around her waist lifted her. A hand cupped the back of her head. A spicy male musk encased her in a hug of familiarity as her face was pressed against a muscular chest.

"Easy."

It was Slade who held her.

She turned her head to the side, easing the pressure on her nose. The shaking she'd been holding back commenced when his hand moved to her waist, anchoring her against him.

"Slade."

"I've got you."

"I was just trying to give him the gun," the man who'd called himself Caleb said.

She didn't look over. What would be the point?

"Shut up, Caleb."

Caleb. "That's really your brother?" Jane asked.

"Yeah."

She couldn't see anyone's expression. She was really glad they couldn't see hers. For once, the darkness was working for her. "Oh my God, I almost shot your brother."

"Serves his ass right for sneaking up on you."

The muscles under her cheek flexed as Slade reached beyond her, but his hand didn't leave her head, just held her to him in an odd combination of possession and comfort.

"As soon as I get my muscles unlocked, I'm putting you over m y knee."

The threat rumbled under her ear, over her head.

"For what?" What century did he think this was? "I never said I would leave you here."

"Not to mention almost taking out Derek here," Caleb interjected dryly.

That sounded way too serious. "I was saving Slade's life."

Slade's fingers tightened on her braid and tugged. She looked up into twin flames, glowing eerily in the dark. His eyes?

"You don't ever risk your life, sweetness. Not for me, not for anything."

She'd had enough. "I'll do whatever the hell I want, but I assure you, I'll not be risking it again for you."

Another chuckle. This time from Caleb. "You met her when?"

"For real? Last night."

"For real?"

Jane felt Slade's shrug against her cheek. "We've been chatting over the Internet."

"You met your mate through an online hook up?"

"Mate?" Jane asked incredulously.

"Mate?" echoed Slade.

"Seriously," Jane snapped, "What century do you all think you're in?"

"The century doesn't matter," Derek said, suddenly closer. "A mate is a mate is a mate."

"Good God, I need to go home." Grabbing the flashlight, Jane flashed it up at Slade. "You don't believe in this, do you?"

There was no missing the shock on Slade's expression.

"Oh my God, you believe this."

"I swear, you Johnsons are slow on the uptake," Derek muttered.

"And you would have known sooner?" Slade shot back.

"Hell yes. A wolf would have known on first contact."

Yes, a wolf would have, Slade realized. Whereas he had had to have Jane's mysterious importance to him put into perspective. Slade blinked. Then smiled. Jane was his mate. That explained everything. The sense of rightness when he focused on her, the perfection of her scent, the wildness that surged inside at the thought of anyone hurting her. The fact that he was willing to sacrifice his family for her in that wild impulse to let her go . . . Hell, he should have known right then. Nothing came between a Johnson and family. Only a mate could do that. A mate was everything to a vampire. Because her life meant more to him than anything. Her life was his.

"You're looking a little shell-shocked, Slade. The scientist in you having a bit of trouble with reality?"

"Shut up, Derek."

"I think you should all know," Jane interrupted, "that I don't like the turn of this ridiculous conversation."

He just bet. Against him, Jane still shook like a leaf. The kind of shaking that came from running too long on nerves and fear. From pushing oneself beyond the point of endurance. Exhaustion, adrenaline, and fear were taking their toll. He should have known she wouldn't have left him. Jane wasn't the type to cut and run. "Did you sit on top of that box all day, sweetness?"

"I couldn't let them get you."

"Let them?"

"It was all my fault."

"What was?"

"I found the transceiver. I didn't think until afterward that just anybody could pick up the call."

"Only Caleb would pick up."

"Well, I didn't know that, did I?" she snapped. "I don't know anything about the technology, and then there was this horrible growl. And you said the werewolves were coming, and I realized I might have led them straight to you."

And she was shaking all over again, just thinking about it. Slade opened his hand over Jane's back, feeling the fragility of muscles and bone. Finding the thread of her energy, he followed deeper, until he could slow the flow of adrenaline and regulate her metabolism, while his own mind raced, the ramifications of her confession weakening his knees. She'd thought she'd signed his death warrant, so she'd stayed to cancel it. Her delicate body pitted against vampire fangs and werewolf claws. They would have cut through her human flesh like a hot knife through butter.

"You should have run right then."

"Right." Her voice was tight with tension. "And leave you alone and helpless?"

"Yes."

"No." The syllable ended in a squeak.

You're hurting her, Slade, Caleb pointed out mentally.

He looked down. His hands were digging into Jane's sides. *Shit.* He never lost control. He eased his grip. To Jane he said, "Sorry." To Caleb he snapped, "Who the hell growled at her?"

Caleb's features were very stark in the black and white of his night vision. Caleb shrugged. "Derek didn't like what she had to say at the time."

Jane's body jerked slightly. Slade knew that she strained to see through the dark. "The giant's a werewolf?"

"Yes."

Shit. "You could have given her time before revealing that."

"Maybe." With a tip of his hat Jane couldn't see, Derek smiled. "One of the good guys, ma'am."

"Oh."

Jane didn't relax. Slade couldn't blame her.

"The bad guys are coming, though. We ran into a couple on the way over."

The last was phrased causally for Jane's benefit. It didn't stop her panic from flicking across Slade's senses. He brushed his lips across the top of her head, inhaling her scent, letting the rightness settle into him anew. "It's okay," he whispered to her before asking Caleb. "I assume you've got that under control?"

"Not much to control, but enough of an amusement that a couple of the D'Nally pups decided to indulge."

Derek touched his hand to the transceiver in his ear. "We need to go."

Trouble. The warning from Derek whispered in his head.

Slade nodded, taking another breath, inhaling again the scent that was uniquely Jane's, that slid so perfectly over his senses. Spring. Hope. Perfection. She was all those things. How had he not recognized earlier what she was to him? "Sweetness, I'm going to pick you up now, and I don't want you fighting me."

She swatted at his hand with typical Jane exasperation. "Good grief, I don't need to be carried."

Yes. She did. He was hiding her weariness from her through

their mental connection, but her legs were just too weak to carry her at the speed they needed right now. Bending, he slipped his arm behind her thighs. "I know."

She stopped him with a hand under his chin. "Maybe you didn't hear me correctly. I'm not going to be carried like a child. Especially in front of your brother and a werewolf." The way she said "werewolf" held more than a hint of disgust.

Derek snorted. "You been filling her head with tales, Johnson?"

He'd implied they were dangerous predators and connected to Sanctuary. Deadly. Jane didn't have the night vision to see any difference in Derek. In truth, Derek's handsomeness equaled his lethal talents. But women didn't see the latter. At least at first glance. "The truth was scary enough."

"Shine that flashlight over here, cutie," Derek ordered.

"I think I know all I need to know about your kind."

"I assure you, ma'am, women swoon when they see me."

Slade shot Derek a glare. "And he insists it's not from fear."

"Though we're abstaining from comment," Caleb added. "Don't want to bruise his fragile ego."

Jane being Jane had to see for herself. She flashed the light in Derek's direction. Of course, the damn bastard was smiling his prettiest.

Jane gasped. "He's handsome."

Slade snatched the flashlight from her hand. "The hell he is!"

Derek laughed. "The McClarens are a very handsome pack." With a jerk of his chin he motioned to Slade and said, "And for sure, before you commit yourself to that one there, you might want to check us out."

To Jane's credit, all she did was blink.

"She's not checking you out in any manner," Slade shot back.

"That's true," Jane snapped. "And the only thing I'm committing to is quitting my job."

"And we're more than willing to help you with that," Caleb interjected, "but we need to leave. Now."

Slade looked over at Caleb. "How close?"

"Tobias said the sentinels are down, but they got a message off. They'll be behind us soon."

"Then we've got to move."

He tipped Jane's face up. "Where'd you put my transceiver?"

While Jane couldn't see him, he could clearly see the nervous dart of her eyes to the right. Amidst the dirt and rock and bits of straw there were pieces of plastic.

"You smashed it?"

"I didn't know if it had a tracking device."

It had. His brother just hadn't needed it to find him. Their mental connection assured, with a little hunting, they could find each other. It was going to take weeks to build a new one. The hardest part would be getting the parts. Sanctuary had started tracking electronic parts orders to track him.

"Shit."

Jane took the flashlight from his hand. "You can build a new one."

Turning the flashlight on Caleb's face, she gasped. "He does look like you."

"Just more handsome," Caleb tacked on.

Jane tipped her head to the side to assess the claim. "Your features are more even, but they're not as compelling."

This time it was Caleb's turn to blink. Then he laughed and grabbed up his pack. "Don't think I've ever heard anyone put it quite like that before."

"No doubt." She pushed away from Slade, her fingertips pressing into his chest, heat from her touch sinking deliciously into his skin even after the contact broke. "I'm not going with you."

"The hell you're not."

Reaching over, she grabbed her bag off the ground. "You risked your life for me, I saved yours." She took a step back toward the door. "We're even."

There wasn't a prayer in hell she was wandering off by herself. "Technically you didn't save mine, because I wasn't in any danger."

"I called your brother. If I hadn't called your brother, the sentinels would have gotten here and you would have been dead."

"She's got you there," Derek pointed out.

If he didn't take charge, the woman was going to fall flat on her face. "Shut up, Derek."

"Just agreeing with the lady."

Slade slipped his arm back around Jane. On her other side, Caleb took her hand, steadying her as she weaved.

"Sorry. I got dizzy there for a second."

A quick mental check revealed she was hypoglycemic.

"Did you bring food?" Slade asked Caleb.

"Allie sent a snack. I tossed it in your SUV."

"Good." Slade took a step forward. Immediately, Jane stepped away. Just as quickly, he scooped her up into his arms, holding her despite her squeal. Or maybe because of her squeal. There was something infinitely appealing about pulling decidedly feminine sounds from the ever-practical Jane. Her arms came around his neck, and then, as if she realized what she'd done, dropped to her chest. "Put me down."

"In a minute."

"I can walk."

"I can carry you faster."

Her nails dug into his chest in warning. "I'm not going with you."

He smiled down into the face of her determination and shook his head. She had a lot to learn about him. First off, that he took care of what was his. "I wasn't aware I was giving you a choice."

❧ 6 ❧

"**Y**OU knocked her out?"

Sitting in the backseat with Jane in his arms, Slade met Caleb's gaze in the rearview mirror. "Yeah."

"Afraid she's going to rip you a new one for tricking her?"

Slade smiled. Jane in a temper. He'd never seen that. He'd bet she would be all fire and reason. "Nah."

"Then why?"

Because he needed to think.

"She needs rest before she faces the rest of what's coming."

"You think she's going to shatter like a piece of china?"

"Hell," Derek turned in the front seat. "From the way she sat guard on Slade, that's one tough woman. Too tough to shatter."

Jane stirred against him. Slade ran his fingers through her hair, mentally soothing her disquiet.

Rest.

Jane would like the world to think her tough, but Slade had seen inside her mind. He'd seen the pain she hid, the sensitivity she guarded, the fear she battled. "She isn't."

Her cheek snuggled into his chest. The fabric of his shirt was an intolerable barrier between her skin and his. His claws extended with the need to rip it away. Caleb's mind brushed along his—a subtle check to see if he was okay. Slade gave him the answer he sought. As soon as Caleb accepted the lie and withdrew, Slade dropped the shield.

He wasn't okay. He was trying to cope with the fact that he had a mate. A woman. A wife. A partner. A responsibility. A liability. A mate wasn't something that he'd ever anticipated. But Jane was here and she was a Sanctuary target. Walking away wasn't an option. Sanctuary would rape her mind and leave it an empty shell. That incredible mind of hers that rattled along like a machine, ricocheting between logic and emotion. That incredible mind that was a perfect match for his. *That* could never be sacrificed, but would be if he let his vampire rule. He'd never let his vampire rule.

"Slade?" Caleb asked again.

Shit. No doubt, his emotions were spiking hotter than Jane's.

"Just catching my breath."

"Finding a mate does have a way of knocking a man off balance."

"Yes, it does."

The low rumble of agreement from Derek was more pain than sound. Unlike the Johnson men, who'd spent more than two centuries as vampires, never expecting to find a mate, Derek had been born knowing his existed. And he'd had to give her up to keep her alive. Because of Sanctuary.

"So what's our plan?" Caleb asked.

"We need to get Jane back to the lab."

"Why?"

"We need to show her Joseph."

Caleb's head whipped around. "She can't be trusted."

"Yes, she can."

"What makes you so sure?"

Slade stroked a hand down Jane's head, preserving her peace. He'd learned a lot about Jane the last few months. "She spent her whole life trying to find a cure for world hunger. The minute she sees Joseph, it's going to be every aspiration she's ever had, every bit of determination she's ever experienced, brought to one pinpoint of need."

"For a vampire baby?"

Slade understood the scoff in Caleb's tone. Bending, he slid his lips over the top of Jane's head, skimming the ridge of her part for a heartbeat, feeling the heat of her skin in a subtle caress across his lips. "Jane won't see a vampire baby. She'll just see Joseph."

"What the hell makes you so sure?"

"We've been talking for months."

Caleb cursed. Derek growled. "And you didn't tell us? That's a breach of security."

It had been risky, but his time with Jane had been . . . unique. "Considering I *am* security, we'll probably survive."

"You should have brought her in earlier."

Probably. But he'd delayed, allowing himself to toy with the possibilities. "She's here now."

Another curse. "Before you follow your instincts, keep in mind that she's been working for a Sanctuary corporation."

Slade met his brother's gaze in the mirror. "She doesn't even know what Sanctuary is."

"That's an assumption on your part."

"No assumption."

"You've been in her mind?"

"Deep enough to know that."

"Deep enough isn't good enough for me."

"Adjust."

Derek shifted in the front passenger seat. Leather creaked as he turned. "If you're thinking on getting nasty with the woman, Caleb, the McClarens will offer her sanctuary."

Caleb cut him a glare. The McClarens wolf pack and the Johnsons were allied, lived in the same compound. Derek offering sanctuary was the equivalent of the Johnsons offering sanctuary. Which effectively tied Caleb's overly protective instincts.

"Since when?"

"Since she parked her ass on that box and drew down on whatever was coming to protect your little brother."

"Hell." Caleb smacked the wheel at the reminder. "Sometimes, Derek, you make me regret saving your ass."

"The feeling is mutual."

Derek and Caleb had been friends since Caleb had saved Derek's life early on in his vampire days, back when the Johnsons hadn't known that vampires and werewolves were supposed to be enemies. Not that Caleb would have cared even if he had known. The Johnsons weren't the conforming sort. Never had been. Likely never would be. That friendship had evolved into an alliance that was forged in steel. The Johnsons and the McClarens had each other's backs. Even if they didn't always agree.

"I appreciate the offer, Derek." Leaning back against the headrest, Slade closed his eyes. He was aching and tired. The last twenty-four hours had been a bitch.

"Anytime. So, what's the plan when she wakes up?" Derek asked, the lazy humor in his voice indicating that he was pretty sure Slade had one. "You going to hog-tie her to the crib, or keep a gun pointed at her?"

"Neither." He pulled her up against him, brushing the hair off her cheek, shifting her hand out from between them when she frowned in discomfort. "I figured I'd appeal to her sense of injustice."

"Does she have one?"

More than she should. "Oh, yeah."

"So you're telling me she has a hero complex?" Caleb asked.

"No." He watched the scenery pass. "What I'm telling you is that I think she's an empath who's driven to make sure she never feels those feelings again."

Derek cast him another look over his shoulder, taking his attention away from the outside. "So you're thinking of mating to a woman who doesn't want to feel emotion. Nice."

It probably would be merely "nice" if she succeeded, but Jane was nothing but logic and emotion, the two uncomfortably coexisting. And he wanted both. He wanted that calculating mind and that passionate heart. In order to get through her defenses, Slade would have to be honest with her, and all he had to give her right now was lies.

"I didn't say a thing about mating."

Derek snorted. "I find it amusing that you Johnsons always start a relationship thinking there's a choice."

"There's always a choice."

"Then how come you didn't give her one?"

"She doesn't know what she's facing."

"Did you tell her?"

"Yes."

"And yet you still forced her to come along against her wishes."

"Shut up, Derek."

Derek chuckled. "It should be interesting when she wakes up."

No. It was going to be straightforward and as uncomplicated as he could make it. "Not if you follow orders."

Caleb arched a brow as he looked at Slade in the rearview mirror. "You're giving orders now?"

"I always give orders. You just hear them as suggestions. Makes you more pliable."

"Uh-huh. Well you might take a minute to figure out how you're going to *suggest* to Allie that she go along with kidnapping a woman."

"Allie won't care if it means Joseph's life."

"Have you met my wife?"

"Many times."

"And you still believe she has a selfish bone in her body?"

"She loves her son."

"Yes, but she won't go along with this."

"She will."

A mother's love was predictable. Reliable.

Caleb snorted again. "Uh-huh."

"**I** am not participating in kidnapping the woman who might save my child's life." Standing on the wide, covered porch of her house, hands on hips, Allie tossed her head, causing the soft brown fall of her shoulder-length hair to swing about her expressive face.

"Allie, be reasonable," Caleb cajoled. "We need her."

"I am being reasonable. You're being reactionary." Allie shook her head. "Kidnapping a woman. Caleb, what were you thinking?"

"Hell, what makes you think it was my idea?"

Allie searched his gaze before turning slowly toward Slade, shaking her head. "I thought you were the reasonable one of the brothers."

"I'm always reasonable."

Just not always as balanced as people believed. But that was his secret.

Slade looked toward the small cabin to the right of the main house where Jane slept in the big brass bed. Even separated by walls and a hundred yards he was drawn by that inner hum of rightness to touch her energy, to feel it close around him. He succumbed to the temptation, reaching out with his mind. Her energy was soft now, peaceful, free of the stress and worries that haunted her mind. At least he'd been able to give her that.

"Not everyone is as open-minded as you," Slade said. "And Joseph needs her."

Allie turned in Caleb's embrace and leaned back against his hard chest. The way his brother loomed behind her, his muscle backing her stance wasn't an illusion. Caleb would always have Allie's back. From the day he'd met her, she'd been his focus. At first, he'd thought to hold himself back from her, knowing there was no future for her without conversion, but Slade and his brothers had taken the decision from his hands the night Caleb had almost been killed by a rogue D'Nally were. Allie was their brother's anchor to this world, and they'd used her to keep him here. He'd just barely worked up to forgiving them.

Allie cocked her head to the side, studying Slade with those big blue eyes. She was such a strange mix of optimism, determination, and new age openness that he could never tell what she was thinking. "Jane is a scientist. Which means she deals in hard facts and proof and only finds questions interesting as long as they remain unanswered. Why don't you appeal to that?"

"Because I ran out of time."

"Another man?"

Allie had always been astute, and today was no different. She'd felt his interest.

"Lots of them."

She let out a huff of air. Caleb stepped in and let him off the hook.

"We're not sure how innocent she is. She worked for a Sanctuary company."

Allie brushed that aside with a wave of a hand. "If there was a taint of Sanctuary about her, she wouldn't be here, but that doesn't absolve you." Pointing her finger at Slade, she said, "You promised me you'd find a cure for Joseph and I'm holding you to it. But not at her expense. We're not Sanctuary. You need to get her cooperation the right way."

"I'll get it."

"Without lies."

"I can't promise that."

"You have to."

He settled his hat over his brow. "No, I don't."

Joseph was his nephew and he'd fight with everything he had, but unlike Allie, he didn't have a qualm about kidnapping a scientist who might have the answer Joseph needed. He'd never been that good-natured.

"But speaking of the devil, where is my nephew?"

"He's sleeping."

"He go down late?"

"No."

It was four a.m. Joseph usually went down at one a.m. and got up at two thirty a.m. Three hours was a long time for Joseph to nap. His constant need for food functioned better than any alarm clock. "Did he seem lethargic when you put him down?"

Worry flashed across Allie's expression. "No. Why?"

Slade hated being the one to add to her worry. "It's a long time for him to be without food."

Panic flared across Allie's expressive face, draining what little color exhaustion had left in her cheeks. "I was just happy he was resting."

The worry immediately echoed in Caleb's energy, the way it would with any mated pair. What one felt, the other did, too. Only in Caleb's case the pain of worry was amplified by the agony of his guilt. Caleb blamed himself for his son's illness. It didn't matter what Slade said to the contrary. Caleb was stuck on the fact that Allie had not been fully converted when Joseph had been conceived. Never mind the suspicion that he never would have been conceived if those unique circumstances hadn't existed. Caleb knew what he knew. "I'm sure he's fine, Allie girl."

Slade closed his eyes and touched his energy to Joseph's, something he could do only when close, and only because he'd taken his blood. "He's fine."

Allie's soft mouth twisted with the truth she couldn't change. "All things considered, right?"

A straight "yes" would have been cruel. "Don't worry, Allie. I promised you I'd fix this, and I will."

Even if it killed him. He ran his fingers through his hair. He just wished he had a clue where to start. He checked Jane's energy again, finding a curious blankness instead of the warmth he sought. The light in the cabin came on. The door opened. Jane stumbled through the opening, fingers rubbing at her forehead.

"Thought you said you put her out." Suspicion edged Caleb's tone.

"I did." And she should still be out. Jane groggily walked to the edge of the porch, gripping the rail, bare feet planted firmly in a pool of moonlight. Light from the interior shone through her borrowed, rumpled nightgown, highlighting the full curves of her hips to all who glanced her way. And more than a couple weres were glancing at the sensual image. Including Derek, who joined them on the porch just in time to enjoy the view. A growl built in Slade's chest.

"I think you underestimated the little lady."

Slade didn't like the speculation in the other man's voice. Jane was his. "Not in any way that counts."

Derek shifted his rifle on his shoulder, blond hair gleaming in the pale light, teeth flashing in a quick grin as he stepped down the stairs, reminding Slade that the were had always been too handsome. "It looks like she has a few questions she needs answered."

This time Slade's growl was louder. Derek didn't look back. "She's not yours yet, vampire. That means it's a clear shot for every man willing to make a move."

Like hell. With a leap, Slade fell into step beside the big were. "I thought you already found your mate."

There was only the slightest break in Derek's stride. "Maybe I'm tired of waiting for her to see the light."

Or maybe he just wanted to get his goat. Either way, Slade found it didn't matter to his vampire side. He didn't want the good-looking were anywhere around Jane in any kind of mood—good, bad, happy, or sad.

"Bullshit."

Derek shook his head. "Sure enough, it is. I'm just damn sick of hearing my mate scream when she sees me."

"She only did it once."

"Though she doesn't remember her time in their hands, I'm still tied in her mind to the horror Sanctuary put her through."

That had to be hell. Wolves waited a lifetime for a mate, lived to find one. And Derek couldn't get near his. "So let Tobias alter her memory."

Derek's snarl was a feral warning. "No one's raping her mind."

Like they'd raped her body. The latter remained unsaid.

"It's not the same." Slade didn't hold his breath that Derek would listen this time anymore than the last time he'd said that. He was right. Derek spun around, canine's bared, eyes glowing. "Go near her that way and I'll rip your throat out."

Slade kept his voice even and his hands down. One thing he was learning about wolves was that they were damn touchy when it came to their mates. "No one would dare go near her. Not with the guard you put around her."

Derek blinked. The battle fire left his eyes, but the tension remained in his shoulders and his features had yet to return to normal. "That's the plan."

Jane was watching them, her gaze locked on Derek. Slade couldn't tell if she was ready to run or ready to battle, but her weight was on the balls of her feet. She was definitely ready for something. "Do me a favor and don't turn around until you're back to normal."

"This is normal."

"How about human then?"

All Slade needed was for Jane to see Derek half morphed and any negotiations would go out the window.

"Is your mate watching?"

"Like a hawk."

Derek took a breath. "It would serve you right if I showed her a bit of canine."

Slade arched his brow. "Now why would you want to do that?"

"Because it strikes me as damn convenient that you put that fear of wolves in her mind."

"It was a necessary warning at the time."

"That doesn't make it any less convenient, seeing as you're bringing her back to a compound full of wolves."

Had he done it on purpose, knowing that bringing any female to the compound would spark the male wolves' interest? Though the Johnsons were vampires who'd taken up with werewolves after their conversion, common interests, common views, and Jace's alienation of the other vampires nearby had pretty much made it an easy decision. But there were some key differences in the two. "Maybe it doesn't, but it doesn't change the facts."

"And they are?"

"She's under my protection, and we need her cooperation."

"And you're going to get that how?"

Slade smiled reassuringly at Jane over Derek's shoulder, just in case she could see them. "I'm going to charm her."

Derek followed the direction of his gaze. "Good luck with that."

"You think I'm going to need luck?"

Derek's canines were almost retracted. "To hear your brothers tell it, charm is not one of your strong suits."

Maybe not, with most women of his day. He was too blunt, but this was a different century. "Jane's a scientist."

"And you think somehow that makes her less of a woman?"

"No." He was just hoping it would give him an opening to work through before any of the too-handsome, sweet-talking weres made their inevitable bid for her attention. Hell, maybe he *had* given her the fear deliberately. "But we speak the same language."

Derek shook his head. "Hell, I've got to stick around for this courtship."

"What do weres know about courtship? You just jump in and claim."

"Shows what you know. A were woman gives herself totally over to her mate on claiming. It's up to the man to prove himself worthy before the bonding can take place."

That was news to Slade and explained why Derek hadn't just claimed his woman. Well, that and the fact that it was forbidden for a werewolf, especially an Alpha, to marry a vampire. Even one who'd been recently turned to save her life, at that Alpha's direction. "That's still not that modern an approach to relationships."

"Werewolf society is not that modern."

"You might want to start changing that."

And claim your woman.

For the first time Derek didn't come back with an emphatic *no*. Instead he shrugged. "Maybe."

Change for wolves often meant battle. "Hey."

The other man looked back, a question in his slate blue eyes.

"You know the Johnsons will support you. Whatever you decide."

It had always been understood, but for some reason, Slade felt it needed saying this time. Maybe because of the set of Derek's chin, which spoke of trouble coming. Maybe because common sense said the man was hurting.

"Thank you." Nodding toward the porch where Jane stood clutching the post, he said, "I think your woman has frozen to the railing."

"You might be right." Slade opened his senses, feeling Jane's energy pour in as smoothly as silk, a foreign softness that filled a void he'd never known he had. Along with the energy came emotion. She was scared, confused, and she wanted to be held. Not by him, but by a man from her past. Anger surged. It was his right to hold her. His right to soothe her. His arms should be the ones in which she wanted to shelter. Not some male who wasn't here and hadn't ever been there for her. A growl rumbled in his chest. Derek laughed. "Oh yeah, she's going to be charmed."

Slade bared his fangs at Derek. "Don't you have somewhere else to be?"

"As a matter of fact, I do."

From the neutrality of his tone, it wasn't hard to guess what he needed to do. "Mei can still only accept your blood?"

"I don't know."

"How can you not know?"

Derek's grip on the gun tightened to white-knuckled. Much more and the barrel would bend. "Because I'd kill the first man she even approached for food."

It was an extreme reaction from an intense man, but looking toward the porch, imagining any other man touching Jane, Slade could understand it.

"Then maybe you'd better get back and take care of her."

"And maybe you'd better brush up on your charm."

If he didn't want the haunted look in Derek's eyes to take up residence in his own, maybe he'd better. "I'll do that."

"The sight of Slade Johnson putting on the charm might just be worth bringing Mei back from her hidey-hole to see."

Mei's hidey-hole was in town among the humans to whom she no longer belonged. It was the first time Derek had put into words what they'd all thought. Derek was the leader of a powerful pack. He couldn't keep leaving. Mei had no people in this world. The only thing that made sense was to bring Mei here and to hell with all the complications that would bring. Slade settled his hat more firmly on his head as a wind kicked up.

Yup. Change was coming, and it wasn't all going to be good.

❧ 7 ❧

THIS couldn't be good. Jane clung to the railing, battling the fuzzy cloud enveloping her brain. It felt as though she'd taken some sort of drug, but she knew she hadn't. Taking a deep breath, she fought the haze—mentally locating the heavy areas and imagining them lifting away. The next breath went the way of the first. Function without feeling. *Damn it!* She knew the air had to be cold. She could see the fog when she breathed out, but she couldn't feel it. Pressing her fingers against her temple, she rubbed. She needed to concentrate on feeling it. That was all. She just needed to concentrate. Looking out into the night, she could see nothing beyond the porch. Just black. Where the heck was a streetlight when she needed one?

She took another step. The world spun out of focus. Closing her eyes, she leaned against the post. Porch light lingered in a golden haze beyond her lids. She couldn't drive like this, which essentially curtailed her plan to sneak out, hot-wire a car, and escape. Not that she knew how to hot-wire a car, but she knew from the movies the basic process and the rest was purely deductive.

Ice crackled beyond the light. Leaning her cheek against the cool wood of the porch support, Jane squinted into the darkness. A shadow moved, took shape. Broad shouldered, lean hipped, determined. She'd know that stride anywhere. Slade. In the distance, a horse whinnied. Where was she? The man moved with a fluidity that made it seem as though he flowed through space rather than strode. She licked her lips as she watched him, vaguely conscious of renewed sensation, even resenting it as he came into the moonlight. She really wished she could be content to be his prisoner. A man like Slade had a lot to offer a woman who'd been too long without a relationship. Heck, he had a lot to offer any woman. There was sensuality in his features, promise in his movements that said his grace wasn't restricted to walking. No metro-sexual there. Slade was all man.

A second shadow stirred in the darkness, vaguely familiar. Derek? Fear rose, hit an invisible wall, and then . . . disappeared in the resurging haze. She released her breath on a shivery sigh. At least the werewolf was staying back. She wasn't up to handling Slade and the wolf. Slade was wolf enough for her.

"I'm no wolf."

She blinked. There was only one way Slade could know what she was thinking. "You can read minds?"

"Some."

Some. An understatement, she bet. She grabbed the post with both hands, forcing herself to look into his too-knowing gaze. "Well, stay out of mine."

Slade stopped in front of her. "You don't look up to a fight."

"You'd be surprised." She would really like to tear something apart. As soon as she could get her muscles to listen to her mind.

"You also look a little cold."

"Do I?"

His gaze dropped to her chest. Her glance followed his. Her nipples were peaked. He could believe that was from cold. That worked for her. It was better than the truth—that he was a walking fantasy and she couldn't stop thinking how he'd look without that shirt on.

Stop. It's just the hormones talking.

Unfortunately everything feminine in her refused to listen to the warning her mind kept screaming. It kept trying to sidle up to him and make friends. To catch his eye. Damn hormones.

Slade's gaze came back to hers. A slight smile quirked his lips. "Absolutely."

"Well, I'm not."

"Then what are you?"

Confused. She was very confused. If she could just push the haze away, she was pretty sure she could come up with a clear answer to the questions in her mind. She licked her lips. Her tongue stuck to the dry skin. Yuck. "Thirsty. I'm very thirsty."

His head cocked slightly to the side as he studied her.

"What are you? Some kind of warlock?"

He stepped onto the first porch step, bringing him level with her. Taking her hand in his, he placed it on his shoulder. His gaze caught hers. He had such beautiful eyes. Gray with flecks of green and blue that seemed to shimmer. His hand came around her waist, drawing her away from the post. "We've already established what I am."

He made it so easy to lean into him that she was doing it before she even recognized the impulse. A memory nudged the edges of her consciousness. "You're a vampire."

He swung her up in his arms as he climbed the steps, taking her with him back into the house. "You got it in one."

"I always get it in one."

"You don't sound too happy about that."

"It can be a curse."

It was easier for her to let him carry her, easier to rest her cheek against his shoulder and breathe his addictive scent, than to protest.

"How so?"

She yawned. "It scares men off."

He chuckled. "You need to start attracting better quality men."

The haze around her thoughts thickened. "I don't think there's a man for me."

"There's someone for everyone."

He carried her through the house with a familiarity she knew she should object to, she just couldn't remember why. "Why can't I think?"

He opened the door that led back to the bedroom she'd just vacated. "Because I'm stopping you."

"Why?"

"Because it's almost dawn, and I need to sleep."

She frowned, concentrating, knowing there was a connection between dawn and his need to sleep. It came to her as he laid her down on the bed. She couldn't see much of his expression. That hat he wore shadowed his face. She knocked it off as her head hit the pillow. She could see him then, the ruggedly masculine face, the distinct intelligence, the raw sexuality. She touched her fingertips to the sharp plane of his cheekbone. His skin was very warm. Weren't vampires supposed to be cold? She grabbed the thought and held it tightly. *Vampire.* "You're a vampire."

He smiled as he unbuttoned his shirt. "Yes, I am." With a shrug, he sent it to the floor, revealing a broad chest and well-developed pectorals covered with an intriguing mat of hair. She did like men with hair on their chests.

"I'm glad to hear it."

Had she said that out loud?

He kicked off his boots, slid his belt from its strap, and knocked his hat off the bed. "Move over."

In the aftermath of obeying, annoyance set in. Since when did she take orders from any man? Before she could slide back to her spot in the bed, he was there. The mattress dipped beneath his weight. She tumbled into him. His arm came around her waist, encouraging her closer. It was natural to bring her knee up. The denim of his jeans rasped against the soft flesh of her inner thigh. Her cheek nestled into the hollow of his shoulder. As she shifted, he pulled the blankets up over her. His scent came to her stronger, lulling her with the sense of security that always accompanied it. Safe. He made her feel so safe. A vague alarm bell went off. It was such a foreign sensation that she didn't trust it. She shouldn't trust it. She knew that. She just couldn't remember why.

Slade's other hand trailed over her forearm, her shoulder, to cup her head. He pressed gently. The sense of safety mellowed to a sense of rightness that seemed to sink into her soul along with his scent.

"Sleep, sweetness. We'll talk tonight."

Tonight would be too late. She frowned. Why? Why was tonight too late? She tried to push away. At least she thought she'd tried. "I need to think."

"No." His thumb stroked across her cheekbone. "You need to sleep."

And suddenly, the fog that was hazing her consciousness billowed outward like a light-obliterating sail, flowing past her defenses, obscuring all her concerns, leaving her with just that foreign, longed for, utterly compelling sense of . . . right.

THE house was pitch black when Jane awoke. She couldn't tell whether it was night or day, thanks to the heavy drapes on the window. For the moment, she didn't care. She was warm, secure, and the slow, steady sound of Slade's heart beneath her ear, beating in time with her own, created the illusion that she wasn't alone. She'd always hated being alone. And she'd always hated the weakness that made her mind solitude. But alone was better than trapped. Anything was better than trapped.

Dear God, she was in trouble. Even knowing what she knew about Slade, she was hesitant to disturb this moment. The sense of safety was just an illusion created to trap her. Vampire or not, Slade was very good. It hadn't even taken him twenty-four hours to find her one weakness and exploit it. And worse, she'd let him. At the very least, she should have seen it coming. Jane considered that. Thinking back, she tried to pinpoint the exact moment that Slade had taken over her mind. All she could remember was being tired, that feeling of safety, and then everything going dark. The same way it had last night. Apparently, her defenses were weak when she was tired, and he'd taken advantage of that. She didn't know if he could take advantage when she was rested, but she wasn't going to hang around and find out.

Jane eased her head off Slade's chest—his perfectly sculpted, made-to-be-nibbled-and-kissed chest. Slade didn't move. Neither did she, for a second. Hormones could be a pain. *Vampire.* Damn, it felt weird even thinking the word. Couldn't survive sunlight. Some legends said they couldn't stay awake while the sun shone, which, if she extrapolated from Slade's deep sleep, would make now her best time to escape.

Staying under the covers so as not to wake him with a draft, Jane inched across the mattress, creating as few percussions as she could. When she got to the edge, she just let her legs slide off, feeling for the floor with her toes. The floor was cold. She hated cold floors. Just one more reason to hold a grudge against Slade. As if his taking control of her mind wasn't enough.

Tugging her nightgown down from where it gathered around her waist, she stood. The first order of business was to get her clothes. She held the cloth away from her body. It was voluminous, easy to slip over her head. The question of who'd done the slipping on would have to be addressed later. Her cheeks heated as she imagined Slade taking off her bra. Her breasts peaked. Her breaths shortened. *Oh, for Pete's sake!* This was ridiculous. As if she needed more incentive to leave, the unruliness of her hormones made it imperative.

Opening the top drawer of the bureau, she found a pair of sweats. They were too big, but at this point she couldn't be choosy. Slade stirred on the bed. A frown creased his forehead. His palm slid across the mattress. If she didn't do something to soothe that restlessness, she'd never get away.

Carefully tugging the sweatshirt down over her head, Jane debated her options. There was only one. And it was a gamble, but not so big, because if he woke before she'd gotten a good distance away, there'd be no escape. She'd seen enough of his abilities to know that.

Moving quickly, she took the two steps to the bed. The closer she got, the more right it felt. Was he controlling her mind even in sleep? As abhorrent as the thought was, it didn't dilute the pleasure that pulsed up her fingertips as she touched the beard-roughened flesh of his cheek. He was a beautiful man. She drew her fingers back, rubbing her thumb across the tips, holding on to the sensation. Not a man, she corrected herself as the urge to touch him increased. Vampire, not human. Dangerous. Definitely not for her. He stirred again. It was no hardship to cup his cheek gently in her palm and whisper, "I'm right here."

He settled immediately. She left her hand there until his breathing evened out and his heartbeat slowed. And hers, too, she realized. It was absolutely time to go.

Jane stumbled over her shoes at the end of the hall. The minute it took to tie them felt like an eternity. Every two seconds, she felt compelled to look over her shoulder toward the bedroom, worried that Slade would follow, worried he wouldn't. The latter scared the shit out of her. She didn't depend on anyone. Ever.

Straightening, she took a breath and steadied her shaky nerves. She was pretty sure that everyone expected her to sleep as long as Slade did. Since only he interacted with her, it was likely he was the equivalent of her personal bodyguard. Or maybe just guard. Who knew? Certainly not her. As she felt along the wall, her fingers bumped a jut of smooth wood. Further exploration revealed more wood on the other side, rather than glass. A door, and from the chill permeating the wood, one to the outside. Perfect. She felt along the wall on either side of the door frame, searching for evidence of an alarm system. She didn't touch any sensors. That didn't mean they didn't exist, but she didn't have time for further precautions. This was definitely an all-or-nothing moment.

"You should probably know there are two werewolves on the other side of the door, ready to pounce."

"Jesum Crow!" Jane spun around, clutching her chest, peering through the darkness for the source of that feminine voice.

A light turned on. She blinked, momentarily blinded, fumbled for the door handle, and, remembering the werewolves, reconsidered when she found it.

"If you're not quiet, you'll wake Slade, and neither of us wants that."

Blinking, she said, "I certainly don't."

A woman sat on the three-cushion leather couch. She had shoulder-length brown hair with bangs cut in a fringe above tired blue eyes. Jane's first impression was of a rather plain woman, but then the woman smiled and that all changed. Her smile animated her whole face, transforming it into something else. Something compelling, inviting.

"Good, then get away from the door before the McClarens come in to see what's up."

Jane did, but only because she didn't want to be anywhere near anything werewolf. "Do they know you're here?"

"Nope." The grin that accompanied that statement showed no sign of remorse. "They think I'm tucked up in bed with Caleb."

"They can't . . . sense you?"

"Not if I shield."

"Shield. That's a mental thing?"

"Yes."

"You're Caleb's wife."

"I'd better be his wife if I'm supposed to be kept in the bed with him, don't you think?"

"I don't know. I haven't figured out how everything works around here yet."

"I'm willing to bet you don't even know where *here* is."

That was the truth. "But you'd be willing to tell me?"

"For a price."

Of course. "What price is that?"

The smile left Allie's face. "I want you to meet my son."

"Why?"

"Because I don't believe in kidnapping."

Allie wasn't making any sense, and she did look a little pale. There were illnesses that could leave a person disoriented. "Are you all right?"

Allie smiled. "I'm probably not making a lot of sense to you."

"No, you're not."

"Then let's go in the kitchen and have some coffee."

Coffee sounded heavenly. Allie caught the anxious glance Jane threw over her shoulder at the door. "They won't come in. But they'd probably like some coffee when it's made."

"Werewolves drink coffee?"

"A cinnamon bun wouldn't come amiss," drifted through the door.

Allie smiled and shrugged. "Doesn't really go with the image, does it? But truth is, werewolves have voracious appetites and a pretty severe sweet tooth."

"And we're open to bribes," came another voice through the door.

"They know you're here now." And apparently they also had a sense of humor. "Why do they need to be bribed?"

Allie rolled her eyes. "So they don't tell Caleb I'm over here drinking coffee. He thinks it's bad for me."

"Is it?"

Allie opened the freezer door and pulled out a fancy bag. "Who cares? It's good."

She had a point. "Do you have cream?"

"Of course."

Jane's patience lasted as long as it took the other woman to measure out the coffee. "Why do you want me to meet your son?"

There was the barest tremble in Allie's hand as she poured water into the coffeemaker. "Because he's dying."

Jane didn't know what to say to that beyond, "I'm sorry."

Allie looked up, her eyes burned brightly in her pale face. "I don't want you to be sorry. I want you to save him."

The only other time Jane had felt so helpless was when she'd been working in Africa and a mother had laid her starving child in her arms and as the baby drew it's last breath said, "Please." The only English word she'd known. The woman had learned it, Jane later discovered, because she'd hoped it would persuade Jane to help her. In the end, Jane hadn't been able to help. The little girl had died of hunger in a world where so many had an excess of food and riches. "I'm a researcher not a practicing doctor."

Allie pressed the button on the coffeemaker. "Joseph doesn't need a doctor. He needs a scientist."

"I don't understand."

Allie's hands clenched into fists on the counter. "I'm trying to be strong, Jane, to do the right thing, because the last thing I need right now is bad Karma, but please understand it's not easy. And it won't take much for me to side with my husband, so don't interrupt until you hear me out."

"Side with your husband?"

Allie leaned back against the counter. "You're not real good at just hearing someone out, are you?"

Jane shrugged. "Not without details."

"The Johnsons are very loyal to those they love. They're not above bending the law to get what they want for those they love."

"Like kidnapping me?"

Allie nodded, the tension in her expression indicating that she was fighting tears. "I love my son very much, and I want him to live more than anything, but kidnapping you, threatening you . . ." She shook her head. "I can't go along with that and look him in the eye and tell him he needs to be honorable if he gets the chance to grow to manhood. Might doesn't make right."

"I appreciate that." And she did. She could also hear the "but" Allie wasn't saying, because the woman was obviously wrestling with her conscience. She brought it out into the open. "But you're not a saint."

"No." This time, when Allie looked at her, there were tears in her eyes. "I want you to meet my son, and if after that you can walk away, I'll make it happen."

She wasn't good at walking away. "And if I need help?"

"I'll give it to you."

"Even if it means going against Slade?"

It took Allie a long time to find the mugs in the cupboard above her head. "You've got my word."

She pushed the cobalt mugs toward Jane as she pulled a plastic tray toward her. "Could you fill those please?"

"Four?" She filled the cups "You're seriously feeding the werewolves."

"You don't have to make it sound like we're slopping hogs."

"I've never slopped hogs, have you?"

Allie rolled her eyes. "You're not going to be as literal as Slade, are you?"

"Probably." She wasn't the most socially apt. Allie took two of the cups and put them on the tray along with four delicious-looking cinnamon buns. "Are you really giving them that because you think they'll keep quiet?"

"One, I'm not the one giving it to them." She shoved the tray into Jane's hands. "And two, I'm giving it to them because it makes them happy, and since they're willing to give their lives to protect me and mine it seems like the least I can do."

When she put it like that . . . "Oh."

Allie put her hands on Jane's shoulders and turned her toward the door. It was a very familiar gesture from a stranger. Especially to Jane. Her internal flinch must have communicated her discomfort to the other woman. Allie's hands dropped away. "Sorry. Caleb's always warning me, not everyone likes to be touched."

What was she supposed to say to that?

"You don't have to say anything. It was a statement of fact."

Jane turned back. "I didn't say that out loud."

Allie sighed. "But you were projecting, which is as good as."

Jane struggled to keep her shock suppressed and her mind blank. They could all read minds. Assuming Allie was a vampire.

"Yes. I'm a vampire. Caleb converted me."

This was too freaky. "I'm going to give this to the guards."

She couldn't believe she was running away from a vampire woman to give coffee and pastries to werewolf guards because they suddenly seemed the lesser of two evils. "I have got to be losing my mind," she muttered as she got to the door. Solid wood, it was the last barrier between her and her most recent fear. Taking a breath, she balanced the tray and yanked it open, leaving her facing two very handsome men. Obviously twins, with cropped brown hair, brown eyes, big muscles, and sporting wickedly sinful grins.

"I brought your coffee."

The one on the left took the tray from her hands. His fingers brushed hers. "Thank you."

Her response was knee-jerk. When she would have stepped back, the other caught her hand. He was a good bit taller than her. Probably taller than Slade. And definitely more classically handsome. "We won't hurt you."

They just weren't as appealing. She took a step back. "That's good to know."

The one on the left took a sip of his coffee. "We'd feel a lot better if you believed it."

"Why does it matter?"

"We would like to be considered."

"For what?"

"For mating," Allie said, coming up beside her. "Weres are obsessed with it."

The one the right caught her eye and said, "Only when there is an attractive woman around."

Now she knew they were pulling her leg. She looked exactly like what she was: a researcher more concerned with the next discovery than her appearance. She didn't even have lipstick on, for heaven's sake!

"Jane, may I introduce you to Travis and Torque McClaren. Two of Derek's best warriors."

"Which is which?"

The man on the left took her hand and brought it toward his mouth. She tugged but he didn't let go. "I'm Torque."

"What you're going to be is dead if you don't let her go right now."

Slade's threat came from directly over her shoulder. How had he sneaked up on her? Before she could turn her head, his hard arm came around her waist and drew her back against his equally hard chest.

"She doesn't bear your mark."

Slade stepped back into the darkness of the foyer, taking her with him. "She's under my protection."

"She's fair game."

"She's mine."

The last snapped her head back. "Like hell."

The brothers filled the door. "She disputes your claim."

Digging her nails into Slade's forearm, Jane got him to put her down, only to be shoved behind him as Travis said, "The law doesn't see it your way."

Slade cocked his head to the side, challenge radiating off every inch of him. "Do I look overly concerned with the law?"

"Well, if you're going to ignore it . . ."

The weres squared off, teeth bared in a parody of a smile, revealing their sharp canines.

Fear and exasperation warred for dominance inside Jane. Exasperation won, because this was just too ridiculous to be happening. Apparently men were men, whether they were vampire, wolf, or human. She glanced over at Allie. "Is that offer of coffee still open?"

"You bet."

"Let's go."

"Stay where you are, Jane."

Slade seriously expected her to obey an order barked over his shoulder? "Go to hell."

"You tell him, Jane."

Slade snapped, "Stay out of this, Allie."

"You should know better than to give Allie orders, Slade. It just makes her contrary."

Caleb walked out of the kitchen, dressed in a black shirt and a pair of jeans, a cup of coffee in his hand.

Jane glanced at the door. He answered her silent question. "I came in the back way."

Allie took the cup from Caleb's hand as he came up beside her, dwarfing her. "I thought you were sleeping," she said.

"I thought you were going to leave this to me."

"Your way won't work."

"You don't know that."

Allie glanced at the contents of the cup and her expression softened. She took a sip. "Yes, I do."

Slade grunted and frowned. "Some mate you are. Coffee's not good for her."

Tucking her into his side, Caleb placed a kiss on the top of Allie's head. "Leave her be, Slade."

If Jane hadn't seen the expression on Caleb's face, she never would have believed it—vampires could love. Deeply, because clear as day, Caleb loved Allie.

"You won't say that if she gets sick."

Caleb shrugged as Allie leaned against him. "You'll take care of it."

Apparently, Slade was not only sexy, he was a miracle worker.

"Keeping her healthy would be easier if she didn't get sick in the first place."

Allie placed her hand on Caleb's chest, total trust in the gesture. Jane, to her surprise, felt a pang of jealousy. The ease of interaction between the couple was something she'd never seen, but always dreamed of.

"I'll only have a little."

"Why don't you take care of Allie, Slade, and we'll entertain Jane?" Torque offered in a deep drawl that resonated sex appeal. A sexuality to which Jane, being female, was not immune.

Slade whipped about with a snarl that immediately reminded Jane of why she was standing here in too-big clothes, trying to escape.

"The hell you will."

She took a step back, but that wasn't any good, because behind her was Caleb.

Caleb took the cup from Allie and took a sip while she watched, grimacing as he did. "Don't know how you can drink it with all that cream and sugar." He indicated Jane's retreat with a tilt of the cup. "Do you still think she can't be forced?"

Allie nodded and took her coffee back. "If she was the type who could be forced, Sanctuary would already have the information they wanted."

Allie's perception was as scary as Caleb's condescending attitude was annoying.

"Are you reading my mind again?"

"Nope. Just commenting on the obviousness of your nature."

Great. Now she was obvious to the people who had kidnapped her. Slade turned. She ducked under his hand and angled past Caleb. "I need coffee."

Out of the corner of her eye, she caught the edge of the grin Slade flashed the weres. "I'll join you."

That was all she needed, the distraction of *him* while trying to gather her thoughts. "Don't bother."

The door clicked shut behind her.

"It's no trouble. We need to talk anyway."

❄ 8 ❄

"**F**OR somebody who wanted to talk to me, you're not saying much," Jane muttered three hours later as Slade led the way across the lawn between the houses.

"That's because you've dodged every attempt."

"Are you implying that I've been avoiding you?" Amazing how self-righteous she could sound.

"Well you certainly haven't been running in my direction."

"And why should I? You kidnapped me."

"I rescued you first."

"But now you won't let me go home."

"You've got a point there, but I also have a good reason."

A reason they were on the way to see. Jane kept telling herself the child wasn't her problem, but with every step across the hard ground she knew she was only kidding herself. She had a feeling Slade knew it, too. The man seemed to understand her on a level that wasn't comfortable to a woman used to being anonymous. On the other hand, in any other situation, she might have worked up to finding it comfortable. At least with a friend, as she had begun to think of Vamp Man. Which just sent her back into the hopeless spiral of what she really wanted versus what she should want, compared to what she should do.

She clenched her hands into fists in the pockets of her borrowed coat. How the hell had her carefully crafted simple life gotten so complicated? With every step, the too-big sweatpants pulled at her legs in little tugging pleas to go back. She didn't want to do this. Didn't want to face her demons. Especially when they were manifested in the face of an infant.

She stopped.

Slade turned. "What's wrong?"

"I don't think I'm ready for this."

"It's just a baby."

"You know it's not *just* anything, otherwise everyone wouldn't be insisting I meet him."

"Fair enough."

Rocking back on her heels she asked, "How bad is he?"

Slade glanced at her, all pretense gone. She could tell from the expression on his face that the answer he was going to give her was the one she didn't want to hear. She only had time to dig her nails into her palm before he said, "I won't lie to you. He's not good. He has the thin, gaunt look of poor nutrition—"

"But he eats?"

"Goes at the bottle like a wolf at a spring kill."

Yet he didn't gain weight. Excitement nipped at her reluctance, demanding she find out more. Which would be a mistake, because the more she talked about anything related to her research, the more personal the subjects became. The deeper the failures struck.

The front door of the main house opened. Light spilled into the yard in a yellow flare of invitation. Allie stood there, wearing her hope in her eyes. Jane turned on her heel.

"I'm going for a walk."

To his credit, Slade didn't say what he had to be thinking. He didn't call her a coward. He merely looked over his shoulder with that expression on his face that said he was employing telepathy. Even the word freaked her out. Almost as much as the concept intrigued her.

"You're talking to Caleb, aren't you?"

"Yes."

Looking back, she saw Slade's brother come up behind Allie and put his arm around her shoulder. Between Slade's reasoning and Allie's subsequent pleas, Jane hadn't stood a chance not promising to help. Part of her resented the manipulation. The other part was resigned to it. "Have him tell Allie that I keep my promises. I'll be back. It's just that I . . ."

"Need a minute," Slade finished for her. She could have kissed him for understanding.

There was another second of silence, and then Allie lifted her hand and waved.

Jane smiled. "She's a heck of a person, isn't she?"

"Yeah." Slade nodded. "Allie has principles. She believes in the Karmic good and keeping the balance."

"She says she doesn't believe in might makes right."

"Nope. She and Caleb had problems with that when they first got together."

"You're not going to tell me he brought her around?"

He chuckled and fell into step beside her. "No, I'm not going to tell you that."

"You're not going to tell me *she* brought *him* around?" She could see a lot of things, but the hard-eyed Caleb as a pacifist? Not hardly.

"I'm not going to tell you that, either."

Her hands ached. Opening her fingers one by one, she released the tension. "Good, because that would totally blow my first impressions of the man."

"Yeah. Caleb doesn't bend easily."

Whereas Jane's impression of Allie was that she could bend like a willow.

"They're very different, aren't they?"

"In some ways. But in others, the important ones, they're very much alike. They protect each other, take care of each other." His gaze met hers. "They're both good people. And they deserve better than this."

And he wanted to give it to them. It was becoming evident to her that Slade had a highly developed sense of responsibility.

"But this is what they got."

"Yeah. And it's not a mess to make a meal of."

The old-fashioned phrase made her blink. "How old are you?"

"In this century or the last?"

Turning, she braced her feet and squared her shoulders. "Are you trying to shock me?"

"Just trying to ease into the subject."

"Thanks." He didn't say anything more. She stared at his lips, which were just like the man. Always tempting and never delivering. Yanking her gaze from his mouth, she asked, "How did you all come to be vampires?"

"Way back in 1862 Caleb was out riding fence. Someone bushwhacked him, gut shot him, and left him for dead. A pretty little vampire came along. Asked him if he wanted to live. He thought she was an angel and said yes."

"It must have been quite a shock later when he realized she hadn't been an angel."

"You could say that. Tore up the family for quite a while."

"Was he the one who changed you?"

"Yes."

"Did you ask him to?"

He glanced at her. "That's a sore point I'd advise you not to be bringing up too often, if you know what's good for you."

Apparently she had an idea what was good for her because the urge to throw herself into the man's arms and cry "Take me, fool!" just wouldn't go away. For God's sake, she hadn't even known she had a floozy gene and now it wouldn't shut up.

She started walking again toward the row of houses that formed the edge of the compound, frustration fueling her strides. Between the structures corrals perched. Horses occupied most of them. From all indications Slade's home was also a working ranch. Cowboy vampires? The facts kept getting more strange. Slade kept pace easily, and that just annoyed her more. Did he have to match her at everything? "How can I know what's good for me here, where nothing makes sense?"

"By following my lead."

"You're the man who's keeping me hostage."

"I'm the man keeping you safe."

"From Sanctuary." The mythical evil Sanctuary whose society she hadn't yet figured out. It could consist of just the members she'd already met.

His fingers flexed and his mouth set in a straight line. "Yes."

"If you want me to believe you, you might have to be a bit less . . . reserved in your answers."

"Fine. No. We didn't ask to be converted, but it's always been the Johnsons against the world, ever since our folks died, so it was only right that Caleb brought us over rather than going on alone."

She stopped, planted her feet again, and caught his eye. He had the most beautiful eyes, even when they were narrowed with caution. "Just for the record, so there's no misunderstanding, I don't agree with that. I think people should have a choice. If they say no, it should be respected."

"You didn't have to say that."

Even from here, she could feel Slade's energy reaching out to her and that strange sensation in her mind that she was beginning to realize was his mind touching hers. "Yeah. I think I do. And while we're on the subject, I don't like you frolicking in my mind like it's your personal playground."

"I've never done that."

"Yes, you have. You're doing it right now."

"I can't help it if you project."

"Try."

"I am."

She shoved her hands back into her pockets. "Try harder."

"It's not as easy as it sounds. You're very appealing, and for vampires, sharing thoughts with a mate is as natural as breathing."

There was that word again. *Mate.* As if uttering it explained everything, when, in reality, all it did was complicate things. She wasn't a stupid woman. She didn't buy into the whole "I'm safe" image Slade was trying to project. Beneath that calm logic, there was a definite edge to his personality. A danger that appealed in a way she'd long since thought she'd put behind her. "Work on it."

"Done."

They reached the edge of the yard. She stopped and looked back. "Who lives in all these houses?"

"The McClarens."

"These houses are full of werewolves?"

"Yeah."

"And you're the only vampires?"

"We don't seem to fit in with other vampires."

"I don't understand."

"Vampires are made, not born."

She opened her mouth. He cut off the question with a lift of his hand.

"The rarity of Joseph's existence is one of the reasons that Caleb didn't want you here. He's proof to Sanctuary that vampires can be born. And if they find out how he was conceived, there won't be a human woman alive who will be safe."

From what? "How was he conceived?"

"I can't tell you that."

"Is that because of some kidnapper code?"

He cocked his eyebrow at her. "You know, you could just decide this is an extended vacation rather than a kidnapping."

If she were delusional. "A working vacation?"

"Yeah."

"My imagination's not that good."

"I told Allie you'd feel that way."

"Allie's a smart woman."

"Yeah. All my brothers' wives are."

"All? How many wives are there?"

Slade blinked and then the right corner of his mouth kicked up in a smile as he recognized how she'd taken the question. "Only one each. The Johnsons are a loyal lot."

"I'm sure their wives are glad to hear it."

"Wait until you meet Raisa and Miri."

"Who are they?"

"My brothers' wives."

She didn't want to get that cozy with his family. She didn't really want to get that cozy with the whole situation. She heard a whicker in the darkness.

"You raise horses?"

He took her hand and led her to the right. "Yes. Some of our best are in the corral right over here."

So there was. She could make out the bars of a corral and the shape of a wooden bench. She sat on the bench. It felt completely normal when he sat beside her and took her hand. She removed her hand and rubbed it on her thigh.

"You still haven't told me how you came to be living with were-wolves."

He shrugged. "It's more natural."

"That needs an explanation."

"I suppose it does." He ran his hand through his hair, causing some to fall over his forehead. Her fingers tingled to push it back. "We grew up in the eighteen hundreds. Things were different then. Simpler."

She could appreciate the appeal of simpler. Tugging her jacket tighter around her she said, "I'm listening."

"We grew up with rules our pa gave us."

"Which were?"

"You protect what's weaker. You keep your word. You stand by family."

Jane thought for a moment about what she knew of vampires. Of the powers she'd seen them wield. "And wolves live by these rules and vampires don't?"

Slade shrugged. "When a human becomes vampire, it's like being told there's nothing between you and anything you want."

"Absolute power."

"Yeah, and there's nothing that corrupts more absolutely."

"But wolves don't get corrupted?"

"Wolves are born, not made, and they have a highly structured society."

That made sense. "So you're saying all vampires are corrupt beings."

"No. I imagine there are a few good ones somewhere, but around these parts, they either hooked up with Sanctuary or Sanctuary killed them off."

"Sanctuary didn't kill you off."

"Johnsons are tough to kill. Plus, we kept to ourselves."

"You didn't bother anyone?"

Standing, Slade put his foot up on the corral fence. A big roan came over immediately and ducked its head. He scratched it behind the ears. "We did have to kick a bit of Sanctuary butt when Jace and them had a misunderstanding, but after that they pretty much left us alone." Patting the horse's neck, he added, "Of course, back then, they weren't that powerful."

"When did they get powerful?"

"About fifty years back, when they got a new leader. Smart guy. Genius." He cocked a brow at her, a smile tugging at his mouth. "Your sort."

As if Slade were lacking in the brains department.

"And then it all began to change," Slade continued.

"But they still left you alone."

"Yeah. For the last one hundred and fifty years, we've just been concerned with our little nook of the world, pretending to be descendants of ourselves, doing what we do best—raising horses."

"What happened?"

"Allie."

"Allie?"

"The woman may look serene but she's a hell of a catalyst."

"You'll have to explain that."

"Another time."

Silence fell between them. It wasn't uncomfortable. But she had more questions. "So you joined forces with the McClarens because their values matched yours?"

"And because Caleb saved Derek's life back during the time when we were still bumbling along, trying to figure out what being vampire meant. To tell the truth, I think Caleb was just spoiling for a fight and when he came across five vamps on one werewolf, he decided to even up the odds."

"Protecting what's weaker."

Slade chuckled and patted the roan's neck. "Don't say that within earshot of Derek."

The proud were wouldn't appreciate it for sure. "It'll be our little secret."

He smiled and pushed the horse away. "I appreciate that."

"So, how did Allie's arrival change anything?"

"Vince—"

"Vince?"

"He was the head of Sanctuary."

"Was?"

He cast her a wry glance. "If you keep interrupting, I'm never going to get to the end of this tale."

"Sorry. What happened to Vince?"

"He kidnapped Allie."

A three-word sentence that neatly summed up a very messy end, she was sure. Rubbing her temple, she sighed. "I think I'm getting a headache."

It wasn't a lie. The headache that had started when she'd turned away from Allie just kept building.

"You want me to go on?"

"Yes." She needed to know what she was dealing with.

"Allie got pregnant and that opened a whole world of possibilities to the vampires."

"I'm not following you."

"Wolves are unified through their families and traditions. Strike at one of them and there's a world of hurt coming your way.

Vampires are more apt to fight among themselves than get along. Their alliances are short term and they tend to self-destruct. Strike at one of them, there may or may not be a response, and you can never be sure who's working for whom."

"But the wolves' alliances hold up."

"Wolves stick by family. No matter what."

Just like the Johnson brothers. "No wonder you felt comfortable with them."

"Yeah. It was a bit of like gravitating toward like."

"But the vampires want to change the balance of power?"

"Yes. They've got a two-prong attack planned. Creating their own families will cover that annoying loyalty issue, and having control of the life from conception will give them an edge for their genetic experimentation."

She wasn't so sure about that. Nature had a way of throwing curveballs. "To what end?"

"Vince also believed that, if he manipulated the genetics of the families, he could create his super army."

"Good grief, will men never stop trying to rule the world and instead concentrate on saving it?"

"Not likely. Human nature being what it is, there's always going to be someone who wants to take what someone else has. We're a covetous bunch. Technology just makes it easier to be more creative about how you go about it."

"I suppose you're right. It's still depressing, though."

"I'll grant you that."

The pressure built to stabbing pain. She winced and glanced at the main house behind them. It shone like a beacon with every light in the building on.

"You ready to go back?"

She guessed she was. She took the hand he held out and stood. "Yeah."

"Good, because Caleb tells me Allie is about to come out of her skin."

Jane winced. "I didn't mean to be cruel."

He squeezed her hand. A tingle went up her arm. "I know. You've got your demons and Allie has hers."

"Mine are dead." She started walking, heading back the way she'd come. Jane couldn't shake the feeling that she was walking into failure. A glance back over her shoulder revealed Slade, standing where she'd left him, a tough man making tough decisions in tough times. No matter how she felt about those decisions, she had no doubt he was doing what he thought was right. "What?"

"It just matters that you try."

She shook her head. "No. That's not true. You need me to succeed."

She hoped. The formula worked with various rats with specific food intolerances, allowing them to thrive on food they normally couldn't eat. but there was no guarantee it would work with humans. Or vampires. Or a mixture of the two. With a shaking hand she pushed her hair out of her face.

"Hope springs eternal."

"So does failure."

From one blink to the next, Slade was at her side. "Succeed or don't succeed, you've got nothing to fear."

"Because you think I'm your mate?" Fat lot of good that would do her when faced with vampire parents' wrath and grief.

"No." Slade's arm came around her shoulder, pulling her into his side. Turning so his big body protected her from the wind, he tipped her face up. His eyes looked as dark as the night beneath the brim his hat. "Because I've got your back."

Somebody had to, she decided, because she'd obviously lost her mind.

JANE thought she'd prepared herself for the sight of the baby, but when Slade stopped outside the door to an upstairs room, she knew she hadn't. She took a steadying breath.

"He's in there?"

"Yes."

She reached for the doorknob. Slade's hand covered hers. "Just a minute."

"A minute isn't going to change anything."

"I disagree. A minute can make things a lot more bearable."

"What on earth could make a dying baby more bearable?"

"This."

This was his fingers sliding behind her head. His other hand curved around her waist, lifting her body up against his. Chest to chest, hip to hip. Heartbeat to heartbeat. His scent surrounded her. His breath caressed her mouth. His gaze locked to hers.

"You're going to kiss me . . ." The realization came out in a soft sigh.

"Yes."

"Now is not the time for this."

He leaned in. "Now is the perfect time."

Maybe he was right, she thought as she linked her hands behind his neck. At the very least, it delayed the inevitable.

He leaned in. She stretched up. He was definitely right. This was a perfect time for this. She could kiss him now while hope bloomed untainted with defeat and have a memory to savor. The way he fitted his mouth to hers let her know he wasn't an amateur. The way he held her told her that their first kiss mattered to him.

Soft and sweet, it was a wonderful beginning to the building heat. His head tilted, her lips parted. Rather than taking her mouth, he tended the budding passion, easing her into it slowly, as if she were more than a means to an end, creating the illusion that she mattered as a woman. As foolish as that notion was—the man was trying to secure her cooperation—she was holding on to it, because she wanted this memory. This moment. When it all went bad, she wanted to remember this first kiss between them and smile.

Parting her lips, Jane discovered Slade tasted as wonderful as he smelled. Clean, masculine, and wild. When his tongue traced her lips, she responded by parting hers wider, inviting him in, welcoming whatever he wanted to do, unable to conceive of doing less, wanting the wildness that he promised. The passion. The loss of self. He was perfect. So perfect.

Someone cleared their throat. She jumped. Slade pulled her closer, not letting her go, continuing the kiss because he either couldn't stop or didn't want to. She didn't care which, just as long as he didn't take his mouth from hers because nothing would ever be so perfect between them again.

The throat cleared again.

She had to stop. They weren't alone. But still she couldn't bring herself to part from Slade. *How does he do this to me?* Placing her palms on his chest, feeling the pounding of his heart, she pushed.

Slade sighed and rested his forehead against hers. He breathed out. She breathed in, taking him deeper in a silent intimacy. "Because I want to."

She didn't ask if she'd projected or whether he'd stolen the thought. It didn't really matter right now. It was the answer she wanted to hear. And it would always make her smile.

"I hate to interrupt," Caleb said, "but Allie's developing a twitch."

Again, the touch of guilt. And again, Slade was there with comfort, massaging the muscles of her back as if he understood. Jane pretended he did. Because it made her feel better.

Forcing a smile, she stepped past Caleb. "Well, let's not keep her waiting any longer."

The decor of the nursery made entry bittersweet. Walls painted the bright yellow of sunshine rose to mix with the sky blue ceiling peaking through a puffy white haze of clouds. A little soft sculpture of a baby floating on the moon hung just above eye level. Innocence. Hope. All the things a vampire baby would never see. All of what Allie had given up to be with Caleb. Jane hoped the man was worth it.

"Seems kind of silly, huh? Giving a vampire child the impression of sunlight?"

Bringing her gaze down, Jane saw Allie sitting by the window in a rocking chair feeding an infant a bottle. She quickly looked away. "Daylight's part of who you are. Or used to be. But I agree. Children should know where their parents come from."

"That's what Caleb always said."

Jane cut him a glance. Caleb stood halfway in the room, arms folded across his chest, eyes watchful. "You're husband's a smart man."

And a protective one. Goose bumps chased up her arms. Jane had no doubt he'd kill her if he thought she would hurt Allie or his son. The son she could no longer avoid looking at. Even from where she stood, she could see the telltale gauntness of his cheeks as he nursed from the bottle. Other faces flashed before her mind's eye. Darker skinned, but no less desperate. Children who needed her. Children she'd promised to help.

Breathe, sweetness.

Slade. In her head again. She wished she knew how to kick him out. She wished she knew how to stop seeing the ghosts of failure.

No chance.

Allie pulled the blanket away from Joseph's face. Jane forced herself to focus on Joseph, who was sucking on the bottle as if he'd been deprived for a week. "When was the last time he fed?"

"About two hours ago."

There was a second bottle sitting by the bed. "He'll eat all that?"

"And then some."

"And he'll be hungry again, when?"

"In about two hours."

It was only routine that made her ask. Slade was not a man to overlook the obvious, and he'd briefed her on the details. "You checked for parasites."

"First thing."

That level of consumption was nowhere near normal. Even for a vampire baby, she suspected. A baby eating like that should have plump cheeks and contented smiles. They shouldn't be wasting away. Jane studied the baby. She could see Johnson influence in his face, but there were also bits of Allie in the shape of his eyes and the fullness of his lips. It did nothing to mitigate the sunken hollows that made him appear a wizened ancient.

"He looks like both of you."

Allie smiled. "I like to think of him as the best of us."

Joseph finished the bottle. Allie put him over her shoulder and patted his back. He let out a belch loud enough to shake the walls.

Everyone smiled except Jane. Excessive gas could be a symptom.

Jane held out her hands. "Can I see him?"

"Of course." Allie pushed to her feet on the next forward rock and placed Joseph on the bed. "He's such a good baby, aren't you, sweetheart?" she crooned as she unwrapped the blanket. The look she shot Jane said more than the croon. Allie wanted Jane to know her son was loved before she unwrapped him. She was afraid of Jane's reaction.

And rightfully so. With every layer of blanket that peeled back, more of the baby's condition was revealed. He was very far gone. So far gone that it was probably only his vampire genetics that kept him alive.

Because Allie was waiting and her anxiety was such that Jane could feel it, she looked past the starvation to the child he should be and said, "He's beautiful."

The lie didn't reduce the impact of the devastation of what starvation had done to his body. Even if he wasn't human, the baby didn't deserve this. Nothing deserved this. But this wasn't a famine caused by politics. This was Mother Nature in a hissy fit, and as a result, Joseph was a pathetic-looking child, with spindly legs and a bloated abdomen. All classic signs of starvation. She'd seen starvation many times before—the distended stomach, the sunken cheeks, the abject misery, but every new confrontation always hit her like a punch in the gut. Too many times, she'd taken the chance, fought the battle, cried by the grave when she'd lost.

His foot twitched in an aborted kick he didn't have the strength to make. "How old is he?"

"Three months."

Three months and he wasn't even the size of a healthy newborn. Touching her finger to Joseph's big toe, Jane asked Slade, "Which tests have you run?"

"Everything I could think of. I've recorded the results."

"What did you find?"

"Nothing of which I can make sense."

"And you think I can?"

"I think what's on those printouts will make a lot of sense to you."

"What makes you think that?"

"Because of what I've seen of your research."

He hadn't seen much. She'd made sure of that, which meant he had to be extrapolating.

"What? Hacking my computers didn't solve all your problems?"

"How long do you intend to hold a grudge about that?"

She tickled the bottom of the boy's foot. No reaction. A newborn should jerk its foot away, indicating normal brain and nerve response.

"You violated my privacy." Her inner space where she never let anyone intrude.

"I tapped into your work file. I didn't rape you."

It had felt like it when she'd first discovered the intrusion. "Plan on forgiveness taking awhile."

"Shit."

Goose bumps raised on the boy's skin. Allie scooped him up, cuddling him against her breast protectively as Caleb came up behind her. His foot hit the rocker, setting it in motion. It rocked on, empty. Lost hope in a room reflecting sunlight. *Oh, damn.*

"Are you going to help?" Allie asked in a whisper laden with tension.

How could she? How could she not? She looked at the rocker. There was something so sad about an empty rocking chair. Rocking chairs were built to be soothing, bonding. She remembered how Allie had looked feeding her child. So happy. So content. For a brief moment while mother and child had rocked together there had been beauty. No despair. Just love. But all too soon the rocking would stop and it would be over.

If someone didn't do something.

Panic gathered in her gut. Sweat broke out on her skin. Slade's arm came around her waist. Strong, supportive. She licked her lip. The rocker tipped one last time before it settled back into stillness. She whispered, "Yes."

✢ 9 ✢

THE woman took risks.

Slade admired the slenderness of Jane's hips and thighs as she walked across the compound toward the lab. He catalogued that unexpected aspect of her personality, surprised at his reaction. And she was loyal. He hadn't expected that kind of loyalty from a woman like her. He'd counted on her fear kicking up her survival instinct when he'd fallen unconscious after getting in the box, had taken comfort in the fact that she'd be miles away before Sanctuary found him. He'd had every intention of finding her again, but had wanted her to be safe. Instead, she'd opted to stay and protect him when she thought danger was coming. Not only did the woman take risks, she also had a foolish courage.

Jane reached the inauspicious front entrance to the lab and turned. "Is this it?"

Her eyes were very blue in the faint glow from the security light, which highlighted the delicacy of her cheekbones beneath the pale beauty of her skin. One blow from a Sanctuary hand and her bones would shatter. One rake from Sanctuary claws and her flesh would be ripped from her bones. But she'd stayed, pitting her small, fragile human body against horrors she couldn't comprehend. To save him. He closed his eyes and took a breath to balance the welling rage. Her scent invaded his senses, settling along his need for her, coating it with determination. He would never let anything happen to her because of him. Never.

"Slade?"

He opened his eyes, knowing they were glowing by the way Jane shrank back against the door. He didn't care. A little fear of vampire power would do her good. "Next time I tell you to run, you do it. No matter what."

The words came out practically a snarl. She pushed off the door, her breasts brushing his chest as she went toe-to-toe with his aggression.

"You do not tell me what to do." A stab of her finger to his chest punctuated the declaration. "And I'll thank you to remember it."

Desire expanded along with the anger, pushing away concern. He took a step forward and pushed her back against the cold metal of the door. "The hell I don't. You're on my land."

"And you're in my space." Her palms flattened on his chest. "Back off."

Holding the door handle, aligning his forearm to the flat surface, he smiled tauntingly, the image of what could have happened to her not leaving his mind. "Make me."

"Do you think I can't?"

The muscles in her thighs tensed deliciously against his. "You're welcome to try."

Leaning in, he bent his knees slightly so his torso fit along the length of hers. Her curves snuggled nicely into the hollows of his body. The puff of air she released in surprise breezed across his throat and shivered down his nerve endings. "But it won't do you much good."

"Want to bet?"

A challenge in the midst of fear. The woman had style. Slade had often wondered about his brothers' fascination with their wives, but experiencing it firsthand with Jane, he didn't know how Caleb had kept his hands off Allie as long as he had, how Jace had endured the loss of Miri, and now he fully understood how Jared's love for Raisa made years of hatred disappear like water under the bridge. There was something purifying about finding one's mate. Something that wiped the slate clean and recentered priorities. An illogical thought for a very logical man. Caressing her cheek with the back of his finger, he murmured. "But in the end, when it comes to things you don't understand, that's how it's going to be."

"Then you'd better get damn good at explanations on the fly."

He couldn't help but laugh. The woman acted as if safe was all she wanted, but when faced with backing down or rising to the challenge, she rose. As did he. As did any Johnson. Which made her about perfect. Except for the fact that she was human and he was vampire and without conversion they had no future, but that critical difference didn't stop Slade from wanting to engage her brain, or her lips. Those soft, supple lips that burned the longing for the forbidden into his soul. He wanted that burn again. Him for her. Her for him. It could never be reality, but in this moment before he lost her to the research waiting beyond that door, he wanted the illusion. He tipped up her chin.

"What are you doing?"

"If you can't tell, I've lost my touch."

She rolled her eyes, provoking a genuine smile. "Now is not the time for kissing."

"Name a better one."

Without hesitation, she snapped, "On my front porch after an intimate dinner in a wonderful restaurant known for its chocolate mousse."

She had him there. "Hell, that would be better."

"So let's get moving."

Slight pressure from his fingertips drew her closer. So close. "Not yet."

With another roll of the eyes she muttered, "A kiss is merely a meeting of mouths. It proves nothing and wastes time."

"There's always time for a kiss."

"Are you back to that mate thing again? An intelligent man like you has to realize that predestined mates doesn't make any sense whatsoever."

"Yup." He pushed a strand of hair away from her eyes, savoring the flex in her energy as his skin grazed hers. She was as aware of him as he was of her. "Makes no sense at all."

"I do not like you like this."

The frown deepened at that. He smoothed his thumb over the pleats between her brows, watching the supple skin relax, hiding the truth in his eyes. He was a sucker for the impossible.

The first subtle tease of her desire slid over his. "Yes, you do."

Pushing against his chest, she grumbled, "Not like this."

The halfhearted protest would have been more believable if she hadn't stopped pushing, hadn't slid her hands over his shoulders, hadn't curved her fingertips in, hadn't pulled that tiniest bit. Hadn't stolen the last of his good intentions. "Oh yeah, especially like this."

"That's contrary . . ."

No, it was a betrayal of what should be, what could be, but it was what he had and he was damn sick of having nothing but lab equipment in his hands. "No, sweetness. It's us."

And it was no good. Even if she was one of those rare humans that could be converted, he wouldn't do that to her. He'd promised.

Slade shook away the thought before dipping his mouth to Jane's, feeling, even before his mouth touched hers, her passion reach out to tempt his, tugging him closer, leading him deeper. It was what it was, and it was too easy to take advantage of the protest that parted her lips, to slip his tongue between, to know his desire blended perfectly with hers. To know that, with the slightest push from his mind, he could have what he wanted. Her compliance. Her obedience. Her. The bite of her nails into the nape of his neck stung in an erotic invitation. Hell, he wasn't a saint. He'd take this.

"Slade."

He accepted with a low growl. She responded with a shivery moan. Sliding his hand around her waist, he pulled her tighter into his embrace. A spike of passion and fear flooded his senses, arcing from her to him in a demand for more. He gave it to her, opening his mind to hers. Her lashes fluttered against his cheek, her muscles tightened. The fear intensified. Too much. It was too much for her. He had to pull back. Away from all that feminine sweetness, from that connection that went so much deeper than the physical.

"You're afraid."

"Not of sex. Sex is easy. It's what comes after that's hard."

"Then don't think of after."

For two heartbeats the tension lingered, but then she relaxed into the kiss, her tongue met his—teased, stroked, encouraged. He growled again when her foot rubbed up his calf. Hell, had he thought that "don't think" or had he projected it? Shit, did he even care?

Cupping the back of her head in his hand, he held her to him, to the power of their attraction. He wouldn't scare her, but he wasn't going to let her run away, either. This was them together. Turbulence. Heat. Uncertainty. It had nothing to do with logic, but it was still good.

Jane's nails dug into his chest, pinpoints of erotic potential. Within her, the tension increased. A thought penetrated the maelstrom of emotion pummeling him.

Can't breathe.

Groaning, he left her mouth. She needed to breathe. He could give her a moment to catch her breath. There were other pleasures he could indulge. Like exploring the smooth hollow beneath her ear. Her scent was stronger there, holding the faintest hint of her favorite perfume, a spicy mix of floral and cinnamon. Inhaling, he touched his tongue to the pulse point, adding her flavor to the mix sinking into his bones with that particular sense of rightness that only came with her. She jumped.

"Easy girl. This is right."

"Let me go," she gasped even as her nails dug into his chest, raking in unconscious eroticism as he took her earlobe between his teeth and bit down gently.

"You don't really want me to."

"That's an incredibly arrogant thing to say."

There was a bit more strength in her voice. She really didn't understand vampires. "I can feel your emotions, sweetness. I know how much you're anticipating my mouth."

She went stiff in his arms and braced against him. "Stop."

He didn't want to stop. Here in the cool embrace of the night, he wanted to move the collar of her shirt out of the way, cut the buttons from her blouse, expose her breasts to his eyes, his mouth.

"I'm warning you, Slade."

Even her human growl struck him as sexy.

"One more inch and you'll never kiss me again."

He stopped immediately, torn between laughter and a groan. He rested his forehead against hers. "Hell, sweetness, it's not fair, pulling out a big-gun threat like that."

"I mean it."

"I can see that." Which was why he'd put a few inches between them, willing his vampire under wraps, trying for something he hadn't had in a long time. A human's concept of limits. "I'm more curious as to why."

"Because, one, I'm not here as some sort of vicarious thrill for the other men to get off on."

He glanced out of the corner of his eye. Shit, there were wolves watching. Not with the vicarious lust she worried about, but with the amusement of a species that regarded the finding of a mate as one of the most perfect moments in a man's life—and they cut him a lot of slack as a result. "And two?"

Not by a flick of a lash did Jane's gaze flinch from his. "I don't like being forced."

"Good, because I don't believe in forcing women."

"Then what do you call what happened between us just now?"

Her lips were rosy from his kiss, her breath still caught, and her pupils still dilated and she had to ask? "Desire."

The second syllable didn't even get past his tongue before she was shaking her head. "I'm not like that."

It didn't matter what had been before. Only what was now. "Maybe not with others."

She blinked at him, her lips pressing to a thin line. The scent of fear tinged the air. Not the arid release of adrenaline but the kind that said it scared her that she felt that way about him. Good. She should be scared. He grabbed the door handle.

He sent a sequence of energy pulses to the lock on the door. The lock gave and the door opened. He caught her when she would have stumbled backward. "What part bothers you more, being out of control, or being out of control with me?"

After a slight pause, she pulled her coat tightly around her and turned, head up, shoulders set, and entered the lab.

"Both."

The wolves laughed. Slade flipped them off before following, a smile tugging his lips. At least she was honest.

HONESTY was about the only thing Slade had to be grateful for in the next hour. Jane in the lab was different from Jane out of the lab. Jane in the lab was confident, particular, one might even say bitchy in her need for order.

She pointed to the left. "That needs to be over there."

There was absolutely no reason for the refrigerator to be anywhere but where it was. But then again, there hadn't been any reason for the ten other things she declared inappropriately placed to be moved, other than that Jane wanted it.

"Why?" He asked the question more to pull her out of her single-minded focus than because of any actual concern. She barely spared him a glance as she turned and studied the lab. No doubt looking for something more to move. "Because it makes more sense."

"Of course."

Jane turned back, narrowing her eyes. "Was that sarcasm?"

Slade bent and unplugged the refrigeration unit. "Nice of you to notice."

Her eyes narrowed further. "That was definitely sarcasm."

The unit wheeled easily across the smooth tile floor. "Might be because I'm irritated."

He had to move the workstation that fit the unit. Metal screeched across tile as he gave it a shove.

"Why?"

The way her arms folded across her chest clearly said she knew why. The refrigeration unit fit neatly in the space. "Because I'm humoring you."

"I told you that I am particular about my lab."

The plug was under the adjoining table. He had to lean way in to get the right angle to insert it. "But this is *my* lab."

He glanced up in time to catch a flicker of something across her expression. A second later emotion brushed his in a silent entreaty. Panic?

She licked her lips. "I can't work in chaos."

He was particular, too, and nothing in his lab was in disarray. "So I gathered."

The agreement didn't relax her any. "I have to have things in order."

That emotion was still tapping at his. He took a step toward her. "I told you, I'd give you anything you wanted."

She nodded. "To save your nephew."

"I don't remember qualifying it."

Her chin snapped up. "I want my freedom."

She was still coming out of her skin. That kiss outside might have been a mistake.

"No."

"See, there are limits."

To how much she could take. He understood that. Another step, and that push-pull of emotion got stronger. She was scared. She wanted comfort but didn't want to expose the vulnerability that made her so nervous. He caught her hand as she stepped back. "No, but maybe I should have added a qualifier or two." A tug and he pulled her away from the stack of sterilized beakers. "Care to share what's got your bloomers in a knot?"

"I just like order."

"I'll take that as a no."

She licked her lips. "I need the lab organized to work."

"I thought that was what we're doing."

He tugged again. The tips of her sneakers bumped the toe of his boots. He slid his hand up her arm. Jane didn't step away, but the expression on her face fluctuated between indignation and longing. Curling his arm around her back, Slade pulled her forward so that she leaned against his chest.

"I'm a perfectly competent adult."

"Uh-huh."

He brushed his lips across the top of her head, noting that while she stood stiffly in his arms, she wasn't pulling away.

"I don't need to be coddled."

"I know that."

"So why are you—"

"Hugging you?"

"Yes."

"Maybe because I need to be coddled?"

Her snort was eloquent. Threading his fingers through the silky strands of her hair, he speculated, "Maybe I'm just making excuses to hold you."

"Why?"

The immediacy of that question struck him as significant. "Because you're the sexiest thing I've ever seen, and you have the most fascinating mind."

"You think I'm sexy?"

Apparently her brilliance was a given, but her sex appeal was up for grabs. "Very sexy."

There was the slightest movement of her head, but then she settled her forehead against him as naturally as breathing. "Are men who think they're vampires hard up?"

Fisting his fingers in her hair, Slade coaxed her face up. "Any man would count his lucky stars to have you in his arms. You know it and I know it, so don't be playing that game with me."

"If this were a game, the rules would be that I am not most men's first choice."

"Well, you can consider yourself on the highly desired list twenty-four/seven from here on out."

Rolling her forehead back and forth, she sighed. "Has anyone ever told you you're crazy?"

"A time or two."

She licked her lips. "Have they ever mentioned you have the patience of a saint?"

With another brush of his lips across her hair, Slade eased Jane away. "Maybe I'm just using you as my guinea pig."

"Good grief, this is you experimenting?"

"Don't sound so appalled."

She took a step back. Too many emotions were coming at him too fast for him to sort them out. He had no trouble reading her anger, however.

"I hate men who are good at everything."

Reaching out, he knocked a beaker off the shelf in feigned clumsiness. It shattered with piercing shrillness.

"There."

Jane looked at him, and then the beaker, and then back to him. "What does that prove?"

He didn't look away. "That I'm not perfect."

Neither did she. "Maybe it could be better if you were."

He didn't have an answer to that.

* * *

"WHERE'D you get this blood?" Jane asked, looking up from the microscope.

Slade stopped searching the filing cabinet to see which slide she was talking about. "It's Joseph's blood."

"The other blood is his parents?"

"His mother and father, just like it's labeled there."

"This isn't like any blood I've ever seen. There are things in there that shouldn't be there."

He sighed and pulled out a folder. "Only if you're running on the assumption that those are human samples."

"This blood is similar to human, but it has some important species-level differences."

He was tempted to flash his fangs. Instead, he smiled a smile that looked as tight as it felt, if her expression was anything to go by. "Yeah."

She grimaced. "Vampires are a legend."

"Most legend is based in fact."

"If this is fact . . ." She held up the slide. "Then this might hold the key to eternal life."

Slade went back to rummaging. "That's what Sanctuary believes"

"But Sanctuary members are vampire."

He shrugged. "Vampires can be killed." Pushing the spare chair away from the second filing cabinet with his foot, he clarified. "They're looking to close that loophole in nature's law."

And God help them all if they succeeded.

"What, *almost* being immortal isn't good enough?"

"Not for Sanctuary. They'd like to improve on vampirism."

"In what way?"

"Well, first off, they'd like to fix it so they can't be killed. Second, they'd like the ability to create life, not just change it."

"So they can have a secret vampire army?"

"Yes, or maybe they just want to touch base with the humanity they left behind. The best of both worlds. I don't know." He pulled another folder out. "Nobody understands Sanctuary."

"Have you tried?"

"You ever tried comprehending what a rabid coyote is going to do?"

"No, but we're talking people, not animals."

"Uh-huh."

"Nobody's all bad."

Slade took Miri's file out of the pile and tossed it to the table in front of Jane. Sometimes convincing was better left to pictures. "That's Miri's medical file. She's my brother Jace's wife."

Pulling it toward her, she asked, "Should you be showing this to me?"

"She wouldn't care." He motioned with his hand. "Go ahead. Read. I'll wait."

It was a very thick file compiled from his images and the ones they'd salvaged from the rubble of the stronghold from which Miri had been rescued. Jane opened it tentatively.

"What you're reading is her account of what happened to her after being kidnapped by Sanctuary. Backed by the best documentation I could provide in the way of forensic evidence."

After she finished reading the entire file, she carefully closed it and pushed it back to him. Her face was pale. "Why?"

"Why did they torture and experiment on her? Because they feel might makes right."

"So do you."

"To a point, yeah." Turning to the photo section, he shoved the file back at her. "But not like that. No one has the right to do that to anyone."

Reflexively, she looked down and touched on one paragraph in particular. Opening her palm over the paper, she stroked it, offering intangible comfort to a woman she'd only read about. "Is she all right now?"

It was the photo and caption describing how Miri had gotten the permanent scar on her face. It took a hell of a lot to scar a wolf permanently. A lot of pain delivered to the point of near death. Pain that had to have been sustained over time as the body was defeated in its effort to heal. His hand closed into a fist. Miri carried the scars on her soul as well. And there were times when even his brother and her daughter couldn't fight the black memories, but those episodes were getting further apart, though he doubted they'd ever totally leave. "Jace is helping her through."

"What happened to her daughter, Faith?"

"Jace brought her home."

After a lot of suffering on everyone's part, but Jace had promised Miri, and a Johnson never broke a promise.

"Where does Jace live?"

"With Miri."

"But not here?

"Nah. Jace went wolf on us."

"Meaning?"

"Jace always leaned toward the wild side, but after he married Miri, it became more evident. He's heading up one of the D'Nally clans now. He fits right in with the wolves."

She glanced at the slides and then the files. "I need to meet him and his family. If his daughter isn't having issues, her blood may hold the answer we need."

"Or maybe theirs?" he asked.

"At this point I'll take everything I can get."

"They'll be coming in tomorrow."

"You'll let me know when they arrive?"

"I don't expect there's any way you'll avoid it. He and Miri will likely come in under heavy guard, and that always kicks up a ruckus."

"Why?"

"Jace's pack is particular as to whom comes near their Alphas. They don't acknowledge the McClarens' claim of family, so, in their eyes, they're in hostile territory."

"Would the McClarens hurt them?"

Stir their irritation a bit. Taunt their overprotective instincts, maybe, but hurt? Slade recalled Ian D'Nally's size, hawkish features, and intense personality that commanded absolute loyalty. Hard to imagine anyone being able to hurt the D'Nally. "No."

She shook her head. "Then why?"

Slade shrugged. "Wolf culture is very insular. The D'Nallys are old school, even for wolves. They view the McClarens as modern."

"They think Derek is modern?"

Slade smiled. "Maybe even downright revolutionary."

"Good God."

"Yeah, it does boggle the mind. What's your family like?"

"Dead."

It was his turn to blink. One word. No emotion. No more explanation. And if he just went by her facial expression, no impact on her emotions, but the energy that flared outward in the split second before she responded contained everything she was suppressing. Grief. Hate. Rage. One hell of a lot of rage. Interesting.

Jane motioned toward the file cabinets. "Are there any other files I should read?"

"Little Penny's, and Faith's."

"Who's Penny?"

"We don't know much about her. She was a victim of a Sanctuary experiment."

Not by a blink of an eyelash did Jane reveal the nausea he could feel rolling through her as she asked, "You said 'little Penny.' Just how old is she?"

That kind of control only came with pain. A lot of it. Slade tossed a file in front of Jane, reaching out mentally to soothe her discomfort.

"Penny is a little over a year now."

Jane skimmed the first page before looking up. "You couldn't fix what they'd done?"

"No." The answer rapped out with all the frustration Slade felt inside.

"Where does that leave her?"

"With the D'Nallys, the McClarens, and the Johnsons standing at her back." And with a very uncertain future. Being neither wolf nor vampire, her altered physiology held untapped secrets many would like to exploit. "We've made no secret of our protection."

"Her family wouldn't?"

Was that a flash of empathy? Slade settled his hip on the side of the desk, tapping her energy as he explained, "In wolf society, children are gifts from God."

She tapped Penny's file. "So how did this gift get misplaced?"

"Wolf culture is also full of myth."

"And?"

"One of those myths is that a child born deformed is more than a genetic anomaly, it's—"

"Bad luck," she finished for him.

"Yes."

"It's a shame that every culture—human, vampire, or wolf—seems to have beliefs in omens and bad luck."

"Yeah."

"So, what myth put Penny in Sanctuary hands?"

That was definitely anger emanating from Jane, but too strong to be impersonal. "Deformed children are almost unheard of among wolves. Without Marc—Penny's real father—knowing anything about it, his wife followed ancient custom and took the child into the woods, leaving her to die."

"What would drive a mother to do such a thing?"

"Fear for her family's reputation. Selfish worry for her status." Slade ran his hand through his hair. "Hell, a thousand things that make no sense to anyone."

"Didn't anyone look for her?"

"When Marc came back from a hunt and went to look for her, he couldn't find her."

"Because Sanctuary had taken her." Jane sighed heavily before asking, "Who found her?"

"Jace did. Many months later. Hooked up to all kinds of devices, undernourished, filthy, and afraid of contact."

Especially mental contact, but Slade didn't reveal that yet.

"And?"

Slade shrugged. "What do you think? Jace brought her home to the Circle J."

"That must have been hard."

"Not for Jace. He made that little girl a promise in that hell hole."

"I meant for Miri, since her baby was still missing."

"It was hell, especially with the little one so changed."

"Changed?"

"The experiments Sanctuary performed changed her from werewolf to something between were and vampire."

Mutant.

The thought projected from Jane to Slade. Hard, angry, protective. None of that showed in her analytical question. "Were you able to undo the damage?"

"No."

"But you tried?"

Six ways to Sunday, but he hadn't been able to alter Penny's chemistry one iota. Not one. "Yes."

Jane's fingers curled over his fist. Her energy smoothed over his with the same comfort.

"At least you tried."

Apparently Jane wasn't the only one who projected. Opening his fist, Slade took her hand in his. Her energy immediately flicked away from his. Had the connection been unconscious? "Eventually I'll succeed."

Withdrawing her hand, Jane asked, "What does being different mean for Penny in regard to her future in the pack?"

"I don't know, but Jace, Marc, and Miri will see to it that she's fine."

"The father is in the picture?"

"Yes."

She drummed her fingertips on the desktop. "And Jace allowed it?"

"Why the hostility? Marc didn't know what his wife was doing."

Anger pulsed off Jane in tempo with her fingers. "How do you know that?"

"Because I know Marc."

"And that was it? They just handed Penny over to the man who lost her in the first place?"

Slade shook his head. "Jace took vengeance in that little girl's name. The war between Sanctuary has definitely kicked up a notch after discovering Penny in that dirt cellar."

Jane drummed her fingers faster on the file and eyed Miri's picture. The anger that had been there before built to rage. "It must have been hard for Miri to give Penny up. It would be like losing her daughter all over again."

"By Wolf law, Miri didn't have to give Penny back."

"But she did?"

"Yes, she did, though it about killed her."

"Then why did she?"

"Because she's Miri, and the pack's female Alpha, and it was best for the pack that Marc recover his daughter."

"I wouldn't have given her back."

Slade's brow arched.

"Would you? He lost her once, with terrible results."

Slade shrugged. "I'm not pack."

"That wasn't an answer."

His gaze met hers. "If you'd wanted her, I would have made sure she stayed yours and to hell with the consequences."

Jane blinked and a bit of that swirling rage faded. "But Jace didn't."

Slade shook his head. "Jace gave Miri exactly what she wanted." A man she could rely on and a man who understood pack.

"But—"

He sighed. "The pack of D'Nallys that Jace heads, the Tragallions, are steeped in tradition and prone to defend their family. Penny was and always will be family."

"Which means?"

"That's the same way Jace thinks, which is why he hasn't transitioned well into modern times."

"Did Marc take Penny away?"

"Hell no. Wolves aren't like that. Children are cherished, in many ways raised by all the pack. Once Jace made the decision to stay Tragallion and take the position of Alpha, Miri didn't have to give up anything."

He pointed to Penny's file. "Are you going to read that?"

"I'm afraid to."

"Still sure no one can be all bad?"

The tips of her fingers vibrated against the folder. "No."

And she hated him for that because she wanted to keep the shield of innocence that said there was a difference between speculating on the existence of evil and it truly existing. He understood that, too.

"I can't believe that all Sanctuary vampires are this sick."

Slade sighed. "Neither could I. I've often wondered if the genetic mutation that takes a man from human to vampire affects certain centers of the mind."

"It didn't affect yours or your brothers."

"Maybe because we're brothers, converted by family?"

"Interesting theory." She tapped the file. "Does conversion affect the women the same as men?"

"There appears to be a gender difference to the way humans react to potential conversion."

Some women went insane. Some died. Some converted. The possible "whys" were multifaceted and intriguing, so he wasn't surprised when Jane's excitement spiked. "Have you done any research?"

Sighing, Slade ran his hand through his hair. "There hasn't been time."

"Because of this war?"

"Yes."

He could literally feel her concentration as her mind raced through the ramifications, feel the excitement surge as she explored the possibilities, feel her energy slow as abstract became reality, feel her fear. Then he felt that indefinable something that removed all emotion from the thought process and left her energy . . . blank.

"Exactly how much danger am I in?"

He wanted to pull her close. Instead, he brushed the back of his finger down her cheek. "A hell of a lot less now."

She flinched away from his touch. "I meant because you have this idea that we're a match."

She'd put that together.

"Don't look so surprised," she said when she saw his reaction. "Putting abstract pieces of a puzzle together is one thing I'm good at, and it only makes sense if two of the Johnson men produced babies in situations where no one else could, that Sanctuary would be especially interested in the women the Johnsons are interested in."

"Your research has already put you in danger."

"But this perceived attraction makes me more of a target."

He owed her the truth. "They're going to be fixated on you now."

Which meant, as long as Sanctuary existed, she was never going to be able to go back to her life. And considering they were immortal, that was a hell of a long time. The realization should have sparked some change in Jane's emotions. Instead, she flipped the files closed and stacked them neatly, as if he hadn't just told her she had no future.

"Then I guess I'd better find a way to make myself unattractive."

"No way to do that."

She looked around the lab, taking in the equipment and supplies. He had a well-stocked laboratory. "I imagine I can be quite toxic when necessary."

Slade's gaze followed hers. Son of a bitch! He grabbed her arm. "You will not experiment on yourself."

An emotion flashed through the blankness. Murderous rage. She didn't like the thought of anyone commanding her. In contrast to the emotion, her voice was soft, almost sweet. "Forbid away if it makes you feel better."

Slade didn't care if she wanted him dead. As long as she was alive, he would deal with it. "I'm serious, Jane."

"So am I."

His rage rose to meet hers. "I mean what I said. I'm not going to let you harm yourself in some mistaken belief that I can't keep you safe."

"I'll keep myself safe."

The hell she would.

She didn't argue, just kept staring at him with that implacable regard that said so much more than words. She didn't trust him.

A knock came at the door. Shit. Slade backed toward it, watching her, his nerves jumping with premonition. A probe of her mind revealed nothing. Son of a bitch! The one person who could lock him out was the one person who never ought to be able to.

He opened the door. Tobias stood on the other side, one of the new guns in his hands. He held it out.

"These have an issue."

As if he needed this now. Looking back at Jane, Slade said, "You need to read Faith's and Penny's files. Like Joseph, they're half vampire. Read all the files. Every word. There might be some help in Penny's if you look at what I did to stabilize her. I used the same technique on Joseph, but without the same success. Faith is healthy. She has no apparent problems."

"All right."

Still sweet as pie. There was nothing to give him pause in the response, but the hairs on the back of his neck stood on end. He wanted nothing more than to walk over there, pull her into his arms, and make love to her until there were no more barriers between them, no more distrust. Instead he turned back to Tobias. "What seems to be off?"

"The beam loses power over distance."

Which meant it lost its ability to kill. "Shit. The refraction must be off."

"Two teams are going out in three days. We could really use these guns."

"I'll have them ready." The tiredness that had been getting stronger for the last year covered Slade in a wave. He pushed it back. Somehow, he'd have them ready.

With a jerk of his chin, Tobias indicated where Jane sat, seemingly absorbed with the files in front of her. "Will she be able to help?"

"I'm hoping so."

"Good. It'd be a shame for Allie and Caleb to lose their little boy."

"I thought you believed four Johnson men were enough."

"With Jace turned wolf, there's hope for the kid."

"Not if Caleb has anything to say about it."

"Hell, Caleb's not far from wolf himself. None of you are."

Slade laughed. "So the McClarens keep saying. Is Jace here?"

"They're on schedule."

"How are they doing?"

"Miri's a little shaken after the last attack. They came right into the compound."

"Sanctuary's getting bolder."

Tobias handed him the gun and smiled coldly. "That's okay. We're getting meaner."

Slade looked at the gun. It was going to take days to fix this. If he put it aside, the wolves would understand, but they were already up against superior numbers. They didn't need to be out-weaponed. Didn't deserve to be. What he needed was more hours in the day. He thought of all the changes in the past year, all the ways he'd come up with to kill the enemy. All the ways the enemy had come up with to kill them. The endless cycle with no end because he couldn't find the edge they needed. But he would. Eventually, he would.

"Yeah. We are."

❧ 10 ❧

CLOSING the door, Slade turned around, the gun in his hand. He looked entirely too natural that way for her peace of mind. Too sexy. He also looked incredibly tired.

"Anything I can help you with," Jane asked, despite her best intentions. She knew how it was to have people relying on you 24/7, to face impossible demands because it meant life or death.

Hefting the gun, he admitted, "I could use a few more hours in the day."

"What? With all your magical powers, you haven't managed that?"

He tossed the gun to his other hand. "I'm working on it."

Damn him for being agreeable. It made it that much harder to hate him. "What's wrong with the guns?"

"One of the refractions is likely off."

"You say that like fixing it is no big deal."

"It'll just take time."

"Time you don't have."

He didn't deny the guess. "I'll find it."

"It can't wait?"

"No."

Paper rustled under her fingers. "Neither can Joseph."

Slade set the gun on one of the long tables. "I know."

Yes, he did. Jane could feel Slade's determination and frustration as though it were her own. It was disconcerting, not only because of the force of the emotion but also because it seemed so natural in its blending with her own. Experimentally, she put her wall around it. There was a start and then a withdrawal. Interesting. She apparently did have some control.

Stacking the files, she pushed her chair back a little harder than she'd planned. She caught the chair with her heel before it rolled past the drawer labeled "Syringes." "I guess you do." Opening the drawer, she said, "I'm going to need a blood sample."

"The one we got from Joseph earlier isn't enough?" He shook his head. "You're worse than a vampire."

"Not from Joseph." She prepared a vacuum tube and needle. "I need your blood."

He flashed his fangs. "I'll be happy to share."

She shook her head and set the tube on the table. "You're going to have to work harder than that to scare me. Give me your arm."

Rolling up his sleeve, Slade took a step closer. "Interesting challenge."

"What makes it so interesting?"

"My options."

Delicious heat poured over her in a wave of energy as she wrapped the tourniquet across the thick bulge of his biceps. "I wasn't aware you had any."

He picked up the tube and handed it to her. His fingers lingered against hers as she took it. The touch was light. There was no reason for her breath to catch, or her pulse to pick up speed, but it did.

"At least two."

Popping the cap off the needle, she asked, "Do I want to know?"

"I don't know. How fond are you of surprises?"

"I know I don't like bad ones." Especially after the last twenty-four hours.

His head canted slightly to the side as she slid the needle into the vein at the front of his elbow. "What about good ones?"

Blood filled the vacuum tube, warming it, giving the impression, for an instant, that she held his life in her hands. Not a responsibility she wanted.

"I don't know. I've never had a good one."

"Really?"

Glancing up, she was in time to catch the speculation in his eyes. "Don't go getting ideas."

Those fingers on her hand drifted over her wrist, sneaked under the sleeve of her shirt. "Too late."

The tube was full. She swapped it for another. Her fingers trembled, every part of her focused on the shiver of sensations radiating up from her arm. Who knew a forearm could become such a sexual focal point?

"Don't you want to know what kind of ideas I'm getting?"

She gave him the truth. "No."

"Why not?"

"I think we've pretty much established that you're out of my league."

The second tube filled. "Who established that?"

Glancing up, she smiled. "My last date was a shy accountant who spilled his wine when I asked him up to my place." Brent was a very nice man, but the night and the relationship had gone nowhere after that. "Trust me, you're out of my league."

As soon as she removed the needle, he brought his arm to his mouth, leaving her with the gauze and tape in her hand, staring as his tongue stroked efficiently over the puncture site.

"That takes care of the bleeding?"

"There's a healing agent in our saliva."

"Oh." She put the gauze on the counter. He took the tubes from her hand. "Be careful with those."

He put them in the rack. "I will be."

"We need to get them sampled."

"What are we looking for?"

"A control sample."

"You think my blood will be close enough to my brother's to provide a control?"

"You know it is. Sibling similarity, converted by a sibling. The similarities are going to be more than the differences, but yours is untainted by any potential changes this . . . mating might bring about."

"Maybe." He stopped her when she reached for the tubes of blood. He stepped in front of her. "In a minute."

"We don't have minutes."

The table creaked as he leaned against it. The chair wheels caught on the toe of his boot, stopping her retreat. He was too close, too big, too male. If Jane could have gotten out of the chair without looking a total coward, she would have.

"I don't like you being afraid of me."

She didn't like the way he said that, his drawl trailing off into speculation. No good could come of him looking deeper into her feelings. Especially when she didn't understand them herself.

"I'm not."

She pushed on his thigh. The movement she meant to be sharp slowed as her palm conformed to the hard muscle. For some reason, she'd expected a bit of give, but there was none. The muscle clenched, her fingers curved. Energy arced between them in a tangible bolt, racing up her arm. This close, it was impossible to miss his arousal. She licked her lips, the sight not as shocking as it should be.

Slade's finger came under her chin, tipping her face up to his. His expression was considering, his eyes watchful. The stroke of his thumb over her bottom lip sent a shiver to her toes. "No, you're not."

She needed to reestablish herself or the man would run roughshod over her. "I believe that's what I said. Now, I need you to bite me."

Not a blink or a twitch of muscle betrayed his shock, but she felt it. Almost as if it were her own. Apparently she wasn't the only one who projected.

"Why?"

As if his thigh wasn't the biggest temptation she'd faced in an age, she reached over and opened the drawer on the other side. Paper rustled as she pulled out another vacuum tube. "Because I need a before and after comparison to see how a normal vampire's blood absorbs the intake of human blood."

"I have slides you can look at."

"How old are the slides?"

"Five or six years."

That would never do. "There might have been changes. We can't risk that."

"I can't bite you."

She arced her brow at him. "Afraid of losing control?"

"Yes."

Good grief, he wasn't bluffing. A little of the fear she said she didn't have came calling. This man, out of control, would be very scary.

"I'll make a point to remind you when you've have enough."

"How will you know?"

"I'll make an educated guess."

It was his turn to cock an eyebrow at her. "You don't really believe in vampires, do you?"

"It's a stretch."

"Do you believe in life on other planets?"

"It would be illogical not to."

He took the tube from her hand and put it on the table beside him, then pulled her to her feet.

"What's the difference?"

"I can't get around the fact that, if vampires were real and they live forever, there'd be so many around by now we couldn't help but trip over them. Especially as each has the ability to create countless more."

"Ah, but there's the hitch in your get along."

"Excuse me."

His fingers drifted up her arm, grazed her shoulder, skimming the goose bumps that anticipation sent racing ahead. "Not everybody can be converted. It's actually a very small percentage of the population that has that possibility."

"What happens to the ones who fall outside that percentage?"

A tug and her braid came over her shoulder and slid down over her breast. The goose bumps spread along with the anticipation. Her breath caught in her throat as his fingers followed its slide forward, grazing the top of her breast. Her lip slid between her teeth. Excitement hummed along beside arousal. He wouldn't, would he? He didn't. His knuckles stopped mid-curve, his gaze holding hers, while her breasts swelled and ached. She couldn't catch a thought. A breath.

"Their blood turns to acid in their veins. They die an extremely painful death. Scalded from the inside out."

Strange lights seemed to glow in his eyes. His hand didn't move.

Two heartbeats passed before she could find a response.

"Wonderful." It still didn't explain the small numbers. "Even an incremental increase would aggregate over time."

"Ah, but you're not allowing for human nature." His hand opened, cupped. "You change someone, give them absolute power, and they tend to want to test the limits of that power."

"You mean they kill each other in pursuit of control."

"Not much else to do but fight when you live forever."

She so wanted to lean into his hand, into the pleasure that had her nipples burning and her knees weakening. "You could cure world hunger."

"Ah, but the vampires aren't the ones going hungry."

"Good point." She looked around the lab. "You and your brothers seem to have done well."

He shrugged. "If trouble didn't come calling, we didn't feel the need to court it."

It was always "we" with him, as if his brothers and he were one unit. "You and your brothers are close."

"Close enough that it won't do you any good running to them for help."

It wasn't help she wanted now. "Uh-huh."

That hand inched lower until he palmed her nipple, shifted until the hard nub was centered, and then pressed. She grabbed the edge of the desk. He smiled. "You think they'd side with you against me?"

"I think they'd do what was right."

Another start. Did he think she hadn't figured that much out? What she needed was something to pull her away from the maelstrom of lust threatening to pull her under. She wanted to melt to the floor, entice him with a spread of her legs. She wanted to invite him into her body, her life. Dear God, she wanted him. Shaking her head, Jane pushed back her chair. It took effort to get air into her lungs. Once there, she held it until the need for air replaced the craving for his touch. "Can you take blood without converting someone?"

"Yes. It's a matter of how much."

She shrugged out of her coat. She needed to get this over with. "Then do it."

His eyes narrowed. "That's not going to happen."

"Why not? I assume you need to eat."

"Every couple months I go out for a bite."

The man was impossible.

"Well, consider this feeding time."

"This is different."

"Why?"

"Because you're my mate."

"You really have to let that go."

His gaze dropped to her breasts. "It's not something that can be wished away any easier than mating lust can be ignored."

"Do you have to make everything sound like something out of a bad movie?"

"You stop making cute faces when I do, and I might consider it."

"I am not cute."

Slade shook his head. That's where she was wrong. She was cute, sexy, and highly intelligent, and if she kept looking at him that way, things were going to get out of hand fast, despite his resolve. He'd touched her to remind her of their connection. To remind himself of his promise not to convert her. To give himself strength. "I guess it's all in the perspective."

"Well, from my perspective, we don't have any choice but to do this now. Not if you want Joseph to live."

Shit, she had him there, but it still didn't sit right, her looking at him with such trust, and him knowing there was a real limit to how much trust she should be putting in him. "There's a good chance I could lose my head and take you with me."

"Where?"

"To the floor."

Feminine desire perfumed the air. She wasn't as adverse to the idea as her expression would indicate. "I think you've got more control than that."

He curled his hands into fists. "You'd be wrong."

"I don't think so, which means you, Vamp Man"—she rolled up her sleeve—"will just have to suck it up, in more ways than one."

When she extended her hand, he took it, cradling it on his palm, tucking his thumb into the softness of hers. Her skin was very fine, very white. The tracery of veins beneath pulsed with the beauty of her life. His mate. His to take. To bind. To do with as he would. Slade shook his head. Jane was right. That did sound wrong. It implied a lack of choice. And he would never take her choice away from her. A man didn't do that to a woman he cared about. His vampire side hissed in displeasure. He smiled at Jane. His vampire could go to hell. "I guess I will."

Even if it killed him.

His expression must not have been as bland as he'd been aiming for. Concern flashed through Jane's eyes as she said, "You're not really in danger of losing control, are you?"

It was little late to be asking that question, in his opinion, seeing as he was already halfway to lost with her hand in his, her pulse under his thumb, her wrist exposed in a submissive gesture that stoked his passion.

"That kiss by the door didn't teach you anything? Or outside Joseph's door?"

"Those kisses were an aberration. They caught me by surprise. I was stressed. That led to moments of . . . weakness."

"And you think, if I kissed you right now, that same thing wouldn't happen again?"

The harsh fluorescent light glinted off the amber highlights in her hair as she shook her head. "Absolutely not."

"Absolutely?"

"Yes. You have too much sense for that."

"And you think passion has to make sense?"

"Everything makes sense if you put it in context."

"And my taking your blood will be defined how?"

"As a means to an end."

She was a lousy liar. Slade tightened his grip on her wrist. "I think it's more than that. I think this is a test."

"Of what?"

"Of how long my honor can hold out against temptation."

"Seriously, I'm not that tempting. I think you can handle it."

He wasn't so sure. Just the thought had him throbbing and hard. "I guess we'll have to see. Just as soon as I get this control sample."

Slade picked up the syringe. A muscle twitched in Jane's cheek. She wasn't as calm as she wanted him to believe. He ought to be able to feel that in her energy, but all he could feel was the simmer of her desire and then . . . nothing. Had she learned to block him?

One look at her face gave him his answer. Her lips were pressed tight with thoughts he couldn't hear. Yet. The stroke of his thumb across her lips echoed in the stutter of her pulse. Holding her gaze, he stroked his calm over the edges of her mind, as he slid the needle into the vein. When he had enough for her to check the sample for changes that might occur post bite, he released her mind, pressing cotton to her vein, while his tongue ached with the need to stroke over her flesh, absorb the taste of the sweet blood he could smell. Addictive. She'd be addictive.

Quelling his vampire, Slade quickly handed Jane the vial and tossed the needle in the sharp tray.

"That part's done."

After a blink, Jane's free hand went to her neck. "Wonderful. Can't wait for the next."

Slade shook his head. "I don't have to take the blood from your throat." But he wanted to. Wanted to be steeped in her scent, steeped in her presence as he took the essence of who she was and made it part of him. "I can take it from your wrist."

It sounded a bit clinical, in the face of the emotion pulsing between them. "I can make sure you don't feel a thing."

Jane was shaking her head before he finished the thought. "I don't want to miss anything."

"Cause you know it's going to be hot, right?"

She blinked. "Because if you really are a vampire, it'll be important I get the details right."

"You still doubt?"

A shrug and then with the efficiency with which she did most things, she shoved her other sleeve up above her elbow, presenting him with a matched set. "How much blood do you need to take for it to impact yours?"

Arousal rose hot and hard at the overt submission. Arm, neck, it didn't matter. She was volunteering her blood to him. His vampire howled in delight. His fangs ached to pierce that white skin. Mate. Wife. His.

"Not two arms' worth."

"Oh."

She debated before thrusting the one without the bandage at him. He brought her palm to his mouth. She gasped. He touched his tongue to her skin. It took a second for what he'd done to sink through her fear. She gasped again.

"This isn't going to hurt, sweetness."

"You're going to bite me, how could it not hurt?"

"There are numbing agents in my saliva." He kissed her palm. "I promise you, only pleasure."

Her fingers naturally curled against his cheek. He set his teeth to the base of her thumb and nipped. She squealed. She was more than a little nervous. He smiled and did it again, just to get her used to the idea. Her thumb rapped his cheek. He looked up.

"Just do it."

"There's foreplay to blood taking, just like there is to love-making."

"I'm not interested in being seduced."

"Now, that is a pity."

Tension entered her muscles. "This is an experiment, Slade. Not the start of a wild weekend."

But it was the start of their relationship. It didn't matter what precipitated the act. The reality was, this was their first bonding. From here on out, a part of her would live in him. A very special first that would open her mind to his if he knocked, lock her emotions to his if he queried. After this, he would be able to find her no matter where she went, probe her mind no matter how much she tried to lock him out. She had a right to know that. He was a bastard for not telling her. "It's a start, make no mistake."

"Just do it."

Holding her gaze, he bent his head, enthralling her, catching her mind, holding it tightly, pulling her thoughts to his. Elation built within him. Vampire lust, primitive and strong, rose right along with the joy. He quickly harnessed it. He wasn't going to convert her. He was just going to torment himself with a taste of her. Not enough to satisfy. Just enough to let him know what he was missing. He had to be insane.

Her pupils dilated. Her nostril flared.

Easy now. This is a taste, not a conversion. Hell, he didn't even know if she could be converted. His brothers had converted their wives out of necessity, life-or-death situations when the decisions were made. This was a choice, not an emergency. Tightening his hold on Jane's mind, Slade slid beneath her fear and untangled the threads of tension, replacing them with calm. His fangs ached and stretched. His mouth watered. Maybe his vampire wasn't as far away from his human side as he'd thought, because nothing inside him was horrified by this. Vampire and human alike wanted to posses her completely, wholly. He placed his fangs at the pulse point of her wrist. Echoes of her heartbeat vibrated along his nerve endings, strumming against the rhythm of his, accelerating it until it matched hers.

"Are you sure?" he asked her, one last time. "Nothing will be the same for you after this."

"Will I be vampire?"

Not if he held on to his control, kept a barrier between their thoughts. "No."

The pink of her tongue slid over the richer pink of her lips. "Then we'll deal with the fallout later."

Moisture glistened on the plump surface of her lips. Damn, was she trying to kill him? "Take a breath and relax for me, then."

If he was truly kind he would tell her to close her eyes, but he didn't want her to close her eyes. He wanted her to see him taking her this way, the same way he was going to want her to see him claiming her the first time they became lovers. He wanted her to know who gave her the pleasure so she'd know to whom she belonged. No doubt she'd call him a chauvinist for the impulse. No doubt she'd be right. He stroked his tongue over her skin. He wasn't born in her time, raised with her values. When he peeled off everything he'd learned over the centuries, he was still who he was. A nineteenth-century man who believed his woman was to be cherished, protected. Owned. He bit down. Hot, sweet spice poured into his mouth. Elation leapt to euphoria. He was helpless to contain it. Inside, his vampire cried *more*. And more came at him—her senses, her emotions, her thoughts. She wanted to be horrified, but a part of her sensed the rightness of this sharing between them. And that did horrify her. Slade could have told her nothing was ever easy, especially this. That it was inevitable and beautiful in its own way. If one had centuries to adjust to the idea.

Three swallows, he told himself. He'd allow himself just three. As he took the first, the scent of her arousal rose up to embrace him. Heady. Powerful. And sweet. Everything about her was sweet. On the second swallow, passion weakened her knees. Catching her with a hand behind her back, he coaxed her into his embrace.

Come here, sweetness. Come here.

The compulsion for more was stronger now, too potent to resist. He was surrounded by her scent, imbued with her pleasure until nothing existed but his desire for her, hers for him. It was all around them. The promise of what would be. What should be.

Jane.

Slade.

The whisper of his name slipped into his mind. As sweet as her desire, as potent as her touch. Tendrils of her need wrapped around his, drawing him closer. Elemental. A longing for the physical as well as the emotional. Alone, she'd been alone for so long. She didn't want to be alone anymore. His thoughts twined around hers, holding her tightly, banishing that loneliness. She was ready. He could take her now and all she'd feel was pleasure. And she'd never be alone again. He'd always be with her. He could give her that.

If he took her humanity.

Slade closed his eyes. The third swallow never came. Releasing her wrist, Slade skimmed his fangs across her skin, the sense of loss pushing him harder than logic. A lap of his tongue sealed the wound on her wrist, but nothing could suppress the howl of loss from his vampire. A cry for a mate that would echo in his head far into eternity. Placing his lips on the inside of Jane's arm, holding her close as she shivered in reaction to the caress, Slade whispered the one promise he could make. "You'll never be alone again."

❧ 11 ❧

SHE couldn't be alone.

Slade laid Jane on the bed in their cabin. Her pulse was too fast, her nerves were on fire. Her thoughts were hazed by discomfort and something he couldn't identify. And he didn't have a clue as to what was going on. He'd been very careful to take only a little blood. Nowhere near enough to risk conversion. But from all the signs, Jane was in rejection. Shifting and moaning, she twisted on the sheets, pushing the pillow aside, shoving her hair out of her face with short, jerky, frustrated movements. He pulled the sheet over her shoulder.

"Jane."

"No."

She shoved the sheet down. Slade caught her hands before she could claw at her skin.

"Don't, Jane."

"Itches," she groaned in that same half-conscious tone she'd used since he'd taken her blood.

He pulled the sheet down. A rash was spreading across her body, starting at her wrist and going up her arm, flaring downward from her neck.

Son of a bitch. She was having a reaction to his bite. He shoved her hand down the back waistband of his jeans, trying to keep it out of his way while he checked her back, then grabbed the other one and did the same.

As he lifted her, Jane's breath hissed out between her teeth. He froze. "What?"

"Better."

Better? What the hell could be better about this?

"What's better, sweetness?"

Her palms were inching back and forth on the small of his back.

"My hands. So much better."

Her hands were better. He thought a moment. He was sweating. Could perspiration from his body be soothing whatever was causing the reaction? He'd heard some pretty bizarre conversion stories—good and bad.

Except he hadn't converted Jane.

Caleb's conversion of Allie had been nothing like Jace's of Miri. Of course, Miri had been werewolf and Allie human, but both women had gained strength with the conversion. Raisa had been converted centuries earlier, but had been so sick her whole vampire life that she'd always been on the verge of death, until Jared. His blood had given her strength. Jane might have been right. Maybe there was something about the Johnson blood that made conversions a whole different prospect. And maybe it was that "something" to which Jane was reacting. *Shit*.

Jane twisted on the sheets, her body writhing in a parody of lust. She needed help. All he had to go on was that moment when she'd said "better." Slipping his hand behind her back, he felt the raised bumps of the rash, felt her muscles immediately react as his hands opened—in anticipation of what? More of his touch? Hell, if that's all it took to give her ease, he'd give it. Ignoring her mewl of protest, he eased Jane back before kicking off his right boot. "Hold on a minute, sweetness."

Jane moaned and reached out. It was a beautifully erotic gesture, sensual and vulnerable, but it was the vulnerability that drew him. It was her deep, dark secret, and she'd want to kick his ass for finding it appealing. Shucking his other boot, he shoved down his underpants and jeans in one push. Getting into bed with her, he wrapped them together, skin to skin. She continued to moan, but not as hard. Her hands stroked up and down his arms, her feet up and down his calves, her shoulders rubbed against his chest, her breasts against his forearms. It was heaven and hell.

Slade?

The whisper in his mind was from Caleb. It was immediately followed by softer ones from Jared and Jace. Distance made the latter queries weaker, but no less concerned.

What's wrong?

There was no way to shield his distress from his brothers. The connection that had always been between them had amplified with conversion. They couldn't always communicate mentally, but they could usually sense each other's moods, and distress was one that telegraphed well.

I'm all right.

He didn't know if his brothers got the communication in word or sensation, but he knew they got it. Now to only hope they respected it. They could be a bit overprotective, and they didn't trust the way he was behaving lately. Truth was, neither did he. He wasn't used to anything breaking his concentration, but lately he couldn't find the single-minded focus that was his norm. Work was piling up, his nerves were fraying, and new demands were coming in daily. But he would hold this illusion to preserve Jane's pride. Keeping a restful image in his mind, Slade turned on his side and pulled her tighter against him. She moaned and drew her thigh up his. His cock jerked as his senses opened to her scent, the delicacy of her skin, the proximity of her throat. His fangs stretched and ached. He was only one bite away from the joining he should never have left half done. One bite away from the satisfaction he craved. One bite away from being the monster that would disregard her wishes. Would risk her life for his chance at forever.

Shit! She was only just recovering from the shock of his first bite. Jerking away, Slade thrust his mind into Jane's, giving her one order only. *Sleep.*

Jane went under, and he was out of the bed from one breath to the next. Running his hand through his hair, Slade took a deep breath, quelling the hunger that pushed at his honor. When he thought he had his vampire under control, he bent and kissed her cheek. Immediately his lips burned with want and his senses flared, encompassing all that she was, craving to bind it to him. On a harsh curse, he stepped away, his gaze following the hug of the sheet as it hugged her curves, caressing the tip of her breasts, snuggling into the juncture of her thighs. So womanly. So beautiful. She sighed and turned, as if even in her sleep, she had to diminish her presence. He shook his head. Jane was so much more than she thought. All scientist, but all woman, too. No matter how much she tried to make herself out as cold or lacking in that department. Trailing his finger down a wrinkle in the sheet as it curved over her hip, Slade shook his head. Jane was not a cold woman.

"I hope to hell you appreciate the sacrifice, sweetness."

Not even by a sigh did she acknowledge the comment. She just lay there, trapped in his enthrallment. It would be so easy to catch the edge of the sheet on his finger. So easy to draw it down. So easy to release the desire in her mind. So easy to slip between her thighs. So incredibly easy to take advantage of her.

Another step back. Son of a bitch, since when did a Johnson even toy with the idea of taking advantage of a woman?

Slade?

A need to see him was embedded in Caleb's query.

I'm coming.

As much as he hated to leave Jane, he couldn't be trusted around her. At least he could maintain their mental connection and take the worst of her distress onto himself.

To Caleb he ordered, *Have Derek send someone to watch Jane.*

Done.

Someone good.

Caleb didn't even mentally blink at the insecurity sparking the demand.

Of course.

SLADE had to take the tunnel to the main house. He wished it was night so he could burn off the energy thrumming along his veins. A run through the night air relieved a lot of stress. Opening the door to the kitchen with its blocked off windows, he saw Allie sitting there with little Joseph on her lap. Caleb sat beside her. Across the table sat Tobias, a D'Nally enforcer. All had coffee cups before them. All were watching him with wary, assessing gazes.

Shit again.

The Enforcer's eyes narrowed as soon as he entered the room. The hairs on the back of Slade's neck rose. A fight was good for relieving stress, too.

He nodded to them. "Allie, Caleb." He narrowed his eyes. "Enforcer. What are you doing here?"

"I'm on guard duty."

There was only one reason Tobias would be on guard. "Jace and Miri are here?"

He nodded. "They're upstairs with Faith."

"Guard duty is a little low for you."

"The D'Nallys take the protection of our Alpha and our children seriously."

Slade didn't doubt that, but he was learning there were many levels to everything the Enforcer did. And there was no just being on guard duty for the Enforcer. Enforcers were the special ops of the werewolf world. An Enforcer of Tobias's level had abilities that no one understood. Those abilities came into play only when there was a lot at risk.

"What aren't you telling me?"

Tobias took a sip of his coffee. "Just that you'd better get those guns fixed."

"Trouble coming?" he asked.

"Yes." The wolf's eyes narrowed as he tilted his head back slightly. "You've been with the woman."

It sounded like an accusation.

"I know he has the reputation of being a recluse," Caleb drawled, "but it's not that rare that Slade's with a woman."

"He's been with the scientist. This can't be."

"Why ever not?" Allie snapped.

Tobias's expression didn't change. "She's a distraction."

"No more than I am," Slade replied.

Tobias shook his head. "A lot more, for reasons you don't wish to acknowledge."

Caleb stepped protectively toward Slade. Allie followed suit, countering her husband's warning glare with a "What? He's my brother, too."

Slade didn't want either of them in danger because of him. Caleb had waited a long time for love and peace. Allie gave him both. Tobias's lip quirked in an amused smile that galled.

Slade shifted to the right, drawing the Enforcer's attention. "You don't think we're a match for you?"

The smile didn't fade from the were's mouth, but his eyes took on a cold, white glow. Tendrils of power pulsed just beyond Slade's mental touch. "If I wanted you dead, there'd be nothing you could do."

Not for the first time, Slade wondered at the true depths of the Enforcer's power. And the direction of his loyalty. Balancing his weight on the balls of his feet, he nodded. "I'll take my chances."

"So will I." Caleb growled, taking a similar position.

Allie placed Joseph in the baby seat on the table and stepped forward. Before Allie could open her mouth to chime in, Caleb put his palm over it and shook his head. "*You* never will."

Allie glared and stomped on his foot. It was such a ludicrous attempt to dent his brother's defenses, done with such expectation of success, that Slade couldn't help but smile. Neither could Tobias. Or Caleb. Which just made Allie madder.

As soon as Caleb removed his hand, she was spitting fire. "You're not relegating me to the sidelines, Caleb Johnson. We're married. That means we're in things together."

"Not battle," Caleb countered.

"Not when it comes to fighting," Slade reiterated.

"You have other concerns," Tobias lectured, nodding to Joseph, who was watching everything.

"You don't have to find the one thing we agree on," Allie huffed.

"It's convenient."

Scooping up Joseph, she muttered, "Oh my God, you're worse than mother hens."

"You should work harder to curb her impulsivity," Tobias told Caleb.

"There are times when I find it charming."

Allie rolled her eyes. "This is the twenty-first century, you know."

"But still dangerous," Slade felt compelled to add. And all the more dangerous now that he'd brought Jane here. Not that he'd had a choice.

"And you're married to the head of an important family," Tobias said, reining in his energy until it was once again an intangible shimmer. "That makes you a target."

"We're all targets, but we still have to live, love . . ." Allie glanced pointedly at Slade. "Marry."

Leave it to Allie to point out the elephant in the room.

"The scientist is not for Slade," Tobias said flatly.

Allie's brows shot up. "Who are you to determine that?"

"Yes, Enforcer"—Slade gave Tobias back his own cold smile—"who are you?"

Tobias bared his canines. "The one with the bad feeling."

Tobias's bad feelings were nothing to sneeze at. The hairs on the back of Slade's neck rose. Caleb stepped forward, all signs of challenge gone. "About Jane?"

"Yes."

Slade knew what the were was going to say.

"Shut up, Tobias."

"For heaven's sake, we can never get the man to speak and then when he actually has something to contribute, you tell him to shut up?" Allie grabbed Tobias's arm and tugged him toward the table. "Come have a bear claw."

To Slade's surprise, Tobias went. "You're getting downright domesticated, Enforcer."

"Uh-huh." He took the heavily iced pastry and bit off a chunk.

"What he's getting is my last bear claw!" Caleb growled.

Allie folded her arms across her chest. "You'd just throw it up."

"But I'd enjoy it coming and going."

"Now that's just gross."

Caleb glared at Tobias. Allie glared at Caleb. Slade wanted to silence them all before the truth could come out. Before it became something that had to be dealt with.

"Jane is my business."

"Not in this."

Caleb shook his head. "She's his mate, Tobias."

"She cannot take his blood. There can be no bond."

That snapped Caleb's head around. "What the hell are you talking about?"

The cold clenched in Slade's gut. Reaching out mentally, he blended his energy to Jane's. She slept because he'd forced her to, but beneath the coercion, there was burning pain. *Shit.* He hadn't accidentally converted her. He'd poisoned her.

"Slade?"

The touch on his arm drew him back. Allie was looking up at him, pity in her eyes. They were all looking at him. He felt the brush of Caleb's mind. The calculation in Tobias's.

"What do you know, Enforcer?"

The chair creaked as Tobias sat back. "Sanctuary is coming."

"Now tell us something we don't know."

He wiped his mouth. "For her."

Caleb snapped. "Why?"

"Ask Slade."

Shit again.

"Slade?" Caleb asked. "Something you forgot to mention?"

"Her research is as important to them as to us."

"Shit."

Inside Slade, the vampire rose with the need to protect. His bones ached with the desire to morph. The coppery taste of blood flooded his mouth as his fangs bared for battle.

Allie snatched up Joseph. "How do you know this?"

Shoving Allie and Joseph behind him, Caleb asked too quietly, "Yes, Enforcer, how do you know?"

Tobias cocked an eyebrow at them. "You can smell the need to mate on him. But she couldn't take his bite." Tobias cocked his head to his side. "Was it your saliva that sickened her?"

"Slade?" Allie asked.

Was she so sensitive just his saliva could hurt her. He ran his hand over his nape. "I don't know."

She can't stay here.

Slade turned with a snarl, meeting the Enforcer's mental push with one of his own. "The hell she can't. One foot off this property, and Sanctuary will have her."

Tobias's gaze didn't shift from Slade's. Neither did his energy. "She can be guarded, but not here."

"She stays."

"Slade?" Caleb asked.

"Why does she have to leave?" Allie interrupted.

"To have a mate so close and not take her will drive him insane."

Slade deflected another probe from Tobias, feeling the were's state of surprise that he could. There was a lot his brothers and the Enforcer didn't know about him. A lot he'd kept to himself.

"I'm fine."

"You're not."

Fine enough. "I would never hurt Jane."

"Yes, you would."

The next snarl came from his toes.

The Enforcer stood—tall, broad shouldered, big enough to give even a Johnson pause. "But not because you wanted to. And that's the problem. We can't afford to lose her. And we can't afford to lose you."

"What the hell are you talking about?" Caleb demanded.

"When the pressure gets to be too much, he will go berserk."

"Berserk?"

"Crazy with rage. No one will be safe."

"Slade? Berserk?"

It was a measure of Allie's sweetness that she couldn't see the beast within any of them.

"The McClarens have offered her protection," Tobias continued. "They will fight to the death for her. As you will fight for Slade." Folding his arms across his chest, he finished, "No matter what side wins that battle, it will be Sanctuary that wins the war."

Joseph fussed. Allie swore and patted his back. "That can't happen. Ever."

"No, it can't." The resolution in Caleb's voice sent a chill down Slade's spine.

"Maybe she can disappear."

And Slade can go with her. The projection bled from Allie to Slade. Slade shook his head. "They'll never forget about her."

Caleb set his coffee cup on the table. "Maybe it's time you told us why?"

How much to tell?

All of it.

Shut the hell up, Enforcer.

"The formula she was working on has promise."

"It can help Joseph?" Allie asked with that ever-present hope Slade wished he could fulfill.

"Maybe. But that's not its true value."

"And what would that be?" Jace asked, entering the room. He

had the same square features as all of them, but his hair was longer under his hat, in the werewolf style, and he was flanked by two D'Nally Enforcers. On his cheek was a fading bruise. In an hour it would be gone.

"Hey, Jace. Still settling out the nuances of leadership?"

"Nah, just teaching the rogues technique."

"They must be getting better."

"They're showing promise." He poured a cup of coffee. "So tell me about the true value of this formula."

Slade hesitated. He could normally tell his brothers anything, but Jace was aligned with the D'Nallys now and Tobias had his own agenda.

"Goddamn it, Slade, you brought her here, we have a right to know," Caleb snarled.

He settled for a compromise. "She's a valuable resource, Caleb. We can't afford to lose her."

"Apparently we can't afford to keep her, if Tobias is to be believed."

"Tobias is just taking shots in the dark."

"Accurate ones, if the look on his face is any indication."

The Enforcer had a way of knowing things. His only weakness was little Penny. When he was around that baby, he was a different man. Almost . . . human.

"I know you can't hide it anymore," Caleb said.

Shit. "You know that experiment I've been working on since we became vampires? Finding a way to sustain ourselves without taking blood?"

"Yeah."

"I think Jane's research holds the key."

"The hell it does," Jace remarked.

"You sure of that?" Caleb asked.

"No, I'm not sure. I haven't seen all her research files, but I think it's likely, though the woman doesn't know what she's holding."

Jace tapped his fingers on the table. "Hell, Slade, that would make the woman as brilliant as you."

She was more than brilliant. She was vulnerable and sweet. And his. Until the split second it would take him to lose control, and then she'd be dead or worse. Dying a slow death as her organs dissolved under failed conversion. But he couldn't let her go. Couldn't trust her to someone else.

"That's going to be a problem," Tobias muttered.

Yeah it was.

"Where is this research?" Jace asked, cutting to the chase as always.

"I don't know yet."

That jerked everyone's head up. Caleb swore. "Christ, you've been with the woman constantly and we don't have it yet?"

"What would you have me do, rape her mind?"

"Whatever it takes," Tobias growled.

"How can you say that?" Allie asked, shocked.

Tobias pushed his chair in, his golden eyes sweeping over the Johnsons. It rattled unsteadily. "Because anyone who controls the ability to sustain life, holds the secret to taking it."

"Son of a bitch." Caleb grabbed the chair "They could poison the water, the environment."

"Only if the compound were able to be inhaled or absorbed through the skin," Slade countered.

"Do you know that it's not?"

"No."

Jace shook his head. "You need to get that research, Slade."

"I know."

"You're the closest to her. She trusts you."

"I know," he all but shouted.

Allie pushed past Caleb. "You can't ask him to betray his mate's trust!"

"She's not a true mate if she can't take his blood," Jace interrupted.

"We don't have any choice," Tobias snarled. "We can't risk Sanctuary getting to the formula first."

"And what are you going to do if you get to it first?" she demanded. "What's so holy about your purposes?"

Tobias stood. "Not a goddamn thing, but when the dying's done, Sanctuary won't be waving a victory flag."

With a shake of her head, Allie stepped forward, reaching out for Slade's arm as if her small hand could contain the force of the inevitable. "You can't do this, Slade."

Slade touched his energy to Jane's. Felt her strength, her turmoil. Her vulnerability. Her need and that ever-present rightness that always came with the joining of their energy. His vampire snarled a warning. His human side grieved, but looking around the room, he saw the truth in his brothers' eyes. It had always been the Johnsons against the world. And when the dust settled here, it would still be that way.

"Do you see anyone else who can?"

Allie didn't have an answer for that. Neither did he. Turning on his heel, he pushed past Jace, ignoring it when Caleb called his name. He had a mate to betray and forever in which to grieve her loss. What the hell could anyone say?

$$\twoheadrightarrow 12 \twoheadleftarrow$$

SLADE stood by the bed, watching as Jane slept. She lay on her back, the white sheets pushed down around her waist, one arm thrown above her head as if warding off what she couldn't see. Him. In her head, poised to take what she wouldn't give. What they needed. Just a little rape of her mind. That's all that was required. For the common good. So why was he quibbling?

Her eyes opened and met his. There was no censure in her gaze. No hate. "Because you're a decent man."

The hell he was. "No, that's not it."

Pushing herself up on her elbows, she shook her head. No matter how he tried, he couldn't skim her emotions off the energy around her. All he got was a sense of calm. "No? Then what would you say?"

"I'm thinking, sweetness, that you have undiscovered talents that keep getting in my way."

"Like what?"

"Like blocking my thoughts, reading my mind, and slipping out from under my orders."

She rolled her eyes. "Orders. Is that what we're calling drugging people these days?"

"I didn't drug you."

"Whether you used your mind or a pill, the results are the same."

"Yet you call me decent."

She rubbed her forehead and glanced at the fading rash on her arm. "Yes."

Just yes. Nothing more. He felt the need to explain. "You were in pain."

"I was then." She looked at him pointedly. "What's your excuse for now?"

He hadn't yet lifted the enthrallment, and she knew it when she shouldn't. Interesting.

"An oversight."

He lifted the enthrallment. She sent him a dirty look. "Thank you."

"My pleasure."

He might have lifted the enthrallment, but he hadn't left her mind. He loved her mind. It worked with methodical precision on problems, evading emotion to maintain the focus. Yet somehow it never lost track of the impact of emotion. Like now. She was scared by what she'd caught of his thoughts. Of what had happened when he'd taken her blood, how he'd handled it, but she wasn't letting the emotions rule. She was sorting through the reality, looking for patterns, looking for how he'd accomplished it. Looking for control.

He wished he could summon the same cool detachment. Inside him, emotion ruled, pushing out logic and the why, leaving only the image of what could be with this woman if he'd committed to her in another time and another place. Say two hundred and fifty years ago when life had been less complicated. When he'd only longed for the mental freedom he had now. When he could only dream of the ability to experiment and create. Before he'd had eternity to long and regret. Weariness crept over him, sneaking up on his blind side. Sliding his thumb along Jane's cheekbone, he let his energy blend with hers, not controlling, not dominating just . . . blending.

Above his thumb her eyes widened, the pupils broadening as his mind went deeper into hers, flowing with her energy past the light, absorbing it, delving into the darkness of his soul. Finding the darkness in hers, the pain that didn't end, the silent scream that no one ever heard.

"Jane . . ."

The whisper wrapped around the scream, binding them together; he pulled it into himself, taking the pain, wincing as he bore the weight of what she buried so deeply inside her. Images rushed his mind. A man's face, handsome but for the red-rimmed eyes and beard. Perfect teeth bared in a smile that hurt. He could feel Jane's hurt. Betrayal. The stench of alcohol hit him in the face. A hand approached. A child's scream. So endless. So desperate. Trapped. She was trapped. Fear clawed at him. Hers. His. Theirs.

"Jane."

"No."

She didn't want him to know. She didn't want him to see, but it was too late. She didn't have the strength to block him from this. He wouldn't let her bear this alone.

Her mind pushed at his. "Back off."

"I won't let him hurt you anymore."

I've got it under control.

You don't. I can feel it.

She shook her head. An internal tug signaled her withdrawal. He growled low in his throat. She caught his wrist in her hand, anchoring him to her even as she tried to push him away. Shame. So much shame. "I'm not who you think I am."

"The hell you're not."

He tightened his grip, shifting his thumb to her mouth. The moistness of her breath was yet another bonding. Her eyes narrowed. Anger flared outward, tracing back along his energy, blazing through her eyes. Old anger. The kind of anger Jared had carried for so many years. The kind that threatened to eat a body alive.

Her chin came up. "You don't know anything."

Fear blended with her energy. Foolish woman to think he didn't know. More foolish still to think it would ever matter. "I know you're mine."

"I'm not something you can take."

"Watch me."

That chin came up. "No, you watch me. I won't be controlled."

He caught that stubborn chin on the side of his hand. "And I won't be denied."

She sat up straighter. "You give me hives."

"So I do." But only if he claimed her. He smoothed his thumb over her lips, studying the rush of emotions over her face even as he siphoned them off. He couldn't give her much, but he wanted to give her peace. As the anxiety in her settled, he found a bit of his own calm. "You'll have to make a cure."

"There's no cure for you."

Such a sad statement made in such a sad voice. He wanted nothing more than to deny it. But he couldn't. Even if nothing would come of it. Shit. She was right. It wasn't fair. He wanted what his brothers had. A mate at his side. A woman to spoil. To protect. To laugh with. Fight with. To make up with.

Slade kicked off his boots. They hit the floor, first the right and then the left. Two soft thuds that shouldn't have startled anyone but made Jane jump. This time when her gaze met his, the anger was gone to be replaced by . . . something else. Something that drew him.

Eyeing the boots and then him, she whispered, "We can't."

Sliding onto the bed, he propped himself over her. Her gasp was as soft as her skin. As enticing. He wanted to hear it again, this time roughened by passion. "Who says?" he whispered back.

"You did. Many times."

The curve of her cheek drew his touch. "I was a fool."

"You're never a fool." Reaching up, she caught his hand. "What's wrong?"

Her body was flush against his. Soft and sweet, her curves fit perfectly to his planes. For now there was no Sanctuary threat, no conversion danger. No loss. For now there was illusion. "Not a god-damned thing."

"You're lying."

Turning his head, he kissed the center of her palm. "And you're hiding."

"Is this where I'm supposed to say I'll stop when you do?"

"No, this is where you say you don't give a shit."

She blinked. "I don't." She sounded surprised. "Is that because you're influencing me?"

"Maybe."

Her grip slackened. "Why?"

"Because I'm tired."

Her gaze searched his. "Of what?"

Of hoping, of fighting, of time without end. Pressing lightly, he parted her lips, getting a glimpse of how it would be to have his mouth on hers, to take her breath as his. To eliminate the physical barriers as well as the mental ones. "Of waiting for my something good."

"Something good?"

He nodded, eyeing the free expanse on the big king bed. There was more than enough room for him there. With her. "When my brothers and I were younger and times were hard, we'd start fantasizing about good things, like a pot of stew that never emptied, or a blanket that kept you warm on the coldest night. It soon evolved into a game where we'd list our something good for that week. And whoever found theirs had to buy the others a round."

"I bet you were good at it."

He shook his head. "I got drunk a lot."

"You were that bad at getting what you wanted?"

"Nah, I was just that bad at wishing."

Her gaze softened slightly. "What did you wish for?"

"A simple thing." A woman to love him as he was, with all his strange ways of thinking and his love of tinkering.

Her fingers trembled against his pulse. "And what was that?"

"It's not important."

"Slade . . ."

He loved how she said his name, soft with a husky undertone that caressed his senses with the delicacy of a touch. "What?"

"Back in your day, how often did you do without?"

"Not that much. We grew up fast."

She licked her lips. Her hand dropped to his shoulder. "I was asking about *you*."

Pulling her into his arms, he wrapped a mental wall around the lingering shame she harbored, burying it beneath all the light he could furnish from his own dark soul. "I know, but there are better things to talk about."

"Like what?"

"Like how much I'd like to kiss you right now."

Her lips plumped. Her scent spiced. His cock throbbed. And his soul yearned.

"We have test results to study." She sighed.

He eased his chest to hers. "I'm too tired."

Of many things beyond the pressure the afternoon put on his alertness, Jane was beginning to suspect. She tried to imagine what it would be like to face forever. To outlive all you knew. To say good-bye over and over. To not love because the pain would be too much to bear when they aged and died. To want but never have. To have everything but nothing at all.

"Did you at least store the samples?"

He sighed and rubbed his thumb over her lips. "Of course. I even started a few of the longer tests."

"Good."

"Which means, we've got time to kill."

"So you took care of everything?"

"Yup."

Twisting against him, moving with him when he took a harsh breath, Jane smiled. She did like how Slade responded to her. "You do know how to turn a woman on."

"Oh?"

Scooting over in the bed, she made a place for him. "'Oh'? After nearly two centuries the only response you have to a woman propositioning you is 'oh'?"

Sliding into position beside her, he smiled that smile that made her pulse skip. "Only when they knock me off my feet."

His big body filled the space she'd created, inviting hers to tumble against his. She could have resisted. Maybe she should have, but unlike that time in her life when she'd made sex self-punishment, she wasn't going to wake up tomorrow with regrets piling on top of shame. So she let herself fall, coming to rest against Slade. His arm immediately came around her, tucking her in. No, this wasn't going to be like that.

Linking her hands behind Slade's neck, Jane savored the hard curve of muscle tickling her palms. "Is that a way of saying you don't mind being propositioned by a nerdy professor?"

His torso shifted along hers, gliding with an ease that should've been belied by his weight. It was fascinating. It was erotic. Even more so when he pinned her with a leg across her hips and smiled that bad-boy grin that sent her heart to pitter pattering. "That's my way of saying you've got too many clothes on."

Sliding her thighs between his, she hummed in her throat. "Maybe you can remedy that."

The narrowing of his eyes made her glad she wasn't a shy virgin out for her first journey into love. Tonight was going to be power-ful. Hot. Everything she'd ever dreamed of and never found. Slade was the type of man to test a woman's limits. It was the scientist in him. He couldn't help it. And the scientist in her couldn't wait. The woman was already softening to receive him.

"A challenge?"

"Absolutely."

Catching her hand in his, he pressed them into the mattress above her shoulders. "You should know no Johnson has ever resisted a challenge."

"I don't see how that works out to be a loss for me."

The corner of his mouth twitched up. "Good."

She waited for the shame, but it didn't come. She wasn't punish-ing herself with Slade. Slade was a gift.

His grin softened to a sensual smile. "I like being your gift."

He'd read her mind. She didn't care. Sparks of excitement gathered in little bundles of sensation that wrapped around her senses, bathing her in of wash of anticipation that verged on unbearable. She shivered under the onslaught and kissed his chest through the parting of his shirt. The warmth of his skin was a small balm to her overheated senses. The caress of his energy stole her breath.

"How do you do that?" she groaned.

"Do what?"

She probably shouldn't tell him, but what was the point of being reckless if she didn't go all the way? "Make me feel as if I can't take my next breath if you're not part of it."

"Son of a bitch."

The curse was harsh. Reverent. Hungry. A warning of the onslaught to come. She opened her mouth and her senses. Inviting him in. Nothing in his kiss was reverent. It was a primal claiming. Mouth to mouth. Tongue to tongue. Soul to soul. And she went eagerly, relishing the way Slade plundered her mouth, demanding everything. And everything he demanded, she gave. Willingly with everything inside of her. This was right. So right. Her man. The skirt of the nightgown twisted around her legs, trapping her when she wanted to be free.

It was her turn to swear. His turn to chuckle. In the next second, there was the sound of material tearing before cool air washed over her sensitive skin. Then her leg was free. She stretched it out, shivering as the roughness of his jeans delicately abraded her sensitive inner thigh. She smiled and caught Slade's hand, bringing it to her lips, not flinching at the sight of his talons.

"I do like the way you get to the heart of the problem."

He stilled. "I don't believe in wasting time."

She knew why he tensed. Holding his gaze, she bit the softer flesh at the base of his index finger. He was worried she feared his vampire side. "This is part of you, too."

His gaze darkened as she set to work on his shirt buttons. "I wish . . ."

"What?"

He shook his head. "I wish I'd met you before."

Before he'd become vampire. She pushed the shirt off his shoulders. "I'll make you a deal. You don't apologize for who you are and I won't apologize for who I am."

"You serious?"

"Yup."

"Shit." His hand curled around hers. His talons touched her skin but did not pierce. He was always so careful with her. "You're reckless."

"You like it."

"I do, and I promise . . ."

She shook her head, and put her fingers over his lips. She wasn't a foolish woman. She knew this couldn't last. She didn't want to be converted even if she could be. But she could make memories. "The only promise I want to hear is the one in which you tell me how good you're going to make me feel tonight."

Another laugh and a smile that kicked his mouth up at the corner. His fangs nipped her fingertips. His talons skimmed up the inside of her arm. "Honey, I'm going to spend all night lingering over you. I'm going to make you scream. And make you beg. And when you don't think you can stand it anymore, I'm going to give you everything you ever dreamed of."

"Oh yes!" She wanted that. Her nerves were already leaping, and between her legs, those little flickers of sensation were multiplying, encompassing everything until she ached for the touch of his hand on her shoulder, the brush of his lips on her breast, the tap of his tongue on her clit.

Closing her eyes, Jane projected the longing toward Slade. His breath sucked in. His body tightened, and for an emotion-packed moment, she thought she could actually hear his pulse leap. As experiments went, this one was by far the most stimulating. To be so connected to a lover that your excitement was his . . . She shifted on the bed and held the mental image. It was—

Perfect.

"Yes."

The mattress dipped as Slade changed positions. His lips brushed her breasts. Fire shot to her core. Taking advantage of her shift, he slid down her body, skin caressing skin as he nibbled his way down her torso. Her breath caught and her pulse stopped a second before catching the rhythm of his. She closed her eyes, letting the sensation pour over her, his emotions pour over her. Hot. Demanding. Possessive.

His. She was his.

She pulled away from the thought.

No. She didn't want that. Didn't want forever.

Yes. Feel me. Feel how perfect.

Suddenly, she didn't have any choice. He was there in her mind, there in her senses, tempting her pleasure, feeding her hunger. "Oh God, I want you."

"Good."

Kissing the inside of her thigh, he lingered on that plump spot near the top she'd always thought so ugly. And made it beautiful. Damn him. He was always making things beautiful for her. His fangs tested the flesh. She should be pushing him away. Instead she was pulling him closer. "Don't fight me, Jane. Not tonight."

Emotion stroked over her. Strong. Masculine. Needing. He didn't fight fair. She could have resisted seduction. Fought enthrall-ment, but what could she do with need? The man needed her. So much. Physically, mentally. He needed to be with her. The way she needed to be with him. This wasn't her trying to make something of nothing. This wasn't her fooling herself. This was real. And she was helpless as he before it. With a moan, she gave in.

"No. No fighting tonight." She drew up her leg, making it easier for him to explore further. Wanting him to find whatever limits she held and push her past them. "But please, could you focus some-where else."

He chuckled. "I like this spot. It's soft and sweet and begs a nibble."

What could she say to that? That she didn't want his attention? That would be a lie. His kisses bathed her skin in fire, and she couldn't wait to burn. "You're beautiful, honey. All of you."

She wasn't, but he made her feel beautiful, and such a feeling needed to be nurtured, explored.

She'd never felt beautiful before.

"Now, that's a shame." He touched the sensitive spot with his tongue.

She slid her fingers through his hair, not caring that he was reading her mind. The strands were cool, his lips hot. She held him to her, not wanting the feeling to go away. Not wanting him to go away.

"Slade."

The edge of his teeth grazed her skin. Her breath suspended in her lungs. Was he going to bite her? Was she afraid he would or wouldn't?

"Shall I continue?"

He had to be feeling that she did. "You know the answer."

With a soft kiss he released her from the tension. "With you, I'm not taking anything for granted."

"Then yes."

"Good." His tongue flicked over the crease between her hip and thigh. Hot. So hot. Jane grabbed his head, pulling his mouth to her as she growled, "Just don't make me regret this."

Chuckling, he kissed the pad of her pussy, teasing her with a butterfly touch of his tongue. Every nerve ending in the vicinity turned to liquid fire. "You don't need to worry, honey. I'll keep you safe. No matter what."

He had to, because she couldn't keep herself safe. Not tonight with his breath on her skin, misting over her clit, her hope. His hands slid up her torso, cupping her breasts. Breasts she'd always felt were too small but now felt perfect in the way they fit in his hands. Just right in the way they responded to the stroke of his fingers. Jane shifted on the bed as heat engulfed her. Fire. Everywhere was fire. She was burning from the inside out, but it was the most blissful heat filled with a need that blended with his energy, threading through passion and desire, finding his passion, dragging it toward her. So good. His energy felt so good.

Slade stroked his tongue through the folds of her pussy, not rushing but lingering, savoring. As connected as they were there was no way she could miss how much he enjoyed her taste, her pleasure.

"Sweet."

Yes, it was sweet and hot. So very, very hot. Hotter than she'd ever dreamed. A wildfire out of control. Wrapping her fingers tighter in his hair, Jane pulled Slade close, and when his tongue swirled across her oversensitized clit, pushing him away, not knowing if she could stand this. Not knowing if she wanted to.

"Oh my God, Slade."

"Burn for me."

She couldn't do anything else. Pulling him closer, she pressed up into his mouth, into the pleasure, into the burn. The likes of which she'd never known before. She'd had other lovers, but always with them she'd held a piece of herself back, and she wanted to hold herself back here, but her will was nothing against the pleasure he lavished on her. Slade drove her forward with the lash of his tongue, the pinch of his fingers. Sweet pain bit into her breasts, quickly melting into a pleasure that pulsed outward, building as his tongue swirled around her clit, settling into an ache. Her pussy flowered with need, softened, invited . . .

"Slade."

"That's it, honey. Open for me."

His lips closed gently around her clit, pressing softly as he pinched her nipple again. She arched up into the caress with another incoherent cry as he parted her folds with his finger, easing first one and then another into her tight channel. She couldn't hold back a moan at the intimate stretching, gasping as he sucked gently and eased his fingers deeper. She gave up the last of her resistance with a breathless cry as he did it again, and again, her legs going slack, no longer fighting him, no longer holding him, just laying there letting him take her wherever he wished.

He took her higher. Always taking her higher. The pleasure drew into a tight, explosive ball between her legs as he took her deeper into his mouth, into the passion. Her arms quivered and her breath caught in her throat. Her nails scraped across the sheets in a fruitless effort to hold on as he twisted her nipple harder, thrust deeper, spiked the flames hotter. It was too much. It wasn't enough.

She twisted on the bed. "Slade."

Pleasure tore his name from her lips, her mind. Energy whipped from him to her, crackling around them as he growled his enjoyment. When he tested her clit with the edge of his teeth, the air was suddenly too thick to breathe, her mind too heavy to think, the pleasure too intense to be born.

"Please . . ." She was there, right there, every muscle quivering, every sense tuned to him. Gathering the sheets in her hands, she groaned. "I need to come."

"Not yet."

This time she grabbed his hair and yanked. It didn't do any good. All it got her was a chuckle as Slade kissed his way up her body, avoiding those spots that would've tipped her over the edge. Against her thigh, his thick cock pressed. Catching her hands in his, he pinned them to the mattress above her head. She glared into his face. He smiled down into hers. How could he smile at a time like this?

"Spread your legs."

Defiance rose at the order. This was her life, her moment, and she would not be dictated to. "No."

Instead of getting mad, he smiled. Then leaned down. She couldn't take her eyes away from his lips. "No?"

With a slow twist of his hips he overrode her weakness. His thigh slid between hers, his cock pressed against the crease in her pussy. For the pulse of a second he let it rest against her, letting her absorb the heat, the size, before he slowly dragged the thick length, tip to base, along her swollen clit.

And that fast, her objections died. He could have anything he wanted of her as long as he didn't stop. Her legs spread. Her breath caught.

"That's right, let me in. Just let me in, no fighting."

Her "Why not?" died in a squeak, but they were so connected he heard it anyway.

"Because I'm on the edge. Because I'm vampire and you're my mate and the need to change you is strong in me."

That snapped her eyes open. She wanted Slade, but she didn't want to be vampire. "No."

He kissed her objection into oblivion. "I won't convert you, but we will have this."

This was a settling of his cock into the well of her vagina, heavy and thick. Another tension entered the mix. She didn't know if she could take him.

You can.

She was getting used to the way he slid in and out of her mind. "It's been a long time."

He kissed her lips, softly, an oasis of calm in the middle of the storm. "Then we'll take it slow. Put your arms around my neck."

She did.

Holding her gaze, he eased his body into hers, blending them together in a steady push. She shivered and gasped as delicate inner muscles caressed his thick shaft. It was hot, wonderful. So good. The pressure built as he pressed deeper almost to the edge of pain.

Digging her nails into the back of his neck she gasped, "Slade."

He stopped, resting inside her. "Too much?"

"I can't . . ." She shook her head not able to convey to him what was going on inside, the desire to run. The need to stay. A conflict too big to put into words, but she didn't need to. His mind was meshed with hers.

"Shh. It's all right. We're in no hurry." He continued to kiss her and stroke her and hold her until her fear faded and her inner muscles relaxed. His cocked flexed, stretching her oh so deliciously. Arching up, she took more, shivering as his cock flexed again. Nothing had ever been like this, felt like this. Nothing else ever would.

"So good," she groaned. "You feel so good."

"Very good."

The masculine whisper filled her mind. His energy wrapped around her. Passion. Perfection. He offered it all to her in a steady thrust. She gasped and he held himself still, letting her adjust, before pulling back and slowly, steadily seating himself to the hilt. As his groin settled against her swollen clit in a slow grind, his fingers grazed her cheek in that way that said so much. "Okay?"

She nodded and turned her head, amazed she found her voice amidst the tumult. "Better than okay."

"Good." Leaning down, he sucked at her breasts, nibbling the tip, catching it between his teeth, biting lightly. It wasn't enough. She needed more.

"Oh please. Harder."

"You sure?"

Did he think she would break? "Positive."

His hand slip between them, settling on her clit in a tiny culmination that became something bigger, growing as he rubbed at first gently and firmer, never quite giving her what she needed to come, keeping her balanced on that sharp edge of desire.

She could feel the force of his passion. His need to possess. He needed her like she needed him, yet he was denying them both. Why?

"Slade!"

"Right here."

Wrapping her thighs around his hips, she drew him to her. "No more games."

"I'm not playing."

"Neither am I." Lifting her hips, she took him deeper still, smiling at his groan, at the breach in his energy that signaled his loss of control. Relishing the rush of desire that rolled over her. Relishing the knowledge that he couldn't resist her anymore than she could resist him. Smiling, she met him thrust for thrust.

"That's right, take what you want."

What she wanted was everything. "More," she gasped, twisting up into his thrust. She wanted more. He gave it to her, but it wasn't enough. She needed him deeper, harder. She needed him wild. "Son of a bitch."

In a move so fast it left her blinking, he flipped her over onto her hands and knees. For a second she saw herself through his eyes. Hips white and rounded, looking impossibly lush above her parted thighs and swollen pussy. He loved her ass. She went with him mentally as his gaze followed the line of her spine to where her hair fell away from the nape of her neck, leaving it exposed and vulnerable. She felt Slade's pleasure. Slade's lust as his cock pressed against her. On the next breath the image snapped, and then it was just her lust consuming her, her need. Her pleasure.

His hand came down on her hip in a light spank. "Now."

Spreading her legs, she welcomed his possession, pushing back as he thrust in, groaning as every inch of his thick cock stroked along that certain spot inside that was like striking a match to tinder. He felt bigger this way. Better. Harder.

"More," she gasped. She just needed a little bit more.

He gave it to her, thrusting harder, deeper, slapping her ass when she cried out, doing it again when she begged. The sting blended with the heat. Just a little more. That's all she needed. Just a little.

"Slade," she called his name, needing him there with her when she lost track of herself. "Slade!"

"Jane."

Her name was a harsh curse on his lips. A blessing. An inducement to push harder, to demand more. His fingers wrapped in her hair, pulling her head back, pulling *her* back into every thrust. "More." Oh God! She needed more. "I need all of you."

"Shit yes!"

He came over her back, bracing himself on one hand while his other slid down over her stomach to cup her pussy, anchoring her there as his fingers found her clit, centering her with a pluck.

"Damn it, Slade! Don't tease."

"No, baby. I won't." His breath caressed her nape. "I just want to be sure," he breathed as he tested the tight flesh around their joining. His lips touched the side of her neck. Every nerve tingled. Goose bumps rose over her skin. He wouldn't . . .

Before she could gather a protest, he pinched her clit, rolling it between his fingers as his cock slammed home. Pleasure exploded into ecstasy and she came, crying his name, hearing him whisper in her ear and then feeling his teeth grazed her neck. She froze as another whisper followed the first.

Mine.

"No!" Was all she managed to gasp before his will overpowered hers.

She didn't want to be vampire.

✷ 13 ✷

THE SUV pulled up to her bungalow on its quiet street in its quiet neighborhood. It would be so nice if everything else was quiet, but it wasn't. The energy filling the SUV was tense, almost angry. And it wasn't only because Derek, the big rough military-looking werewolf who was a friend of Slade's, was with them. The man radiated hostility in a restrained it-would-just-take-one-little-thing kind of way. He was a perfect example of suppressed rage eating a man from the inside out. All the werewolves were tense.

As if he heard her thoughts, Derek turned and ordered, "Wait here."

Opening the door, she got out. The look he shot her would have turned her to stone if he'd had the power.

Jane gave him her sweetest smile and hitched her laptop case onto her shoulder. "You forgot to say please."

Slade caught her wrist and pulled her back. There was something both endearing and enraging in the way he was always pulling her away from the edge of her own recklessness.

"I've got her."

Derek grunted and motioned the other weres forward.

As they disappeared into the shadows surrounding her quaint little home, taking their tense energy with them, Jane felt the anger inside her lessen.

"Do you really think the big bad Sanctuary is sitting here at my house waiting on my visit?"

"I think they've got the place watched."

"Not anymore."

Tobias slid up beside them. A shadow shifting within the shadows. Jane couldn't help her jump. The man made her nervous. His energy was such a seething mass of indefinable qualities. She didn't trust anyone who wouldn't fit some pigeonhole somewhere.

"Stop creeping about."

He didn't apologize, just gave her a look that mirrored the one Derek had shot her. No sound came from the house.

"There were only two lookouts," Tobias told Slade.

Were. She shuddered. Slade squeezed her hand. It was an almost absentminded gesture. Like the others, his attention was on their surroundings.

"Did they get notice out?" he asked Tobias.

"Not those two, but it's possible there were others. It was foolish for her to come."

Jane slammed the door closed. *Her?* "What is your problem with me, Tobias?"

He looked at her over the roof of the car. "You keep secrets."

"So do you."

"Your secrets could get people killed."

"And yours won't?"

Slade's grip on her arm tightened in warning. "Are you questioning my mate's loyalty, Enforcer?"

"She's not your mate in fact."

"As far as you're concerned, she is."

Jane wanted to push them both aside. She had had her fill of arrogant men.

"That true?" Tobias asked.

He was trying to back her into a corner. Did he really think she was that easy to manipulate?

Yes.

Good God! He was in her head. "Go to hell."

"We're all going to be there soon if you can't bring in the promise of your research."

"I can bring it in." Just maybe not in the time Joseph needed. She pictured the baby's wan little face. Nothing short of his plight could have forced her to reveal her hiding place, but without her notes, she couldn't attempt his cure. So in a blind leap of faith, she'd agreed to this trip. "But it does seem to me that if I can't pull this off you're simply back to where you started."

"There's no putting the genie back in the bottle once it's out."

"What does that mean?"

"For the rest of your life, you're going to be hunted," Tobias informed her.

She glared at Slade. She had him to thank for that. If he'd just left her in her lab, none of this would have happened. "Thank you."

"You're welcome."

The urge to kick something, or someone, increased.

"But we can keep you safe," Tobias promised.

"Really?"

"Yes."

"Would you stake Penny's life on that?"

Tobias didn't give her the satisfaction of a response. "We're wasting time."

"Did I strike a nerve?"

"Control your woman, Slade," Tobias snapped.

Jane rolled her eyes. Like there was anything Slade could do to control her.

"Enough," Slade drawled obligingly.

She looked at Slade. "That's your attempt at controlling me?"

With a pointed look at Tobias, he answered, "That's my attempt to make you see reason before I have to take charge of someone."

"You think you can take me, Johnson?" Tobias demanded.

Slade didn't back down an inch. "I think we're about to find out."

Gravel crunched under Derek's feet as he emerged from the shadows. "I told you, Tobias, beneath that lab coat the man is a fighter."

"We don't need him to fight. We need him to get the information from her before it's too late. If he can't, he needs to step aside and let someone else do it."

Jane felt a probe at the edges of her mind. Potent energy just beyond her boundaries, coiled and ready to strike.

She took a step back. Tobias.

"Don't." Slade's warning was couched in a savage growl. When Jane glanced over, she saw Derek had Slade by the arm. Slade's fangs were exposed.

Derek glared at Tobias. "You've said enough."

"We don't have much time."

"Then we'll make it," Slade shot back.

"Make it fast." The energy withdrew. Turning on his heel, Tobias vanished back into the shadows.

Jane rubbed her hands over her arms. "I do not like that man."

"He grows on you," Derek said.

Slade put his finger to the transceiver she knew was in his ear.

"Why don't you just talk telepathically to everyone?" she asked when he was done.

"Because I can't talk mentally with a werewolf unless I've bitten him, and biting a were gets complicated."

"Politics?"

"A shitload full."

"Tobias is a were."

"We're not sure what Tobias is."

"He's more than a werewolf."

"Yes."

He didn't offer any more information.

"If you did take a were's blood, would they be able to read your mind, too?" Jane asked.

"Not necessarily. Only if they had psychic power before they were bitten."

"Is it the same with humans?"

Slade shook his head. "If a human survives being converted, he becomes a vampire with some level of vampire power, but those powers do seem tied to whatever latent tendencies they have as humans."

"Really?" That was interesting.

Slade nodded, though his attention was clearly not on her but on whatever was being whispered in his ear.

"Why can't I have one of those earpiece things?"

He glanced at her but didn't answer. She knew what that meant. She was being excluded from the earpiece conversation "for her own protection."

With a "Got it" he dropped his hand. He motioned her behind him. "Let's go."

Finally. "To the house?"

"Yes."

Now that it was time, a sick feeling settled in her stomach. No one was that tense and on guard for no reason. "They've been here, haven't they?"

"Yes."

He took her hand. His energy smoothed over hers. How sweet he was worried about her. "I'm not going to fall apart if they wrecked the place."

"Good."

"They didn't find the flash drive."

His eyebrow cocked at her. "You sound sure."

"I am." Because no doubt they'd been looking in the house. She didn't say that to Slade because she wanted to see her home. Everything about her life right now was so surreal, all the threats she never felt supposedly there. She needed evidence that the bad guy still existed. That the threat hadn't been eradicated at the parking garage that day. She needed to know this wasn't a figment of her imagination, that she hadn't eaten some bad mushrooms or something. She let Slade escort her to the house, bracing herself for the worst.

And the worst is what she saw when she got inside the door. She looked around the shambles of her once neat little bungalow and sighed. They hadn't just been searching for her notes. They'd been venting their spleen on the place where she kept the few things that mattered to her. The place she'd created into her sanctuary was now a victim of war.

"They made a mess of things."

"I'm sorry," Slade murmured.

"Thank you."

From the way Slade's men were spread around the room, they'd been doing a bit of searching of their own. "Did you find what you were looking for?" she asked a younger man with brown hair and light brown eyes.

He shrugged and looked to Slade. Clearly he was tossing her

complaints up the chain of command. Turning to Slade, she asked, "What would you have done if you'd found the research?"

"Spared you this."

"And then?"

"Asked you to work with it."

"After you'd analyzed it yourself?"

He didn't lie. "Yes."

"So maybe you wouldn't need me anymore."

"Jane, I'm always going to need you. But only one person having the information this vital is not good strategy."

"Maybe not for you, but that research is pretty much my life insurance."

He smiled that bad-boy smile and caught her chin on his fingertips. "Sweetness, I told you that first night, I'm your life insurance."

She wanted to jerk her chin away, but she knew what came next. She was such a sucker for bad boys. This one in particular. "Because you're the badass vampire that can kick Sanctuary butt?"

His fingers skimmed down her neck. Flickers of lightning raced down her spine. His eyes narrowed and his mouth softened. He leaned in. Hot and potent, his energy wrapped around her. She shivered and bit back a moan. His lips touched the delicate flesh just beneath her ear. She felt the moistness of his breath. The graze of his teeth. The force of his passion. Goose bumps raced up her arms. Her knees went weak.

His chuckle as he caught her was positively wicked. "Exactly."

JANE supposed Slade was her insurance policy in many ways, but she hadn't gotten this far in life by relying on others. She wasn't going to start now, especially when so much of the threat was in shadows. She looked at bits and pieces of her life tossed about the room. Her once orderly existence now in disarray. A lot like how she felt inside when she looked at Slade. He wanted from her what she'd never given anyone. Complete trust. Complete faith. A hot, sexy bad boy with a mission. She could still feel his touch on the sensitive skin of her neck, the subsequent kiss. Her own personal kryptonite. She was in so much trouble.

A dish toppled off the debris scattered across the counter. It hit the floor with a sharp crash, splintering into tiny pieces. It'd taken her months to settle on that china pattern. And every time she'd added a new place setting to the set she'd felt the same sense of satisfaction. And now the set was ruined. Stepping past the soldiers, she bent down and gathered the pieces. A splinter cut into her palm. She licked her lips, feeling the last of her disbelief shatter with the same catastrophic effect. She'd been kidnapped by vampires, was guarded by werewolves, and hunted by some combination of the two. And a little boy was dying for want of a cure she might be able to provide. She brushed her palms off on her pants. She couldn't afford denial anymore. Either she let that boy die or she put her faith in Slade and his version of the truth.

Porcelain crunched as Slade approached. She watched him as he knelt down beside her. She expected him to say "leave it." Instead, he gathered up a few more pieces and held them out. "We'll replace it."

She shook her head at the irrelevance of replacing china if everything else he'd been telling her was true. "It's antique."

"So am I."

Was he trying to make her laugh? She grabbed an empty plastic grocery bag off the floor "Yes, you are."

He cocked his head to her side. "You're not saying that with a smile."

"I'm not feeling like smiling."

He motioned to broken pieces of china. "I'm sorry about this."

She held out the bag. He dropped the pieces in. "It's not your fault."

"I'm still sorry."

Looking into his eyes, she believed him. But believing that he was sorry didn't change reality, didn't ease the decision she was about to make. Sorry wasn't going to fix the catastrophe that could happen if she put the bits and pieces of her research together and the wrong hands got hold of it. Sorry had its limitations.

"Thank you." Tying a knot in the top of the bag, she set it on the floor and dusted off her hands. Looking around the shambles of her home, she realized there was nothing she wanted to salvage. Slade helped her to his feet.

"I told you they would have been here," Slade said.

She'd understood that. It was only logical that someone hunting information she had would search her home. "Yes, you did. But knowing it and seeing it are two different things."

His hand on her shoulder startled her. The destruction of her home had affected her more than she'd anticipated. Whereas before she'd felt safe, she now saw demons in every shadow.

"You need to get your notes."

"I know.

"You need to get them *now*."

To further emphasize Slade's "now," Tobias spoke up from his position at the door. "There's no doubt they're watching this place, and those two Sanctuary spies we found aren't likely to be the only ones."

"You said your guys took them out before they got a message out?" Jane asked.

Tobias nodded. "Those new pups have Jace's efficiency."

The new pups were young men with long hair and an edgy energy that made Jane think of wild animals chewing at their chains. She was not the least surprised they killed efficiently. "All right."

Grabbing a set of tongs out of the debris and shouldering her backpack, she headed for the back door.

"Where are you going?"

"To get my notes."

"You said they were here," Slade countered

"And if you remember back to the first night, I told you they weren't in my home."

"Then why are we here?"

Opening the door, she looked over her shoulder. "Because it's my home."

And she'd needed to see what they'd done to it.

A hand grabbed hers and yanked her out. Derek. The man's face was as dark as any thunderstorm beneath the short cropped blond of his hair. The inflection of his voice never changed. It was always on the edge of rage. Slade said he could tell a mean joke. She couldn't see it.

"Squabble later. I don't have much time."

"You have some place better to be?" she snapped, tugging her hand free. The man had scared the bejeezus out of her.

Without preamble he retorted, "Yes."

"We won't keep you from your mate any longer than necessary," Slade said.

The flicker in Derek's energy, which could only be described as agony, surprised her. "Good."

There was so much here she didn't understand, beginning with this newly acquired sensitivity to energy. She'd always been the fig-urative island before, apart from everyone, her life neatly compartmentalized. Now, she was buffeted from all angles by emotion and thought.

"You vampires are rubbing off on me."

Slade tensed. "How so?"

She shook her head. There was no way to explain what she didn't understand. Immediately, men fell in around her like perversions of her shadows. The men kept a respectful distance. Only Slade was in her space. He was always in her space. She should mind.

"What's wrong?" Derek asked. The growl in the question raked over her nerves.

"I'm about to change the world. Pardon me if I take a moment to contemplate the ramifications."

"It'll be okay, honey."

Maybe. She eyed Tobias and Derek. But what if they didn't need her after she gave up this information? Would they be her killers?

It was Slade who answered the unspoken fear. "No. And, Jane, I'll always need you."

Great. Needing her would just get him killed. The fresh air felt good on her cheeks. She hadn't realized how stressed she was until that moment. She'd painted the small deck off the back door a cheery white and yellow with a daisy pattern on the floor because she'd wanted nothing but happiness in this house. In the dark the pattern was invisible, taking on a sinister cast as shadows blended with the darker paint distorting them. Perception. She realized. It was everything.

Slade caught up to her easily, his long legs eating up the distance between them. "Where are we going?"

"To the happiest place on Earth."

"I read that on your laptop notes."

When he'd been hacking her system. "And you didn't think it sounded out of place?"

"I figured it was a clue."

But he hadn't been able to figure it out. Apparently, his ability to read her mind wasn't as complete as he would have her believe. It was reassuring.

"What's that little smile about?" he asked.

"Oh nothing."

"Sure."

She stopped at the base of a small tree at the edge of the yard. It stood just within the light thrown from the spotlight above the deck.

He looked at the tree. "This is it?"

She touched the side of the bluebird house precisely six feet off the ground, just as the article she'd read said was important. Before she'd done anything else after she'd moved in, she'd put up the birdhouse. It symbolized everything she'd hoped for her future. Everything she'd wanted her research to accomplish.

Slade shook his head. "The bluebird of happiness."

"Yes."

"The flash drive's in the birdhouse?"

"Yes."

When he would have taken the box off the tree, she grabbed his wrist. "No. There's a bird on the nest."

"We'll only disturb her for a minute."

"We have to get it without disturbing her, otherwise she'll abandon the eggs and the babies will die."

"She'll build another nest. Lay more eggs."

Surprisingly, it was Tobias said, "But those lives won't replace these."

"No," she agreed. "They won't."

Derek stepped forward. "I'll take care of it."

She wasn't about to let him wreck this little home any more than she was about to let Slade. "Get back."

He brushed her aside as if she were nothing. The strength of these men was all the more irritating for the way they combined it with gentleness.

A strangely focused energy came off him. Peaceful even. Inside the box, the mother's restless chirps calmed.

"When I tell you to, slowly and gently reach in with those tongs that you brought and get that flash drive."

"You're putting them to sleep?"

"*Her* to sleep," Derek corrected. "It's a female."

The box was quiet. Keeping his hand on the top of the box, fingers spread, Derek stepped to the side. "Do what you need to."

It was awkward getting the tongs in the hole, but she'd placed the bag on the bottom right side just in case this scenario occurred. Plastic rustled as she caught the edge. Very gently she pulled. It was hard to tell whether she had it. Flash drives weren't that heavy.

The bag came out without incident. As she clutched it in her hand, energy bombarded her. All male. All eager. They wanted the flash drive.

Was it her imagination or had Slade, Tobias, and Derek moved closer? "It wouldn't do you any good even if you did take it from me," she informed any would-be thief, her nerves screaming a warning. She fully expected to feel claws in her back at any moment. "It's encrypted."

A twig snapped. Slade was definitely closer. So close her nerve endings started tingling for a whole other reason. He turned her around. Her breath lodged in her chest as his fingers stroked down her cheek. His eyes glowed with that strange light. She couldn't look away. "No one is going to take it from you."

Calming pulses of his energy surrounded hers. She shook her head and backed away, coming up against the tree.

"I won't be hypnotized, either."

"Too bad," Tobias drawled. "That would make things easier."

The energy stopped. "You're not helping, Tobias," Slade barked over his shoulder.

"I wasn't aware I was trying to."

A chuckle rippled among the men. The tension in Jane eased. Slade backed up. She stepped away from the tree.

Not taking his eyes from hers, Slade ordered, "Make sure it's also clear around the car."

All of the men except Slade and one of the "pups" left. The energy coming off the younger man was intense and when Jane focused on it, it struck out like a blow. Controlling her flinch with effort, she asked, "Can I help you?"

Before he could answer, Slade stepped in front of her, pushing her back with a mental shove. Only stopping when her back was once again against the tree. "What do you want, Broderick?"

"They'll be coming for her now."

"We know."

"You're going to need help."

"If we need more guards, Jace and the D'Nally will see to it."

"They don't trust me."

Jane blinked at that honesty.

"With reason," Slade retorted.

"We had no pack. No purpose. It's different now."

"Miri or Jace give you that excuse?"

Broderick went still.

Slade growled in his throat.

Good God, were they going to fight here? Now? "Cut it out,"

Jane snapped, the fragile flash drive suddenly heavy in her hand. "We don't have time for your testosterone moments."

With another mental push, Slade pinned her against the tree as he squared off against Broderick. "That's all this will take, a moment."

She rolled her eyes, a gesture totally wasted on Slade considering he had his back to her. "Not hardly. If you kill him it's going to take forever to find out what he wants."

"Who cares."

For some reason, she did. "I do."

Muscles bunched in Slade's jaw. He was probably gritting his teeth. Derek stepped into the small circle of light with a low growl. Slade nodded and motioned to Broderick. "Have your say."

Derek growled again. If a "make it quick" could be squeezed into a rolling snarl, she'd just heard it.

Broderick looked her straight in her eyes. The impression of youth on fire flowed over her. "They're going to come after you hard now."

"Lovely."

"Shut up."

Broderick ignored Slade. "You don't need pet wolves to protect you."

"True."

"You're going to need wolves willing to sacrifice all."

"Are you saying you're willing to die for me?"

"Not you, what you can do."

That was honest.

"She doesn't need you, pup," Slade snapped.

"You're useless to her in daylight," Broderick snapped back.

That was brutal but true.

Slade took a step toward Broderick. Jane leapt into the small space between the two men, placing her hands on Slade's chest. Fire rushed up her palms. Over her shoulder she asked Broderick, "He'd die for me. What are you offering?"

"My life and the life of my pack."

That was quite an offer. "Why?"

"You can't trust him, Jane," Slade interrupted. "Up until two months ago he was packless."

That might explain the edge to Broderick's energy. Anyone new to a group tended to have a need to prove themselves. "Who is your leader?" Jane asked.

He didn't hesitate. "Jace."

She turned to Slade. "Your brother trusts him."

"Not with his wife."

"Well, you won't be either as we're not married, so I guess that makes this okay."

Slade grabbed her hand. There was no breaking the grip. "No." Slade watched the were. "What prompted the offer, Broderick?"

The big D'Nally werewolf called Creed came back through the yard. In one glance he took in the tension. "This pup stepping out of line?"

Slade's "yes" coincided with Jane's "no."

Jane smiled into the younger were's set expression. "I do believe he's just declaring himself."

"As what?" Creed asked.

"My protector."

❖ 14 ❖

THE shit hit the fan on that one.

Talons came out. Fangs flashed. Energy whipped around her. The porch light flickered as the men clashed. Creed stood calmly in the midst of it all. "That was a poor choice of words on your part."

Jane looked between Broderick and Slade and then back to Creed. "Apparently, but who knew vampires could be so excitable?"

"A woman can have only one protector," Creed explained.

That hardly seemed fair. "Who says?"

"Pack law."

"Slade's a vampire."

"An accident of bite." Creed jumped back as Slade leapt to avoid Broderick's right cross. The thud as it connected with Slade's jaw made Jane wince. If both men weren't hugging the shadows, she would be worried, but if they were in control enough to remember to stay hidden, then they were in control enough not to kill each other. Slade landed a nasty gut shot. She winced as Broderick went flying backward.

"I warned you against dropping that right, pup," Creed called out to Broderick before turning back to her. "The Johnsons might as well be wolf the way they love."

"So?"

"You're Slade's mate."

"I don't believe in mates. In time Slade will move on—"

Creed cut her off. "Being human, you'll move on." He pushed her back against a tree as the men stumbled closer, shielding her with his body. "He won't."

There was a distinct sneer to the word "human." With a start, Jane realized the solemn, contrary werewolf was actually protective of Slade. "You can't know that."

Creed's strange brown eyes with their flecks of gold burned into hers. "I know."

She rubbed her hands up and down her arms. "I don't want forever."

She wanted a bed and a good eighteen hours of sleep, but she didn't want to pay the price she'd have to pay for forever.

Creed cocked an eyebrow at her. "But you want Slade."

It wasn't a question. "Yes."

"Then you need to make a choice."

"I've made my choice."

He glanced at Slade as he circled Broderick. "Then you need to make another one."

"Would you?"

Creed didn't even hesitate. "A mate is worth any sacrifice."

An image of herself as vampire popped into her mind. Face ghastly white and distorted, fangs dripping blood. A shudder went down her spine. Slade's head snapped around. She felt his probe as clearly as she felt his touch. She'd projected her distress.

"Damn."

Slade straightened.

Broderick spat blood and wiped the back of his hand across his mouth. "This mean you're done being reactionary?"

His gaze still on her, Slade answered, "I haven't worked up to a reaction yet."

"Then what was that all about?" Jane asked, blocking his mental probe and the knowledge of the weariness dragging her down. This mission was too important for her to be weak.

Slade frowned, obviously not happy with her success at shielding her thoughts. "A warning."

She rolled her eyes as he got closer. "Good grief. For a logical person you can be so caveman."

"When it comes to you. Absolutely."

With a shake of his head, Creed blocked her impulse to check on Broderick. Putting her hand on her hips, she faced Slade instead. "Well you might want to consider I'm the one who called him my protector."

"He didn't deny it."

"It was probably hard for him to talk with your fist in his mouth."

Slade shrugged.

"I don't want you as my woman," Broderick cut in.

"That might just keep you alive," Slade countered.

Jane ignored the comment. "Is this where I say thank you?"

"Say whatever you want as long as your research continues."

"Watch your tone, pup."

The pup didn't look the least intimidated by Slade's growl. Creed, however, did lose a bit of his nonchalance. Jane didn't want another fight. Angling herself between Slade and Broderick, she asked, "Why is my research so important to you?"

Jane just couldn't help it, Slade decided as she put herself in harm's way yet again. The woman just couldn't stay out of a fight. He pulled her back a safe distance as the werewolf answered, "Because it matters."

The deliberate lack of inflection in Broderick's voice caught Slade's attention. He made a note to dig deeper into the were's background. "It's a little brassy to be demanding trust when you don't give it."

Creed stepped forward. "Are you challenging the honor of the Tragallion weres?"

"Just this pup's."

"This pup is Tragallion. Part of the D'Nally pack."

Shit. That was going to complicate things. "I thought the rogues were on probation?"

"It ended."

About ten seconds ago, he'd bet from the way Broderick tensed. "Does Jace know?"

"It's pack business."

Which implied everything and said nothing. Boundaries had gotten a bit vague when it came to Jace and the pack he'd adopted. It was no longer the Johnsons against the world. It was the Johnsons filtered through the Tragallions, D'Nallys, and McClarens. Cocking an eyebrow at Creed, Slade asked, "You think he's going to spout the party line against his brothers?"

"Yes."

That confidence was irritating. "He's a fucking vampire and a Johnson. His loyalty should be with us."

Creed smiled that smug werewolf smile that just made a man want to punch him in his mouth. "But he's *our* fucking vampire."

It was a reminder. The Johnsons owed the Tragallion weres. And their overpack, the D'Nallys. Jace would be dead except for the Tragallion weres who'd come to his rescue in the battle for little Faith's life. The Tragallions had done more than back Jace. They'd given him a place. After years of senselessly risking life, his brother was alive, calm, and happy. He owed Creed D'Nally and all the Tragallions for the sense of purpose that took all that reckless energy and gave it a focus.

"Shit."

Creed just smiled, which pissed Slade off more. Jane's look said she was out of patience. The voice through the transceiver said they were out of time.

Wiping the blood from his already healing mouth, he jerked his head in the direction of the SUVs. "Time to go."

Broderick took a position behind Jane. Creed took the position ahead. From the shadows came Broderick's fellow rogues. Young men without pack who'd gone wild to fend for themselves. Young men who now wore the Tragallions' fighting spirit with pride. Young men Slade was supposed to trust. Creed met his gaze, those distinctive D'Nally eyes narrowed in challenge.

"Don't worry, I won't hurt your little charge's feelings."

"Oh, for Pete's sake," Jane muttered. "Do you have to antagonize everyone?"

Slade didn't break gazes with Creed. "It's family talent."

"Lovely." Jane picked up her laptop case.

The corner of Creed's mouth tipped up in a smile at Jane's defiance. "Seems to me, Johnson, you'd be better focused on getting your woman to the safe house."

Slade cast the former rogues a jaundiced eye, wondering if he'd ever been that young and that full of fire. He didn't doubt they were trained well. Jace wouldn't have sent them otherwise, but still . . .

they were damned young. Or maybe he was just getting damned old. He reached for Jane's case. She shook her head.

"If we're attacked, they'll go for the case," Creed pointed out.

"If they get the case through all of you, it doesn't matter anyway."

She had a point, but Slade wasn't taking chances with her safety. "Give Creed the case, Jane."

She clutched it tighter. "No."

He didn't have time to argue. It was getting close to dawn and his senses were starting to agitate in that way that said trouble was coming. "Take it."

Creed snatched the case from her grasp. Slade caught Jane's arm before she could go for the were. He palmed his gun, a combination weapon of silver bullets and lethal spectrum sunlight, as the rogues stepped forward. "What the hell is in there?"

Jane didn't take her eyes from the case. "My life."

He could feel her stress. He didn't doubt she was telling the truth. The agitation in his senses increased. "Let's go."

As a unit they moved forward.

"And, Creed?" Slade called.

"What?"

"Don't lose the case."

THE safe house was giving Slade the creeps. Which was something for a vampire. There was nothing about it to signal trouble. It was a small nondescript cape set at the end of a long street populated with equally nondescript capes. To the rest of the world it was abandoned. A property trapped in probate. None of the fortifications made to the structure showed. The filtered glass in the windows. The high-tech cameras. The special energy mat that detected vampire presence. But it was all there. He'd designed it himself. The little house was the safest anyone could be outside the Renegade compound, but every time Slade looked at it, it looked . . . wrong.

If they'd had any other choice, he would have pushed on, but he couldn't take the coming sunlight and Jane flat refused to go without him, claiming no end of troublemaking if he tried to force it. And when he'd called her bluff, the rogues had stepped to her side. Clearly, their instructions were to protect her. He and Jace would have to talk about that when he got back home.

Through the window he could see Jane standing by the kitchen table, her laptop open before her. He couldn't see the screen, but the energy coming off her was tense. In her right hand, she clutched the flash drive. She reached for the keyboard and then stopped, pulling her hand back and rubbing her fingers together. Whatever was on that screen tempted her. Greatly. Whatever was on it scared her. Whatever was on it needed to be revealed. It was a threat, and whether she thought it relevant or not, he needed to be aware of it.

I don't want to be vampire.

Slade flinched at the unvarnished truth. He didn't blame Jane. He hadn't particularly wanted to be vampire himself, but after all was said and done, it hadn't been bad for him. Vampirism had allowed him to live until a time when his way of thinking became appreciated. It had allowed him the time to experiment. To succeed. Once he'd gotten used to the oddities, vampirism had been a gift.

But Jane had been born in a time that embraced her mind and talents. She didn't long for the future to come. She longed for the present. Buried the past. She didn't want to live forever. Even for him.

The horizon lightened. Derek came up beside him, his blond hair shining white in Slade's night vision. "It's time to go in."

"Yeah."

"You don't look too happy about it."

Derek was as close to him as any brother. "Jane doesn't want to be vampire."

"Did you ask?"

"Indirectly."

"Try directly."

"Why?"

"Because forever is a hard concept for humans to wrap their brain around."

"Not for Jane."

Derek cut him a pitying glance. "Maybe not now, but it's a woman's prerogative to change her mind."

There was nothing Slade hated more than well-meant advice. He'd already weighed the pros and cons. "Has Mei changed hers?"

Slade regretted the jab as soon as it left his mouth.

"No."

That one syllable summed up a world of hurt. Derek had ordered his mate converted to a vampire rather than lose her. She hated him for it, but he couldn't walk away. Not only because she was his mate but also because his was the only blood she could take and survive. She should have been able to take Jace's since he'd converted her, but once her conversion was complete, Jace's blood had been as poisonous to her as anyone else's, leaving Derek in an impossible position. Derek shifted his grip on the rifle.

"Maybe Jane can cure Mei."

"Do you want her cured?"

Curing Mei would remove the only bond between the couple. They'd never had a relationship. Derek had found her as she was dying, cut down by a Sanctuary guard. Slade couldn't imagine that.

To wait hundreds of years for a mate only to find her as she was taking her last breaths. It's a wonder the wolf was sane at all.

"I want her happy."

"There's no saying she can't be happy with you."

"I scare the shit out of her."

"Not so much anymore. Heard she tried to shoot you last time you got to arguing."

"She thought I was going to rape her."

Slade cocked an eyebrow the werewolf. "What were you doing?"

"Wiping a smudge off her cheek."

Shit. "Still, shooting is a step up from screaming."

"True." A ghost of a smile touched Derek's lips. The first Slade had seen in a long time. "She's beginning to find her feet."

"Give it time, maybe she'll find you, too."

"Maybe." He motioned to the house with the tip of the rifle. "You need to head in."

Yeah. He did. He was as excited about that as Derek was about Mei's screams.

I don't want to be vampire.

He shrugged off the memory. Nodding to Derek, he headed for the house, stopping in a few feet and turning back as the hairs on the back of his neck rose in warning. "Watch yourself out here. I've got an uneasy feeling."

"Will do."

SLADE opened the door quietly. Jane was waiting for him, her hand clenched at her side, the computer open before her. A strong intelligent woman battling with things above her head.

"Come in."

There was a touch of sarcasm in the invite. She still hadn't for-
given him for his high-handedness earlier in regard to the case.
Closing the door behind him, Slade stepped into the plain kitchen
with its cheap maple-finished cabinets and white tiled countertops.
He still didn't have a good enough angle to see the computer screen,
but he wanted to. Whatever was on that screen was something that
scared her but not . . . really. He couldn't define the emotions that
poured off her when she thought of whatever was on the computer.
They were complex, old mixed with new. Anger mixed with purpose. With anyone else he would have been able to probe for the
answers, but Jane was very good at hiding things from him. Too
good. It was annoying. It forced him to deal with her in ways he'd
thought he'd put behind him. It forced him to deal with her as if he
was human.

"Didn't you watch enough B-movies to know it's dangerous to
invite a vampire into your home?"

She didn't smile. "I'm a slow learner."

She punched a button on the keyboard. He heard the soft click
that said the computer had gone to sleep.

"I doubt that." He nodded toward the keyboard. "Keeping
secrets?"

She didn't deny it. "A girl needs her mystery."

"A woman knows when to come clean."

"Yes, she does."

He tried the direct approach. "What's on the computer?"

There was a hesitation, and then she licked her lips. A sure sign
she was about to avoid the truth. Slade had been reading people's
minds for so long he'd forgotten how intriguing it was to focus on a
person's physical response to understand what was going on inside
them. Maybe there was something about mystery after all, because

it was absorbing having to analyze her outward reactions rather than her thoughts.

"There's nothing on that screen that will affect you at all."

"But it affects *you*."

"Contrary to popular belief, my life did not begin once I met you."

The scent of stress increased. "I'm not criticizing, Jane. But I'd like to help."

She closed the lid of the computer. An answer in itself. "I don't need your help with this."

Emotion flared into his mind, bleeding from her to him. Old. Uncertain. "A long-standing problem."

Though he didn't make it a question, she took it as one. "My own personal moral debate. I think of it as humanizing."

Slade took another step into the room, the tension in her drawing him as effectively as a winch. "You don't find taking up with a vampire humanizing?"

She was close enough to hug. The tingling in his fingers increased, and the heat in his blood rose. She'd likely slap the grin off his face if he hugged her now.

"It makes me aware of the fragility of life."

"Is that a roundabout way of saying you feel threatened?"

"From all sides. At all times."

Hunted. The knowledge flowed along the link between them. This time he didn't check the impulse. He pulled her into his arms. She didn't relax against him like he was used to.

I don't want to be vampire.

The biggest blessing in his life was now the curse it was always supposed to have been.

"It's not like before. You're not a child and you're not alone."

"That part of my life is none of your business, Slade."

He tipped her chin up. "When you put your hand in mine that first night, you made everything about you my business."

"You wanted my formula."

"I wanted you."

Sadness flowed through their connection. Her hair rustled and she denied the claim. "I'm not a fool despite how easily I lay down with you. I watch suspense movies along with B-grade horror. Romance is a tried-and-true method for gaining the confidence of the person whose formula you want."

"Maybe for a human."

"And for a vampire who can't read my mind."

"You know?"

She nodded. "I've been working hard at perfecting my blocking."

"Smart lady."

"Smart enough to stay alive."

"But not smart enough to know when to trust."

Her cheek rested against his chest. "I trust you."

As much as I trust anyone.

The thought escaped her control.

"Then you need to trust more."

Jane pushed away, stepping out of his reach. Head up, shoulders back, looking every inch the strong intelligent woman she was. Feeling to his senses like the vulnerable child she had been. What the hell was on that computer?

"Obviously I need to practice more."

"I haven't noticed that practice helps me any."

Her eyebrows rose and she looked up. "Those stray thoughts haven't been deliberate?"

"Maybe in the beginning." He rested his chin the top of her head. "Maybe not. I don't know what you heard. Hell, I'm even not even sure when I lost control of them."

"So this is new to you, too?"

"To the point I feel almost human again. There's a lot I've forgotten about courting."

The little start she gave at the word "courting" gave him hope. "What makes it 'almost'?"

How honest should he be? "The encouragement I get from your scent."

"I know I'm going to regret asking this. What do you mean?"

He kissed the top of her head, wrapping his energy around her stubbornness, holding her to him in every way he could. "Your scent changes with your emotions. It tells me when you lie. Tells when you're upset. It tells me when you're happy, but mostly it tells me how much you desire me."

"A physical reaction has nothing to the reality of commitment."

He tipped her chin up again. "It does between us."

"How?"

"Because we don't have a choice. Because I'm vampire and you're human. Because it's impossible and we still can't walk away. Something that strong is based in something bigger."

"Are you saying we're made for each other?"

Put like that, it did sound sappy. "I'm saying sometimes when we're pushed in a direction it's not always wise to go another."

"You believe in destiny."

"I know you're made for me."

"And the fact that I have the information to a formula that you want has nothing to do with that declaration?"

"No."

"What if I decide never to reveal it? Are you going to take it from me?"

"It's not my call."

"Bold words."

He shook his head. "You're a woman with a mind of her own. No one, not Sanctuary, not Renegade has the right to rape your brain for their perception of the greater good."

She took a step back, her gaze searching his. "But they asked you to do that very thing, didn't they? Tobias, Caleb, Allie."

"Not Allie. She would never ask that of you."

"But Caleb did."

"It's his son."

"And he believes that makes it all right?"

Slade could offer a ton of excuses for his brother. He was desperate for his child. For his wife. Slade gave Jane the truth. "Yes."

"What about Tobias?"

"He has his own reasons."

"And what about you?"

"I love Joseph."

Her finger clenched around the flash drive. "I envy you that, a strong sense of family. Never being alone."

"It's a mixed blessing."

"Especially now." That was a guess on Jane's part. The conflict in Slade was palpable.

"Yes."

"They told you to get the formula from me however you could, didn't they?"

"Yes."

"Did you agree?"

His gaze didn't leave hers. "Yes."

No matter how she searched his eyes, Jane couldn't see a lie.

The truth hit her like a blow. She'd wanted him to say no. Even hell no. And it wasn't happening. She shouldn't be surprised. It was survival of the fittest in the world. She'd made herself the fittest in her world. Reaching out, her fingers slid over the lid of the computer. The aluminum was cool to the touch. The chill spread up her arm, getting colder as it traveled to her core. They'd asked him to sacrifice her and he'd said yes. She blinked rapidly to control her tears. She didn't know why she'd expected anything different. She was an outsider. The foot of distance between them might as well be a mile.

"Thank you for your honesty."

His finger under her chin was an all-too-familiar gesture. She didn't want to look up. He left her no choice.

"That's the first time I've ever lied to my family."

She blinked. "Why would you lie to them?"

His thumb touched the corner of her mouth. "Because they needed hope."

"Why should I believe you?"

His eyes narrowed. "Because I won't lie to you."

It was a promise. And even without checking his mind, she believed him. "Vampires in real life are so different than in the movies."

"This isn't a movie."

No, it was her life, and it was so completely complicated there was no end to the tangles. Beyond the window, dawn was breaking. Thanks to the specially tinted windows, no harmful rays could get into the house. Somewhere out there the werewolves were on guard. Tobias, Derek, Broderick, and the others. They were all willing to give up their lives for her research. The Sanctuary was equally determined to give up theirs. And in the middle, she was starting a relationship. Leaning her cheek into Slade's hand, she whispered, "What are we going to do, Slade?"

His fingers slid through her hair, pulling her into his chest as his energy entwined through hers. This time she welcomed the embrace rather than fought it. Welcomed the strength of his arms around her. Welcomed the moment of security. It was a big bad world out there, and she was damned if she did and damned if she didn't. No-win positions sucked.

Slade rubbed her back. "We're going to find the cure for Joseph, Jane, and then we'll see where this takes us."

A pretty dream. "I might have already found the cure."

"When?"

"As soon as I looked at the information on the flash drive, I knew what was wrong. We were looking at the wrong protein/amino acid combination. From what I can tell vampires don't so much digest food like humans do as absorb it. Joseph is trying to digest it because his body doesn't recognize blood as a food source but doesn't have the necessary digestive balance to digest it."

"Shit. Really?"

"Yes." It sounded so uncomplicated when she put it like that. In reality, creating the right balance of enzymes, amino acids and protein targets at the right strand of DNA to enable his digestive tract to function had so many variables it scared her silly. Hiding her worry, she smiled up at Slade. "And you didn't even have to seduce the information out of me."

He rocked them gently. "I appreciate you lightening my workload."

"Any time."

Minutes passed. His energy softened and wrapped around hers. He leaned down. "Seduction can be fun, you know."

"I know." Standing on her tiptoes, she met him halfway, keeping the kiss gentle when he would have deepened it. "But as much as I appreciate the thought, what I really want is to go to bed."

He blinked. She let down her defenses, allowing him to feel the weariness dragging at her bones. "I'm so tired."

Shit. "I forgot . . ."

"The limits of a human body?" she asked as he scooped her up in his arms.

"Yeah."

It was a short trip to the bed. Slade sat her on the edge. It took everything she had to not just tip over.

"Go ahead."

For once she was glad he could read her mind. Kicking off her shoes, she lay on her side, sinking gratefully into the mattress. Every muscle in her body heaved a sigh of relief.

"You should have told me."

"Why? We couldn't afford to stop."

"We could have made time."

She yawned. Exhaustion was claiming her fast. "I don't think so. This is going to sound strange, but I've got the feeling time is running out and it has nothing to do with Joseph's health."

He paused in the middle of unbuttoning her jeans. "A feeling?"

"Yes."

With a tug he yanked them off. There was a soft plop as the jeans hit the floor. "Why the hell did you keep this from me?"

"It's just a feeling," she mumbled, closing her eyes. "Probably because I'm so tired."

"Feelings are important." She heard his belt slide through the loops. "If you have feelings, you tell me about them."

"Okay." She yawned. "Right now I feel like I'm about to fall asleep."

He swore. Two more thuds. His boots she realized.

"Goddamnit." The mattress dipped as he slid into bed beside her.

"I'm sorry."

"It's all right." His arm came around her waist, solid and strong. His thighs tucked under hers, cocooning her in his strength. It was such a comforting feeling. She nestled into the pillow. The same comfort sneaked into her mind.

"You're the only man I ever trusted, do you know that, Slade?"

Against her hip she could feel his arousal. He wanted her. She smiled to herself. Really wanted her.

"Maybe you shouldn't."

She shook her head and let sleep take her away, whispering as consciousness faded, "I've always had the feeling I should."

SHE trusted him. Slade stood in the glow of the laptop screen and shook his head, taking in the complexity of what he was looking at. It was always a mistake to trust a vampire. They had no honor.

As he read down the screen, he couldn't help but be impressed. His Jane was a clever woman. A brilliant strategist. Slipping the satellite card in the slot, he activated the connection. He perused the screen as he waited. Everything she needed for revenge sat there all set, ready to go. All she had to do was push the button and the man who'd raped her as a child would lose everything he valued. First his money. Then his reputation, and likely after that, his trophy wife. Yet Jane had never pushed the button. How many times had she sat at this screen and fondled the send button? Savored the ramifications? An exercise in humanity she'd called it. It all made sense now. A self-inflicted test of her moral code. With a grim smile, Slade hit the send button. Vampires also weren't afflicted with a messy conscience and they had a real liking for revenge.

❧ 15 ❧

IT was the scream that woke Jane. Hoarse and inhuman, it reached through the dense fog of sleep and dragged her out. Jane sat up, blinking as she tried to orientate.

Her head felt heavy, and it took too much effort to open her eyes. "Slade?"

No answer, but from beyond the bedroom were other sounds. Distinctive and unmistakable. They were under attack. Stumbling to her feet, she threw on her shirt and jeans before bolting for the door. Only to run straight into Broderick.

"Get back inside."

"My laptop."

"Is safe where you left it."

She'd left it in the kitchen. She tried to duck past him, but he easily blocked her.

Slade!

No answer. Searching for Slade's energy, she ran into a wall of nothingness. Did that mean he was dead? She refused to even think it. "That research cannot fall into the wrong hands."

There was nothing boylike about Broderick now. He was all soldier. And he was in her way.

"It won't."

But it could and then there'd be hell to pay. She'd transferred key data from the flash drive to the laptop. With that data in their possession plus the information gleaned at the lab, the Sanctuary scientists would quite possibly have what they needed within a year. That couldn't happen. "Take me to it."

"Orders are you're to stay in here."

An alarm sounded to the right. A short, high-pitched sound that barely carried. Someone was outside her window. She backed into the room looking around. "Broderick!"

He was in the room in a second, pistol at the ready. She waved toward the window. "The alarm . . ."

"I heard it."

"Can they get in the windows?"

His mouth set in a grim line. "If they have enough time."

Great. "How do we prevent them from getting time?"

"*We* don't do anything."

"You seriously expect me to just sit here and wait and see what happens?"

"I expect you to have faith in your mate. And failing that, the team."

To hell with that. "There's only eight of us. Lord knows how many there are of them."

"There's seven of us. You don't count."

Another alarm went off inside the house. More toward the kitchen where she'd left her laptop. That couldn't be good. "I need to get that research."

"My orders are to keep you in this room."

"Then bring my laptop to me."

"My orders are not to leave you."

She'd had enough of this catch-22. "If anyone from Sanctuary gets a hold of that laptop, within a very short amount of time their scientists will know how to alter your body chemistry and every damn member of your pack's chemistry so that you waste away. Just like Joseph."

His head snapped around. "You said there wasn't anything on that laptop that concerned us."

"There wasn't, but I started getting worried about what would happen if the flash drive got damaged. I didn't have a backup."

He lowered the rifle slightly. His brows took the same downward dip. "So you backed up to the computer."

"Yes, I did."

"Fuck."

"Precisely."

Something thudded against the side of the building. She jumped. Broderick's expression grew even more serious. She pressed her advantage. "We can't leave that laptop out there."

"Son of a bitch." He put his hand to the transceiver and turned away. She could hear the low murmur of his voice. She couldn't tell what he was saying, but his energy was intense, lashing around like the tail of a cat on the verge of attack. She knew he was supposed to be a wolf, but right then he looked like a panther full of lethal energy backed into a corner with no good way to turn. She knew exactly how he felt. She waited while he debated the issue, her nerves crawling beneath her skin. The alarm sounded again in the vicinity of the kitchen.

"Are you sure they can't see in the windows?"

"Yes."

"Would you know if the shielding failed?"

The sense of lashing energy increased. "I assume so."

"There has to be a reason they're focusing their attention by the kitchen."

"Fuck."

"You are if they get that information."

She waited. He held his position. Goddamnit. They couldn't just sit here and let the unthinkable happen. "I'm getting that laptop. You can stay here or come with. I don't care."

She darted out the door. Once in the hall, she slowed down. The house she'd thought so cozy just a few hours ago now seemed claustrophobic.

"Lost your courage?" Broderick asked.

"Did you lose yours?"

He shouldered past her. "What makes you ask that?"

"There had to be some reason they made you my babysitter."

The sound that came from his throat was definitely a growl. She stuck close to his back as he made his way to the kitchen. It was only twenty feet but felt like twenty miles. When she got to the kitchen she could see light beyond the window. Nowhere else in the house was there light. Broderick's curse confirmed her worst fear. "The shields aren't working here, are they?"

"No."

Another thought hit her. If light was coming in the window, that meant it was daylight outside. "Where's Slade?"

With a jerk of his chin, Broderick indicated the door.

"He can't survive sunlight!"

The wolf didn't say anything.

"Why didn't he stay with me?"

Broderick leaned against the wall, checking the perimeter beyond. "The subject was brought up."

"By whom?"

"Tobias. Creed. Derek." He shrugged. "Myself. He didn't listen."

Why was she not surprised? "Why didn't you bring it up harder? Maybe with a two-by-four in hand?"

"He's your mate. He has a right to protect you."

She grabbed the computer off the table. "And how is he going to protect me if he's a crispy critter?"

Broderick moved to the next window, easing the curtains aside. "He's trying out his new sunscreen."

"In the middle of battle?" She headed for the door.

Broderick caught her arm. "Slade's the smartest man I know. And he wouldn't risk you for pride."

"What aren't you telling me, Broderick?"

"We're outnumbered."

She straightened slowly. "That has the sound of an understatement."

He nodded. "Slade has a plan, but for it to work he has to be part of it."

"How did he get out of my bed without me knowing?"

"He drugged you."

"With his mind?"

Broderick shook his head. "That would've been easier, but he said it wouldn't work."

Because she'd learned to block him.

"He actually drugged me?"

She didn't know why she was shocked, but she was.

"A bit primitive for a vampire, but yes."

"That bastard."

"He didn't want you in the middle of things."

The wall of silence on Slade's side of their normally noisy mental connection took on a much more sinister quality. Grabbing her backpack from where it hung on a kitchen chair, she yanked it open. "Well, that's a plan that's about to backfire on him."

Broderick grabbed for her arm. She twisted away. "What do you mean?"

"I'm not leaving him out there alone."

"He's not alone."

"So you say, but if the team is as badly outnumbered as you've led me to believe, and everyone is fighting their battles"—she jerked at the backpack zipper—"then how the hell do you know that he's alive and not down?"

"Jane, you're too important to risk. That's just the bottom line. And if I have to knock you out, I'll knock you out, but you're not going out there."

She scanned with her senses, looking for any indication that Slade was alive. She couldn't find it. There was just that wall of nothingness where he should be. It could be he was blocking her, but there could be another, more sinister reason. He could be down, a victim of his own experiment. He could be burning as she sat here arguing. An image leapt into her mind. An image of Slade lying unprotected in the sun, his skin turning to ash over his bones. His face contorted in a scream of agony. Shoving the laptop in the pack, she yanked the zipper closed and grabbed her shoes. Slade wasn't going to die like that.

In her gut, emotion and determination coiled into a tight mass. The force built. It was scary. It was empowering. So much energy inside her, it spilled over into a shimmer of light around her. Broderick reached out. The motion appeared slow. But it wasn't. She knew it wasn't. Werewolves had reflexes as quick as lightning. She looked into his eyes. The power built. Inside her, the protest built right alongside it. Sound faded. The ghostly light in the periphery of her vision grew brighter.

No.

Broderick froze.

Get back.

He took a step back. She didn't know what she was doing or how she was doing it, but somehow she'd stopped him. A full-grown were. Was it a delusion caused by the drug? Was it real? How long would it last? Hitching the backpack up on her shoulder, Jane glanced at the door. It had to last long enough. She took a step and looked back. Broderick was still standing there, his expression blank. She touched her fingers to the pack's shoulder strap. She couldn't take the laptop with her. Sliding it off her shoulder, she put it on the floor and cautiously shoved it toward Broderick. With every bit of the energy in her, she gave an order. "Protect it."

Not a muscle in the were's face moved. Had he heard?

"Do you hear me?" she asked.

He nodded. Jane sighed. It was the best she could do. Staying low as she'd seen on TV, she opened the door slowly and immediately winced. Her panic was premature. No spray of bullets filled the interior. No one shouted a warning.

She looked back. Broderick was picking up the backpack. Sunlight caught on the gun attached to his hip. She'd need a weapon. Closing the door, she hurried back and quickly took it from his belt. He caught her hand. Her heart leapt in her throat.

Let go.

The fact that he did freaked her out. She backed toward the door, watching him carefully, expecting a trick. Beyond picking up his rifle, he didn't move. She opened the door again. A fly was the only thing that seemed to notice.

She sneaked out into the sunshine. For once, the environment could work for her. Daylight was her natural environment. Or at least it used to be until Slade had forced her to start living in the night. She rubbed at her burning eyes and the tears blurring her vision. She didn't used to be this sensitive.

A whisper of energy trickled over her shoulder. She spun to her left, blinking furiously. Lifting the gun, she pointed it at the monster coming at her. She had the impression of a semihuman form baring yellowed canines before she pulled the trigger. Nothing happened. If a monster could smile, it was a grin that spread across the beast's face as its approach slowed to a stalk. Jane looked at the gun through a haze of tears. In rapid succession, her mind catalogued the pieces. The little lever on the left looked out of place. Flipping it down, she raised the gun again. The monster lunged. She pulled the trigger.

Blinding light shot from the gun. The recoil knocked her back into the wall. A hole big enough to put her arm through blew wide in the monster's chest. She could see daylight through it. Her stomach heaved. He crumpled at her feet, the grin still on his face. There was no blood. No gore. The edges of the wound were seared closed. She tilted the gun to the side and looked at it again. What in hell was this thing?

She took a step to the left, shock splitting her purpose. Half of her screamed to get inside. The other half screamed for Slade. The sun burned uncomfortably on her skin. Hotter than she'd ever remembered the sun feeling. Another residual effect of whatever the drug was that Slade had given her? Or something more? She was beginning to suspect the latter.

She tried another mental probe. *Slade.*

Again no answer, but an inner voice prompted her to go to the right. Inching along the building, holding the gun in front of her, she swore. She wasn't cut out for this. She was a scientist, for heaven's sake. She didn't indulge in confrontation. She just created through research the moral issues that others loved to debate. She stubbed her toe, grimacing as she stumbled. There was a reason she hadn't joined the military. And that reason was, she was a goddamned coward. She didn't like having to face life-or-death reality. She liked being locked up in the carefully controlled environment of her lab where everything went the way she said it should go. So how the hell had she ended up out here in the middle of a war between supernatural beings that wanted to take her prisoner, rape her mind, and then kill her? How did things like this happen to anyone, let alone her? One of *these days she was going to have to seriously talk to God.* GI Jane she was not, and he had to stop putting her in scenarios just because *he* believed she could be.

Energy whipped at her from above. With a mental block she sent it sliding to the side. Dirt spewed in every direction under the impact. She jumped back. The ground exploded again where she'd just been standing. Son of a bitch, there was someone on the roof.

Pressing back against the building, she counted to four. Instinct said she had to cross the clearing. But if she left the shelter of the overhang, she'd be an easy target. Of course, staying here was no better. No doubt that person on the roof had one of those transceivers that Slade wouldn't give her. And no doubt he was talking to all the other monster guys running around loose. While she could talk to only herself. So in about three minutes everybody was going to know where she was. And if everybody knew where she was and everybody came for a party, she was not going to escape. Which meant once again, she had to do something.

Please, Lord, let them see me for what I am, the wussy scientist about to pee her pants, and not some sort of badass that needs shooting. I could use the edge.

Turning around, she pressed her elbows against the building.

Don't see me. Don't see me. Don't see me.

On the count of three she backed up into the open, blindly aiming for her rooftop target. He was standing there looking around. She pulled the trigger. The same hole exploded in his torso. And just like the last monster, he dropped. Before she could lose her courage, she bolted for the woods. Slade was in there somewhere. She heard a shout. It sounded like Tobias. An order burst into her mind.

Get in the house.

She fired back along the mental channel, *Leave me alone.*

To her surprise there was no response and no one came running toward her. She made it to the woods. As soon as she stepped under the sheltering branches, she realized her mistake. She couldn't see anything beyond the next tree. Here the monsters had all the advantage. They could be above her, below her; they could be waiting on the other side of the next bush.

"Damn it."

It sucked being a human in a world of paranormals. It wasn't as if she could go back, though. Which left only one option. She had to find Slade. She headed deeper into the woods, letting her instinct guide her. Thirty feet in, she had an option. Up or down. Her gut said down. She followed the muddy streambed down the hill, every step taking her farther away from the house. Farther from the team. Hopefully, farther from the monsters. Her heart pounding in her chest, she resumed her mantra.

Don't see me. Don't see me. Don't see me.

The couple minutes she walked felt like forever. Through the breaks in the underbrush she could see the house and the monsters that stalked it. She could hear the sounds of battle, but no one seemed to see her. No doubt they were too focused on killing

Tobias and the others to notice a lone woman creeping down a streambed. Which was good. At the next curve of the stream, the path was blocked by a fallen log. From the hollow beneath the log poked . . . a boot? She knew that boot.

"Slade!"

Pulling back the branches, she stepped over the log. It was Slade but he was all but unrecognizable. His hands and face were an ugly blackish red. Blisters bubbled under his skin. A gaping wound seeped a steady stream of blood from his side. She didn't have to be a doctor to know it was bad. But she *was* a doctor and she knew what that wound meant. There was no way Slade hadn't suffered massive internal damage. She didn't know how much blood a vampire could lose and survive, but Slade had to be getting to the limit.

Don't see us. Don't see us. Don't see us.

She couldn't stop the chant even to scream for help. Reaching up, she moved a strand of hair off Slade's face. His beloved handsome face. She wanted to stroke his cheek but as burned as he was, his skin would come off in her hand. She shuddered and pulled her hand back.

"Some badass vampire."

Something stuck to her fingers. Looking down she saw they were stained with the same reddish black of his skin. He wasn't burned. He was covered in sunblock. The relief was staggering. "Damn it, Slade, only you would have your sunblock mimic a burn."

Resting her forehead against his, Jane let herself relax just for a second. She'd found him. And he was alive. But for how long? Sitting up, she cupped his face in her hand. "You hold on, Slade Johnson."

Not even a flicker in his energy. She wanted nothing more than to lay down beside him and hold him until help came, but she also knew help wasn't going to come. Not in the time Slade needed. And if the Sanctuary monsters overpowered the team, then not at all. She set the gun on his thigh and lifted his shirt away from his wound. Her gorge rose and clogged the scream in her throat. For a moment her litany stopped. From afar she heard a shout.

Oh God! Had they been found?.

Don't see us. Don't see us. Don't see us.

With a shaking hand, she rested her palm on his stomach. She could see his intestines through the hole.

"What were you doing so far from everyone else?"

He didn't answer.

"It's just your bad luck that I'm the one that found you. I don't know what to do to help you."

She tried probing his mind, but it was as if he'd already left his body. The anguish that struck her was unimaginable. She felt as if her soul were being shredded. Placing her palm over the gaping wound, she tried to hold him together. She wouldn't lose him like this. Not like this.

Then you need to make another choice.

Creed's words came back to haunt her. She'd been so confident in her decision, so focused on what she wouldn't be she hadn't realized what she would be without Slade. A woman without her soul.

Bracing her hands on either side of Slade's chest, she angled up, placing her lips on his cold unresponsive ones. "You don't get to be right at the expense of us."

Focusing all her energy, she sent one thought into his mind. *Live.*

His mouth felt foreign beneath hers. Like a stranger's. With her sleeve she wiped the smear of sunscreen from her lips. Leaves rustled in the breeze. A crow cawed. There were no sounds of battle, but beyond the one that had woken her up, there really hadn't been any. At any other time, she would have been impressed that so vicious a war could take place so far below human radar. But right now she was just panicked. And she needed help.

Slade needed blood. Vampires self-healed if they had enough blood. That's what all the best movies decreed. She rubbed her neck and then her wrist as she considered her options. Her stomach heaved as she knelt beside his head. Fear raged right alongside hope. She really wasn't GI Jane, and she really wasn't good with pain. She hated it. "Don't bite my hand off."

Closing her eyes, she put her wrist against Slade's mouth and raked his fang against her skin. Biting her free hand, she smothered her gasp. It didn't just hurt, it burned like acid.

She kept her hand there, letting her blood drip on his tongue, horror and determination vying for dominance.

Slade didn't take the bait.

"Goddamnit, Slade, drink." There was no flux in his energy or his muscles. "I don't know how long I can hold them off."

Just saying it freaked her out. She wasn't Wonder Woman. She didn't have supernatural powers, but she couldn't shake the feeling that she was the one making them invisible. It could be yet another residual delusion courtesy of whatever Slade had used to knock her out, but there was comfort in thinking she had some control, so she didn't completely dismiss the notion.

Pressing her hand against his mouth, she tried again to get through to him. "I'm not an outside kind of girl, you know. I'm more the kind that sits back and asks someone else to fix things. But, seeing as there's no one else around, you're going to have to help out here, Slade, because I don't know what I'm doing and you're dying." Tears clogged her throat. "And I can't live with that."

"But you expect him to go through forever without you."

Tobias. Jane never thought she'd be so happy to see the enigmatic werewolf. Wiping her tears on her sleeve, she sat back. "He's dying."

"I know."

Catching her arm, he lifted her away from Slade and turned her toward him, keeping her arm elevated so she couldn't catch her balance. Men come out of the woods, forming a solid wall between her and Slade. Those strange eyes of his studied her from head to toe.

She yanked at her arm. "Don't look at me like that."

He cocked an eyebrow at her. "Like what?"

"Like I'm some strange species of bug you've just discovered."

He let her go. "You definitely have hidden talents."

Rubbing at her arm, she muttered, "That wouldn't come as a surprise to you if you didn't automatically assume you knew everything."

"I'll keep that in mind."

Try as she might Jane couldn't see what the men were doing. She wanted to pick them up and hurl them aside. She wanted to scream at them to move. More than anything she wanted to see what they were doing.

"You don't need to see." Tobias had been reading her mind.

"You don't know what I want."

"You want him to live."

Duh! "Will he?"

Tobias shrugged. "He's still alive."

"How do you know?"

Instead of answering, he knelt beside Slade. Men moved aside, giving him room. It was a gesture of faith and trust. She wished Tobias didn't irritate her so. She could use a bit of that confidence right now. Tobias ran his hands slowly over Slade's torso and legs, searching for something. Whatever it was, she hoped he found it. The men fell back in around Slade, blocking her view. She needed them to move. Inside, the energy built.

"Don't interfere if you want him to live," Tobias ordered.

"I'm not doing anything."

His head cocked to the side. "You don't know, do you?"

She just shook her head.

"That means it's new."

"What's new?"

The only response he gave was a cryptic. "Interesting."

"I can't even feel his energy," she whispered.

"He's got it blocked," Tobias answered, his tone as even as always. Reaching into Slade's pocket, he pulled out a small metal device with a green light on the tip.

"Brace yourself."

Before she could ask "For what?" he pressed a button. The light died out. Energy blazed into her mind. Slade. She almost sobbed as the void filled with Slade's pain, Slade's confusion, Slade's worry. She covered her mouth. Even stretched out within kissing distance of death, the man was worried about her. And he was alive.

Tobias passed the device to her. "Hold this."

She took it. It felt oddly heavy.

"Now turn it on."

"Why?"

"Humor me."

She did. Her eyebrow cocked up.

"Interesting," Tobias said again.

Jane shot him an angry look. "You need to be helping Slade, not irritating me."

"Am I irritating you?"

"Yes. And enjoying it if your expression is anything to go by."

"You don't read people well, do you?"

"I do fine with people. It's werewolves that give me trouble."

As if on cue, Derek stepped into the little clearing. Like Tobias, he had presence. And like Tobias, he was intimidating, but unlike

Tobias she knew he loved Slade. Tobias stood and made room for him. She watched as he knelt beside Slade. Sunlight gleamed off his blond hair. She reached for his energy. And found nothing. So either he had a device or he could block her, too.

"He's lost a lot of blood," she called.

"They can see that," Tobias interrupted.

"I told you before, leave me alone."

"You don't have to worry. We won't let him die."

"Pardon me if I don't take your word for it."

Derek rolled up his sleeve. The men leaned in, Slade's pack, Slade's family all gathered around him. There was room for all of them at his side. But not for her.

She blew out a breath. "I hate this."

To her surprise, Tobias took her hand. "I know."

Comfort flowed over her, dampening her panic and replacing it with a sense of . . . calm. She left her hand in his.

"Are you sure he's going to be all right?"

"We got here in time."

"Good."

Again he gave her that strange look. "What are you thinking?"

"That I don't do Wonder Woman well."

"Oh, I don't know about that. I was just thinking you had potential."

She pulled her hand from his. "Then you'd be wrong."

Because, once again when it had mattered, she hadn't been able to do a damned thing.

❖ 16 ❖

THEY were picked up by a convoy of heavily armored vehicles. No one spoke, which was fine with her. She was exhausted, shell-shocked. She'd killed two men—things. Almost lost Slade, and had a few home truths shoved down her throat by the events of the day. If she were an ostrich, she'd be standing with her head in the sand. Instead she was riding on the floor in the back of one of the vehicles, holding Slade's hand, pretending she didn't feel the censure of the others. She wasn't alone in her assessment that she'd failed Slade.

By the time they were halfway back to the compound, Jane realized everybody was also looking at her strangely. She didn't care. She was too worried about Slade. He lay across the backseat too quiet. Too pale. His energy a mere echo of the force she was used to. She brought the back of his hand to her lips.

Live, damn you.

Tobias turned around from where he sat in the front. "You know a Johnson is too damned stubborn to die from a flesh wound like that."

"Two attempts at consolation in one day? Be careful, Tobias, or I might start thinking you're a good guy."

"We wouldn't want that."

She threaded her fingers through Slade's unresponsive ones. "What was he doing out there alone so far from everyone else?"

Leather creaked as Tobias shifted position. "He was pretending to be you."

"Please."

Tobias ran his hand through his hair. "Your mate is a very intelligent man, capable of many things. And what he's not capable of physically, he finds a way to do mechanically."

"In other words," Jace said from the far back, "he was able to project your presence."

"How would something like that work? I mean, as soon as somebody got close enough to . . ."

"See," Tobias finished for her. "Yes, but we didn't need them to believe it forever."

"If they thought we were sneaking you out, it would bring them all to one place," Jace explained.

"And give you the advantage you lost by being outnumbered," she finished.

"As I said, your mate is a very intelligent man."

And devoted to those he loved to the point he'd sacrifice his life without batting an eye. Stroking the backs of her fingertips across his forehead, she whispered, "He's a scientist. He shouldn't have been out there at all."

As soon as she said it, she knew it was wrong.

I'm the badass vampire who can kick Sanctuary's butt.

Tobias snorted. "He's a Johnson. They're more outlaw than anything else."

Outlaw. Such an old-fashioned term. But then again Slade had been born one hundred and fifty years ago, and the majority of a person's personality was formed in their first years of life. Slade's had been formed in the Wild West where survival depended on a person's ability to adapt. Slade was a master of adaptation.

"I don't really know him, do I?

"You know what you need to."

"Which according to you is that he's my mate." She waved her hand in the air. "This mythical concept that disregards reality, circumstances, and events."

"Comforting, isn't it?"

She shook her head. "Not if you don't believe in mates."

"A month ago you didn't believe in vampires," Jace offered quietly.

"Has anyone ever told you that being logical during an emotional moment is irritating?"

"Not recently."

"Well it is, and I can't make a decision when I don't agree with the concepts."

"I thought your decision was already made."

The SUV hit a bump. She jumped right along with it. Even though she was surrounded by Renegade soldiers, she still couldn't shake the feeling that Sanctuary would be on them at any minute. With a trembling hand, she smoothed back the lock of hair that fell over Slade's forehead.

"I can't do this, Tobias."

"Do what?"

Again, she made a wave of her hand. The car hit another bump.

She felt the touch of Slade's energy. Stroking her fingers down his cheek, she debated turning off the energy masker that was still in her pocket.

"They're never going to stop coming after me, are they?"

"And we won't stop stopping them."

War. Never-ending war and always at the end of it the potential for destruction of an entire species. Because of her.

What could she say except, "Thank you."

CALEB was waiting for them as they came into the yard. The look he gave her as he opened her door wasn't strange, it was flat-out angry. It made for a refreshing change. Jane could deal with hostility.

"What is it?"

He held out his hand. She put hers in it. He half hauled, half helped her out of the SUV. Then he reached for Slade. A muscle in his jaw bunched as he worked his hands under his brother and then slid him across the seat. Standing, he cradled Slade in his arms, his love for his brother etched in the anguish on his face. It was such a human moment, one that had been captured on camera time after time by war correspondents. And here it was playing over again. With vampires. More proof love wasn't species specific. A horse in the paddock whinnied uncertainly.

With a sharp nod of his head, Caleb turned on his heel and carried his brother toward his house. When Jane would have followed, Jace caught her arm.

"Joseph is worse."

Out of the corner of her eye she could see Caleb reach Slade's porch. In a minute she'd hear the squeak of the screen door.

"How do you know?"

"Allie just sent it over the system."

Clenching her fists against the need to bolt after Slade, she snapped, "I want one of those transceivers."

"You'll have to ask Slade."

She couldn't ask Slade anything. The screen door squeaked. They'd taken him away. "How bad is Joseph?"

"Bad."

She stood there torn. Her heart said she needed to be with Slade. Her conscience pushed her toward Joseph.

Jace's tone softened. "Caleb will take care of Slade. He just needs time to heal."

"Maybe."

"Joseph needs you now."

Triage. She understood the concept of treating the most severe cases first. She was just having a hard time accepting it.

"Joseph is dying."

The anguish in that statement brought her head up. Looking into Jace's hazel eyes, she was struck by the realization that there was more than the warrior to the man. He was also an uncle. "You love him."

His head jerked back with surprise. Looking down his straight nose, he informed her, "Of course. He's my nephew."

It was easy to see Slade in that gesture. "I'm sorry." Running her fingers through her hair, she massaged the tension in her neck. "I'm just more used to seeing you as a soldier."

"Soldiers have families, too."

Yes, they did. And Jace and Joseph were Slade's family. She really didn't have a choice.

"Take me to Joseph."

With a jerk of his chin, Jace indicated she should follow him up the path to the main house. She did, feeling that sense of déjà vu as a horse whickered a greeting from the corral. Her sneakers made little noise crossing the big porch. By the door, a board squeaked. Opening the front door, Jace waved her in.

As the door closed behind him, Jace said, "Joseph is in the nursery."

The nursery was the third door on the right at the top of the curved stairway. She knew that from her previous visit. Stopping just inside the high-ceilinged foyer, Jane stood motionless and absorbed the energy of the house, mentally preparing herself for what was to come. "I just need a minute."

"I'm not sure Joseph has it to spare."

She forced a smile. "Then let's get going."

Jace caught her arm. "Do me a favor."

"What?"

"Don't smile like that in front of Caleb and Allie."

"Not coming off confident?"

"Not at all."

She nodded. "Then maybe we should nix the smiles."

"I would." He led the way up the stairs. Caleb's comfortable house. A house built for laughter. Joseph's room was no different. Painted in pale yellow with accents of white and blue and a gingham crib set, it was a room reflecting the hopes of proud parents. But there was no laughter here. Just sadness. It echoed in the walls and from the rocker by the big windows. Allie sat in the rocker with Joseph, her cheek resting on his head. Looking completely normal in blue jeans and a pale blue tank. On the table beside the chair was an untouched bottle. Not looking up, Allie whispered, "He's dying."

Yes, he was. Jane could feel it in the uneven fluctuation of his energy. "I'm sorry."

"Can't you do something?"

Controlling the anger at the pointlessness of this life leaving too soon, and the fear that she wouldn't be able to stop it, Jane crossed to Allie's side. Kneeling beside Allie, she pulled the blanket back from the baby's face. His parents loved him so much, were going through so much to keep him alive, and he was over here in his own corner of the world fighting his own private battle. And he was losing.

The old anger came back. She'd seen too many babies die, seen too many mothers look at her as Allie was right now in that warring combination of fear and hope. She'd felt this anger too many times. She didn't know what to say. She touched Joseph's cold little cheek. So pale and sunken, as if death felt the need to advertise its imminent arrival. Jane stood. Allie looked at her, the hope she couldn't relinquish filling her gaze. No mother could give up that hope. Vampire or human, it didn't matter. Jane couldn't find the words Allie needed to hear. Turning on her heel, she left the room.

"What the hell are you doing?" Jace demanded as she passed him at the door.

"I'm going to the lab."

His fingers sank into her arm. With a jerk, he spun her around. "You leave the room without a word to Allie? You are one coldhearted bitch."

Yes, her heart was very cold. "What do you want me to tell her? She already knows her son is dying."

"I want you to tell her you can do something about it."

Jane shook her head, brushing her hair off her face. She'd thought earlier when she'd put together the mental formula for the potential cure that it was going to be so easy. A series of tests narrowing the options, a few experiments, some educated guesswork when it came to dosage, and voilà! A cure. But that all required time that she didn't have. Now, she had one shot to get it all right. One impossibly long shot.

"And give her false hope?"

"You need to give her something."

With the odds being what they were, she didn't have any right to give Allie any hope. And Jace had no right to take her to task for it.

"Let me go."

Jace dropped her arm with a look of disgust. She pushed past him. When she got to the lab, she closed the door behind her and keyed in the code. The locks slid shut with a satisfying clank. Walking over to the desk, she set her backpack on it. Her hand shook so hard she could barely open the pack. After three tries she got it open and set the laptop on the desk. Pushing the power button, she waited for the gong. The glow of the screen welcomed her into its embrace. Clicking on the folder holding her data, she concentrated on the numbers and notes. A little of her tension eased.

She took another steadying breath. The familiar scent of the pristine lab soothed her nerves a bit more. This was her world. There was no life and death here. No chaos. There were just abstract problems to be solved. She let the sterility of the environment wrap around her. But no matter how hard she tried, she couldn't erase the feel of little Joseph's cheek from her fingertips. She'd touched death twice today. Now, she had to figure out how to defeat it.

FOUR hours later, Jane had her formula. Whether it would work or not was a whole other question. The only way to know was to try it. Rolling the chair back from the desk, she rubbed the tension from the back of her neck. She had no idea where Caleb was, but she needed him in the lab ASAP. Picking up the phone, she hit the whole compound intercom.

"Caleb, I need you in the lab now."

Five minutes later there was a knock. Punching in the combination, she unlocked the door. Almost immediately, the heavy door swung in. She took a step back. Caleb stood in the entry, his expression stony. Jace and Jared flanked him like guard dogs.

She motioned him in. "I need your blood."

He ripped open his sleeve, and then, with one of his talons, sliced through the exposed flesh of his wrist with the same efficiency. "Take however much you need."

When she looked into his eyes, she saw the same desperation she'd seen in Allie's. Father, brother, leader, warrior. Like Slade, Caleb wore many roles.

"Thank you." Putting pressure on the wound, she led him to the chair. "Keep pressure on this while I get the syringe."

He motioned to the dripping blood. "This is faster."

"If you had waited two seconds I could have told you I needed it from the vein to avoid contamination." She opened a syringe packet. "Besides, what if I hadn't needed blood?"

"You're a scientist like Slade. You'll always need blood for some test or another," Jared cut in.

Pulling the protective cover off the syringe, she asked the one question she needed an answer to. "How's Slade?"

"He's holding his own."

Caleb nodded. "Good."

Jane motioned to his arm. "Please close that wound." Caleb did. "And roll up the other sleeve so I can get a sterile sample."

While she waited, Jared drawled, "It's nice of you to ask about Slade."

"Would you by any chance be lecturing me?" she asked as she slid the needle into the vein.

"Slade deserves better."

Blood filled the vial. "Slade and my relationship is none of your business."

"He's our brother."

"And my lover."

"You all might want to save this conversation for when the woman doesn't have a needle in my veins," Caleb pointed out.

"You'll survive," Jace countered dryly.

"Slade damn near died saving your ass," Jared growled.

Jane counted to ten, reaching for patience. She missed. "He came near death protecting the information that I have that you need."

Caleb tipped her chin toward him. The gesture was so reminiscent of Slade that she couldn't blink back the tears fast enough. Caleb's gaze searched her expression. "Make no mistake, he risked his life for you."

"Really?"

"Yes."

"And that has you concerned?"

"He's been taking a lot of risks since he met you," Jared interjected.

"Is that why you sent him out to betray his mate in order to get the information you wanted? Because you respect his feelings and the concept of mates so much?"

Caleb winced. She exchanged the full vial for a fresh one. "We had to think of the greater good."

"A funny thing about the greater good. It's a moving target whose significance changes according to whom you speak."

"We were wrong to ask that of Slade."

"Is that an apology?"

"Yes."

"I don't know if I accept it."

"We didn't want Slade to get hurt," Jared explained.

"If you cared so much about your brother, if you were so worried about his happiness, you wouldn't have asked him to betray me."

"He can't mate with you. Hell, you're allergic to just his saliva. About the only thing being with you can do for him is send him insane." Jace pointed out with his usual bluntness.

Jane withdrew the needle from Caleb's arm, and then asked him, "If you could never touch your wife again, would you just walk out of her life without a second glance?"

"It's not the same thing," Caleb answered.

The hell it wasn't. "Let me put it another way. If one of these Sanctuary whack jobs snipped off your penis, would that be the end of your emotional attachment? Would you be any less committed to Allie's well-being?"

"Of course not."

Jared snarled in his throat.

She tossed the syringe into the trash. "I'm getting darned sick and tired of you sanctimonious bastards growling at me. You love your brother. I get it. Well, guess what. I love him, too. And from where I'm sitting, I'm not the threat. You are. You keep him in this lab twenty-four/seven as if his life is the lamb you sacrifice to your ambitions."

"Slade loves his lab." Caleb snapped.

"Slade loves *you*, and he has an overgrown sense of responsibility that doesn't allow him to say no when you produce yet another demand for the impossible."

Jace took a step toward her. "We're at war."

"But you have wives and children to go to at the end of the day. Loved ones who demand your time and give you balance. Slade doesn't. And you're so thrilled by what he can do, it doesn't even occur to you that Slade might want the same."

"Of course it occurs to us," Caleb said.

"Really? I don't think so because if it did you'd consider how much time it takes to give you what you want and how much of his life he gives up to produce the next gadget that you want. I mean honestly, when did you expect him to find this mate if you keep him locked in this lab?"

Tension filled the room, building on energy already there. The brothers exchanged a glance that told her they were communicating mentally amongst themselves. Good. Let them talk. "Face it, you use him. You use his brains and you use his love."

Caleb jumped to his feet. She caught the flash of his fangs. "The hell we do."

"The hell you don't. You don't do it out of spite or malice, but you do."

Jared and Jace took a step in. Too little, too late. She was way past the point of intimidation. Jane took the energy-damping device and put it on the table.

"I've been in Slade's mind in a way none of you probably can. As much as you love him, he loves you back, and he *will* drive himself into the ground to give you what you need. All you have to do is ask, but I can tell you right now there's one thing he's *not* going to give you." She jabbed her thumb toward her chest. "Me. I don't know what Slade and I are going to do from here on out, and neither do you. But none of you, not Tobias, not Derek, not you or your wives are going to manipulate it. Do you understand me?"

"Or what?" Jared challenged.

"I swear to God if you even try, if you interfere in any way, whether it be under the guise of brotherly love or the greater good, I'm going to lock myself up in this lab and create the most effective torturous compound I can come up with."

"You're serious?" Jace asked.

"Slade is my mate. My man. I've been a bit off balance, but today has put me back on my feet."

Reaching out, Jane put her hand on the energy-damping device. "Your game ends now."

With a flick of her thumb, she switched it off. "Stay out of my relationship and stay out of my life."

Caleb towered over her. "If you hurt him, we'll toss your ass to the first Sanctuary pack we find," he countered in a drawl that sounded like a snarl.

She stepped into his space. It'd been one hell of a day and she was done being afraid. "If I hurt him, then Slade and I will deal with it. I repeat, our relationship is none of your business."

"She's right."

Jane spun around. Slade stood in the doorway, leaning against the doorjamb. His face was ghastly pale, but his energy was brilliantly alive. And he was as pissed as hell.

"Slade," she whispered.

With a flex of his fingers he summoned her to his side. She went eagerly.

"What the hell do you three think you're doing?"

"Jane needed blood," Jared explained, that smile still hovering on his lips.

"And you all just had to wander over here to provide it?"

"Slade . . ."

"I might be your little brother, boys, but I'm a grown man, and this for-my-own-good shit? It ends now."

"We're worried about you, Slade," Jace said. "You spend more time in the lab than you do in the world and—"

"I'm in this lab so much because things need to be done, not because I'm afraid of the world."

"You don't know what you're letting yourself in for," Jared added.

"Just get the hell out." He stumbled. As one, his brothers rushed forward. With a flash of fangs he drove them back. To her he said, "In the future when a vampire threatens you, I expect you to run."

She was done with being threatened. "Before you flash those fangs at me again, I should warn you I'm in a pretty mean mood myself. One more threat from any of you, and I'm going to bring my rotary tool to the party. We'll see how tough you look with those nasty fangs filed flat."

"Hell," Jared muttered.

Caleb rolled his sleeve down and eyed her speculatively. "You know, we may just have been sticking our noses where they don't belong."

"May have?"

Caleb's energy snapped out at her. "Don't push it."

The energy was gone as fast as it had arrived, replaced by a sense of calm. Slade had deflected. "Back off, Caleb." he snarled.

Caleb held up his hands. "Done."

Closing her eyes, Jane savored the sensation of having the old Slade back. But as he was just coming off an injury, she did a little emotional smoothing of her own. She knew she'd succeeded when Slade's muscles relaxed and he dropped a kiss on the top of her head.

"What's going on with Joseph?" Slade asked her when the tension in the room had abated.

She glanced at Caleb. He didn't say anything, leaving her to break the news. "He's not doing well."

He probably had another day before he passed the point of no return, but Caleb didn't need to hear that.

"What have you done?"

"Not enough," Caleb bit off.

Slade held her to his side when she would have moved away. "We're working on it, Caleb."

"Son of a bitch, I know." He ran his hand through his hair. "But I want a guarantee."

Jane flinched. Slade didn't. "Life doesn't come with those."

"Yeah."

"But if you all get out of here and let us work, I'll see what I can do."

As one, the brothers headed for the door. As they drew abreast, Caleb stopped. He glanced at Slade and then at her. Slade took her hand. Caleb looked up.

"About what you said earlier about your relationship being your business?"

She nodded.

"I'll think about it."

"Thank you."

When the doors closed behind his brothers, Slade tugged her down onto his lap. She made a token protest. "We have to get to work."

"In a minute."

"We don't have a minute."

He tipped her head back. His gaze met hers. "I need this."

Come to think of it, so did she. She rested her cheek against his shoulder. "Your family doesn't like me."

"My family doesn't know what to make of you."

Linking her fingers behind his neck, she smiled softly into his eyes. "But you do."

"Uh-huh." The skim of his hand down her side snapped her nerve endings to attention. His fingers curled around her hip, sinking into the softer flesh. Hot and familiar desire thrummed through her veins. Turning her face into his chest, she whispered, "I thought I'd lost you."

His lips brushed her hair. "Never."

But he lived with the daily knowledge that he might lose her.

"How do you do it?" she asked.

"I focus on what I have."

She wasn't good at that type of thinking. As if reading her mind, he added, "And if I can't do that, I focus on my work."

That she could do. "I think I've figured out the formula."

"So why the tension in your voice?"

"It's got to be right this first time. I didn't want to say anything in front of Caleb, but Joseph is too weak to hold on much longer."

"And?"

"What if I'm wrong?"

His lips brushed her hair. "Then no one in this world would get it right."

Maybe. Maybe not, but all that mattered right then was his faith in her.

"We need to figure out the delivery system."

He arched that eyebrow in that way that made her heart leap in an inner smile. "Are you inviting me into your research, Jane Frederickson?"

With a start she realized she was. She who had always worked alone was actually inviting someone into her "inner sanctum." And she wasn't the least bit nervous. "Yes, I believe I am."

❧ 17 ❧

A FEW minutes passed, and with each one, the tension within Jane eased.

"You were right, you know," Slade said, breaking the silence.

She tipped her head back. "About what?"

"About this being only between you and me."

She rested her finger on his cheek, tracing the slash of his cheekbone. "Because it's already so damn complicated we don't need any third parties?"

He grinned wryly. "Because they'd just mess it up."

She nodded. "And we're going to do a good enough job of that ourselves."

"Yeah."

His energy pulsed around her. Weaker than normal, but still so much stronger than hers.

"I was so scared when I found you."

"I bet."

"I couldn't feel your energy. I could only feel the nothingness where it should have been."

"I'm pretty impressed you thought to trace that back."

She feigned arrogance. "I am a genius."

"Not all geniuses have common sense."

"Very true . . . Slade?"

"What?"

"I would love to sit and cuddle with you, but Joseph really doesn't have the time."

His head snapped up. "He's that bad?"

"You haven't seen him?"

"No, goddamnit."

"Well, I saw him a few hours ago."

"How long have I been unconscious?"

"Not that long, but—"

"Shit. Why didn't anyone wake me?"

"If you'd look in the mirror, you'd know why."

"That's an easy fix."

"You need more blood."

He glared at her. "Don't even think it."

She rubbed her hand on her thigh. "I wasn't about to."

He let the lie slide and changed the subject, for which she was grateful.

"You took Caleb's blood because you needed the protein?"

She nodded. "But what we really need is a way to synthesize it, and then maybe we can regulate the dosage and store it."

"Where are you now in the process?"

"This sounds entirely too simple. But you know how lactose-intolerant people just need to take a pill? I think that's all Joseph needs, too."

"But we have yet to make the pill?"

She nodded again. "Yeah. He's going to need it for every meal."

"That's going to be complicated."

"I know."

"I think down the road, I'll be able to synthesize the protein, but right now we're working with it raw."

"What delivery system are you going to use?"

"I don't think an injection will work. I think the protein needs to be in his stomach at the time he eats."

"So liquid."

She nodded and slipped out of his lap, heading around to the big table upon which she'd spread her notes.

"How much?"

"I don't know." She studied the percentages on the paper. "I don't even know if too much will cause other problems."

Slade stood. "He can't afford another problem."

She spun back around. "Slade, stop telling me what I already know. Okay. I realize this is life and death. I realize if I get this wrong I kill this kid. Okay? I get it. I get it. I get it."

"Jesus God, Jane!" Reaching out, Slade grabbed her and pulled her close. "Baby, you're doing all you can."

She pushed against this chest "And if it's not enough, what? Do you think Caleb's not going to blame me? Do you think Allie's not going to blame me? Do you think *you* aren't going to blame me?" She shook her head. "They think you walk on water and they expect me to strut right along beside you, but I've done this before. I've lost this battle before. I know how it goes. I don't want another life on my conscience. I don't want this, but I don't have a choice."

Slade's energy wrapped around her, holding her tighter than his arms.

"You have a choice." He took the notebook from her hand. "I can take over."

Jane allowed herself the illusion that that was possible while she let Slade siphon off the worst of her agitation. When she was calm again, she took the notebook back. "You can't. Not in the time frame we have."

She appreciated that he didn't argue, but what she appreciated more was the way he stood beside her. "Then we'd better get to work."

IT was different working with someone who was as capable as she was. An equal, not an assistant. Someone who wasn't afraid to interrupt her thoughts and put forth his own. Irritating, too, but good. At first she fought it, but as they worked she realized how much they complemented each other. Soon they were finishing each other's thoughts, leaping through the process much quicker than she would have on her own. Just another area in which they were compatible. Which was good. They didn't have time for trial and error. They needed a solution. And, three hours later, she held up the little bottle full of clear liquid; they had it.

"Should we call them?" she asked, screwing the eyedropper lid onto the bottle.

Slade looked at her. "How sure are you that this is it?"

"As sure as I can be. How sure are you?"

He leaned back in the chair, looking at the latest calculations. "Sick-in-my-gut-one-shot-at-life sure."

She took his hand and held on. They'd done all they could. The only thing left was to see if it was enough. Slade laced his fingers through hers.

"Then it's time to make the call."

* * *

SLADE led the way. By the time they got to the nursery, it seemed like half the compound was in the hall. Jane walked the gauntlet of hope-filled faces, keeping her gaze centered on Slade's back, her heart in her throat. At the door, Slade stopped.

"You go in. I'll handle the riffraff."

Predictably the riffraff had something to say about that. The attempts at humor did break some of the tension, though. She mouthed a "thank you."

She felt his smile. *You're welcome.*

Taking a steadying breath, Jane stepped into the room. Allie sat on the rocker by the window. Joseph was wrapped in a blanket cradled in her arms. There was no sign of Caleb. On the table beside them was the bottle of baby formula that Slade had prepared. They'd decided it'd be best to simply feed Joseph the liquid protein along with his usual diet. They did not want to introduce any additional variables—they had enough of those to deal with as it was. Everything was set to go.

Allie's smile was tremulous but with that optimism Jane was beginning to understand was so much of her personality. "We're ready," Allie said.

Jane held up the vial of protein. "So are we."

"Is that the magic elixir?" Allie asked.

"Yup." Jane forced what she hoped was an encouraging smile. "This is it."

"It doesn't look too impressive."

"Well, if you'd ever seen proteins under a microscope, you'd know they make this look fancy."

"He needs protein?"

"Not just any protein. A specific one."

"And when he gets it?"

"I think he'll have what he needs to be his little vampire self."

Allie kissed the top of her son's head. "Do you hear that, baby? Auntie Jane is going to have you smiling in no time."

Auntie Jane?

"How much do I give him?" Allie asked.

"That's the catch. I don't know. But you're very connected to your son and that gives us an advantage. So the plan is, you give him a little of the protein, and then you try the bottle. If he eats, we know we're on the right track. If not, we'll try a bit more of the protein."

Allie sighed. "Trial and error."

"I'm sorry," Jane said, kneeling down beside the rocker. How many times had she said that in the past? How many times had she stood and watched a parent's world crumple around them?

Please. Not this time.

Slade's mind touched hers. *I'm here.*

Yes, he was. Not with promises she wouldn't believe and he couldn't keep. But just there. Ready to catch her. Stand for her. Support her.

Thank you.

"I wish I could give you definite amounts," Jane continued, "but we're on uncharted ground and we have to feel our way."

Allie nodded. "And this won't make him worse?"

The only way Joseph could be worse would be if he were dead. "It shouldn't," she hedged.

"It'll be fine," Slade said, coming up beside her. "Jane's a genius at what she does."

"And in case no one's mentioned it yet, we're damned glad she is," Caleb stated, striding into the room behind Slade, looking like a warrior entering the battlefield. She tensed. Slade's fingers tightened on her shoulder.

"I'm glad you made it," Slade said.

Caleb took a protective position behind Allie. "I wouldn't miss watching my son enjoy his first meal."

Slade offered her a hand up. Jane shook her head. "I'd like to watch from here."

Mainly because she was so nervous she thought her knees would give out. Without a word, Slade knelt behind her, wrapping his arms around her and pulling her onto his lap. And that fast, she didn't feel like a scientist out on a limb anymore. Instead, she felt like a woman who was . . . loved.

Slade's lips brushed the top of her head. *It'll be all right, sweetness.*

"So what do we do?" Caleb asked, taking the vial from Jane and unscrewing the lid.

"Give him half a dropper first. Just kind of dribble it in."

The room collectively caught its breath as Caleb slipped the tube between Joseph's pale lips. "Drink this, little man," he said as he squeezed the dropper. "A very nice lady made it. It's going to get you back to rights in no time."

Some of the liquid spilled out of the baby's mouth. The rest trickled to the back of his throat. At least he still had the reflex to swallow. Allie and Caleb looked at her. Jane nodded.

"Give him the bottle," Slade ordered.

Everyone held their breath. Even the flow of energy froze.

The same thing happened with the formula as with the protein mix. Joseph wasn't eating so much as he was trying not to choke, but the liquid was getting down to his stomach, and after a couple minutes his eyes snapped open and he latched on to the bottle. He sucked it down so hard Jane could hear it draw.

"He's eating!" Allie cried out.

"That's it, little man," Caleb murmured. "Drink."

A collective sigh of relief echoed around the upper floor as people released their tension in applause, laughter, or muted cheers.

Jane held back on her celebration. Starting to eat was a plus, but she needed Joseph to continue eating, and after he ate, to keep the food down.

"Don't let him take too much at first," she cautioned. "It's been a long time since he's truly eaten in terms of being able to digest his food and we don't want to overwhelm his system."

Allie rested her cheek against Caleb's hand and nodded, smiling up at her husband. Joseph showed no sign of stopping.

"Do you think he's going to need more protein?" Caleb asked.

Jane shrugged and held out her hands. "I don't—"

"I know," he said with a snap of energy. "You don't know."

"Back off, Caleb," Slade ordered with a snap of his own. "She's saving your son's life. If you want to get picky about the trial-and-error aspect, get someone else to do it."

"We want Jane," Allie cut in. "And, Caleb?"

"What?"

Allie eased the bottle from Joseph's mouth. "I love you, but please be quiet until you get your fear under control."

"Shit." He ran his fingers through his hair, his eyes on his son. "He's getting uncomfortable?"

"He's getting full," Allie corrected.

"Is that all it is?" Caleb asked Joseph in a soft murmur. "Is your tummy full?"

Slade reached out and rested the back of his fingers against Joseph's cheek, his love for his nephew evident. "Going to have to work on that. The Johnsons are known for their appetite."

"I'm sure he'll be beating his father out of bear claws in no time," Allie interjected.

The hope was contagious. Jane smiled. "I didn't think vampires ate."

"He throws them up," Allie explained, "but he does love them."

"It keeps me human," Caleb quipped and with the cares of his world temporarily lifted, Jane saw the charm that would draw a woman like Allie.

"I think he looks better already," Allie said, kissing Joseph's forehead. The stair creaked as the hall cleared, giving the family their privacy.

Jane didn't see a difference yet. "We'll have to keep an eye on him. If he gets sick and has any other abnormal symptoms we'll need to come at the problem from a different angle."

Allie shook her head. "No, this is working." She paused and then asked, "It's because of how we got pregnant that he's having problems, isn't it? I was still human when he was conceived. That's why he didn't get what he needed."

"I don't know." Jane shrugged. "Maybe it's just one of those things. A birth defect."

"Can you keep making this protein?" Caleb asked.

"Yup. As long as Caleb's willing to give blood. Eventually I might be able to make it out of any vampire's blood, but—" She shrugged again.

"It's too soon and you don't know," Caleb finished, but this time without the sharpness.

"No, I don't know. We just have to wait it out."

Caleb stepped around the rocker and held out his hand. Slade lifted her up. When she took Caleb's hand, instead of shaking it, he pulled her in for a hug. It was a little stiff and a lot awkward. She got the impression the man didn't do this much. "Thank you."

Tears she didn't know she was suppressing gathered in her eyes. Caleb stepped back and looked at her. "Hell, Slade," he said, "I think your woman's sprung a leak."

Jane wiped at her cheeks. "I'm sorry. I'm just tired."

"Exhausted would be a better description, I'm guessing."

Turning Jane with a gentle grip on her shoulders, Caleb gave her a little shove toward Slade. "Take your woman to bed."

"Don't mind if I do."

Before Jane could offer a comment one way or another on the brothers' high-handedness, Slade scooped her up in his arms. Once there, it seemed just easier to link her hands behind his neck and rest her cheek against his chest. She really was tired. Around her, the family continued to banter. She absorbed the happy energy, letting it flow through her. The celebration might be premature, but she didn't think so. After the days of fear and negativity, this moment of normal felt good. Very good.

Allie put Joseph to her chest and burped him. He belched loudly, but it was a dry burp. No vomit in sight. Everybody smiled.

"A true Johnson," Slade bragged.

Jane rolled her eyes. "That's the Johnson claim to fame? The ability to belch?"

"It's one of them," Caleb assured her.

"Good grief."

Allie shook her head and rubbed Joseph's back, a smile tugging her lips. "One we'll be discontinuing."

"Don't worry, Joseph," Slade said. "Your uncles will sneak you out from under the women's thumbs and teach you all the important skills of being a man."

"Oh my God. Go before you corrupt my sweet innocent boy."

Caleb laughed outright. "Allie girl, there's not a Johnson born whose been sweet and innocent."

"Now you tell me."

"I bet you're glad to be back in the lab?"

Jane looked up from the slide she was preparing to see Allie standing in the doorway of the lab. One night had made quite a difference in the woman. She looked young and carefree.

"Yes. It's a pretty scary world out there when you know what's lurking in the shadows."

Allie stepped into the room. "Especially with Sanctuary hunting you."

"You have no idea."

"Actually, I do. They held me prisoner for a while."

"I didn't know."

Allie's grimace nowhere near matched the stress flare of her energy. "It was an experience."

"It doesn't show."

"Should it?"

"I don't know, those monsters I saw . . ." She shrugged. "I can't imagine it not leaving scars."

"Fortunately vampires heal."

"Yes." Shoving her chair back, Jane hazarded a guess. "You want to talk to me about something, don't you?"

"I want to talk to you about Slade."

"I haven't seen him since he put me to bed last night."

"I know. What I want to know is why."

"Maybe he just doesn't need me anymore?"

"What makes you think that?'

"His absence?"

Allie rolled her eyes. She had an expressive face. It was easy to see why Caleb loved her. She radiated life. "The Johnson men are stubborn."

Jane smoothed a crease in her jeans. "How is Slade doing anyway, physically, I mean?"

"It's taking him longer to fully heal than he wants to admit, but Tobias said he'll be at full strength in no time."

"Tobias. He's in the middle of everything."

"Yeah, he is. I think of him as a catalyst. Wherever Tobias lands, things change. Whether you want them to or not."

"And you still keep him around?"

"Change is part of life. You can fight it, but it's still going to happen."

Which was not a soothing comment to a control freak like Jane. Picking up a pen on the desk, she asked, "While you're here, can I ask you a question?"

"Shoot."

"What's it like to be vampire?"

"Honestly?"

"I don't think I can take a lie right now."

Allie laughed. "Then I'll save my creativity for later."

"Thank you."

"Being vampire is like being human on steroids. You can do everything bigger and better, even screwing up."

"Great." She gave the pen a swirl.

Allie put her hand on the pen, stopping its spin. "It really is no different than being human. There are things you can do and things you can't do. You fall in love. You make sacrifices. You adjust to your environment. You don't get to enjoy the sun, but there's beauty in the night. Pain is more intense but so is pleasure."

"And you have wars."

Allie shrugged and sat back. "So do humans."

She had a point. Jane tapped the pen on the smooth metal. "What about the blood? And keep in mind you're talking to someone who doesn't even like her meat to be pink in the center."

"I was a vegetarian."

Jane gripped the pen hard, watching her knuckles turn white. "Didn't you vomit? The first time at least?"

"I wanted to."

"Why do I hear a 'but'?"

"Because there usually is one?"

"Nobody likes a know-it-all."

"So I'm always telling Slade. Maybe if you stick around, you can convince him of it."

"I wouldn't hold my breath."

Allie cocked her head to the side. "I can hold my breath for a very long time."

"Why am I not surprised?"

"Because I'm clearly a woman of many talents who was able to get past all the ick factors of vampirism?"

Jane tossed the pen on the table. "How did you do that?"

"I can take only Caleb's blood, and I find it very erotic." She smiled a gamine grin. "Bottom line, for me sex was the great equalizer."

Jane couldn't imagine it.

Allie's grin faded. "So, joking aside, have you thought about what you're going to do?"

"You mean right after I stomp Slade's toes for being such an ass?"

"Yes. Right after that."

Jane sighed. "I have no idea."

"I could play devil's advocate," Allie offered.

"I kind of thought you already were."

"But now we can make it official and I won't have to waste a lot of time delicately broaching the subject."

It was hard to imagine the always-serious Caleb with the irreverent Allie. "You must give Caleb fits."

"I have to. It's in my job description."

"Really?"

"You know, he didn't believe it, either. I had to point it out. It was right there under the clause specifying all the mind-blowing lovemaking he could stand."

Jane couldn't help but laugh. She didn't imagine many people stayed tense around Allie. "No wonder he didn't see it."

She swung her feet. "I was counting on his attention stopping right about there."

"I like you, Allie Johnson."

"I like you, too, Jane Frederickson. And not only because you saved my son's life."

"Thank you."

"And I for one think you're perfect for Slade."

Jane grimaced. "That makes you a fan club of one."

Allie rolled her eyes. "The brothers didn't like me either when I first arrived."

That was hard to believe. "You have got to be kidding."

"Nope, as a matter of fact, they almost killed me on our first meeting."

"Why?"

"They needed to give Caleb a reason to live. See, he was going to be all self-sacrificing and let me live my life unmated."

"What happened?"

"He was almost killed by rogue wolves. I saved him. They slit my wrists."

"Oh my God! How did you ever forgive them?"

"They gave me Caleb, and as I said, things change. But, for the Johnsons, change comes hard, and there isn't a woman that's come into the family that the others haven't put through some sort of test."

"Wonderful."

"On the upside, once you're in, you're in for life. And these are men who know how to love in a way that many have forgotten."

"You're happy, aren't you?"

"I miss my family, but I am."

"You can't see them?"

"I'm working on it. Do you have family?"

"No, there's just me."

"Then that part will be easier."

"You talk like the decision is already made."

Allie gave another one of those shrugs. "Slade's not going to age."

"I will."

"Are you counting on that to diminish his interest?"

"The man's not going to get hot and bothered over a wrinkled prune with breasts down to her knees."

Allie shook her head again. "You so don't understand mates, but for the sake of argument what were you going to do if that happened? Fade off into the distance, a martyr to negative thinking?"

"Honestly?"

"Of course."

"I can't bear to think about it."

"That's because he's your mate. Your other half. The ying to your yang."

"Mate, husband, what's the difference?"

"A husband is a convenience. A mate is forever."

"So everyone keeps telling me." It wasn't helping.

"And everyone would be right. There's a chemical bonding that occurs between a mated couple."

"So you're, like, drugged?"

"No. Of the two bonds I'd say the emotional bond is stronger, but the physical is pretty fabulous."

That was good to hear. "How do you know when you've met your mate?"

"One of the first things you notice is the attraction, of course. But that's the same for most humans. And that overwhelming feeling of everything being right. But then there are more subtle things, like being able to sense where your mate is, catching stray thoughts here and there, feeling their emotions as yours." She shrugged. "I know there would never be another for me if Caleb died."

"Why? Wouldn't you miss the closeness?"

"Yes, but why would I settle for half a loaf when I know what it's like to have the whole thing?" Allie plucked a stick of gum off the desk. "I'm an all-or-nothing woman. Always have been. Caleb fits me to a 't.' "

Jane envied her that confidence.

Allie sighed and turned the gum over in her hand. "I used to love gum. There's something so focusing in that rhythmic chewing."

"You can't chew it?"

Allie held it up to her nose and breathed deep. "It makes me sicker than a dog."

"Bummer."

She dropped it back on the desk. "Yup."

Jane slid her finger alone the base of the rack holding the vials before her. Mate. Was it truly possible?

"I made Slade promise not to convert me."

"Sounds perfectly sensible to me. Taken in abstract, going vampire is a pretty freaky concept."

Going vampire. What a way to phrase it. "I could feel how much he wanted to. I was afraid he'd just do it and I'd have no choice."

"A woman should always have a choice."

"Yes." She licked her lips. "He almost died protecting me."

Allie settled more firmly on her chair. "I've been busy with Joseph, so I missed all the juicy gossip. What happened?"

"Caleb gossips?"

Allie rolled her eyes again. "They all do, though they like to call it"—she made quotation marks in the air—"exchanging information."

"We stopped at a safe house on the way back. He mentally drugged me and when I woke up, we were under attack. Broderick told me Slade was outside as part of his plan, but when I checked, I couldn't feel his energy. I knew he was out in the middle of a battle fighting on a hope and a prayer his latest invention would keep him from frying." She threw up her hands. "Who does that?"

"Don't let the lab coat fool you. That man is the biggest risk taker of all the brothers."

"At last someone that agrees with me."

"Wait until you get a chance to really meet Raisa and Miri. That am-I-crazy feeling will just disappear."

"Can I say woot?"

"Yes, but not too loudly. I don't want Caleb to find me just yet."

"You're hiding?"

Allie held up the energy damper. "I thought we should talk."

Jane shook her head. "He's going to be mad. I get the feeling I'm off limits until Slade comes to a decision."

Allie didn't look concerned, which told Jane that aura of happiness the woman wore wasn't fake. "If he didn't want me to find ways around his edicts, he wouldn't issue them."

"You don't really believe that."

Allie shrugged. "Nope, but I do believe as a grown woman I get to run my own life. Granted, sometimes I have to get more creative to make that happen when Caleb's protective side rears its head, but marriage is all about compromise."

"You're really married? As in human married?"

"Had the whole white-dress affair. It was lovely."

"Why?"

In the blink of an eye, Allie went from amused to serious. "Because changing my species didn't change who I am."

No, Jane didn't think it had. Allie was a woman very comfortable with herself. "I bet giving you that ring was the easiest thing Caleb ever did."

"In the end, I believe it was."

"In the end?"

"No relationship is smooth sailing." Allie hopped off the desk. "So tell me what happened when you found Slade?"

"I thought Slade was too sick or to hurt to feed. I tried to give him my blood, but he blocked me out. He would have lain there and died rather than risk converting me by taking too much blood after I had that reaction."

"A man of honor."

"Yes. But what kind of person am I? He almost died and all I could think of was how grateful I was that he'd been strong enough to keep his word."

"Not everybody can be vampire."

Jane's gaze went immediately to the vials of blood. "Will you keep a secret?"

"I like that you don't ask if I can, and yes, I will."

"I think I'm already halfway there."

"What?!"

She motioned to the vials of blood samples in the rack. "That's mine."

"I thought you said Slade didn't convert you."

"From the procedure everyone's described, he hasn't. But"—she tapped the paper in front of her—"there's no denying my blood chemistry has changed."

"Oh wow." Allie leaned over the paper. "Did it change in vampire ways?"

"Yes."

Her gaze met Jane's. She covered her hand with hers. Sympathy flowed along the connection. "This is huge. Does Slade know?"

"No. I'm scared, Allie. I don't want to live long enough to see the things that will change."

"You're a scientist."

"I don't want the responsibility of fixing things forever."

"Ahh. Like with Joseph."

"Yes. Because it's not always a win and the losses add up."

"I bet they do, but what makes you think you have to?"

"I've seen how you are with Slade."

"So have I in the last few months. It can't continue. We lean on him too much."

"You don't have a choice."

"There's always a choice if you look for it. We've just been a bit lazy looking for it."

"You're a dyed-in-the-wool optimist, aren't you?"

"I prefer to think of myself as practical."

"I don't think I was cut out for this career. I got caught up in the puzzle and didn't look where it would lead me."

"Where did it lead you?"

"To starving villages all over the world."

"And you watched people die."

"Yes. Over and over, sometimes because I couldn't help, and sometimes because I wasn't allowed to."

"You couldn't keep your distance."

"No."

"That's not a bad thing."

Jane closed her eyes against the memories of the faces, the hope, the tears. "Sitting here, no. Sitting there, yes."

"But you're not there."

"No, I'm here. And there's no walking away from Renegade problems."

Allie slid off the desk. "I don't think I'm the person you need to have this conversation with."

"I disagree. You've been where I am."

"Not quite. I wanted Caleb from the minute I saw him. Hell, I even wore a Wonderbra for him."

Jane chuckled. She couldn't help herself.

"I would have done anything to spend forever with that man," Allie added. "There are only two things I regret about my conversion. One, I didn't get the kick-ass powers others have."

"You were gypped?"

"Yes, I was. I'd been looking forward to that."

"What was the other?"

"I didn't get to make the choice of my own free will."

Like you. The unspoken hung between them.

"I think your way is easier," Jane said softly.

"It would seem that way, but you and Slade have an opportunity to work things out your way. To proceed without resentment. That's the way it should be. I don't know what's going on with your blood, and I don't know what's going on between you and Slade, but you need to find out. Life, even vampire life, is too damned short for stupidity."

"I apologize for my wife," Caleb said from the doorway.

"I've really got to start setting the alarm," Jane muttered. Her glare was wasted on Caleb. His attention was completely on Allie. His expression was stern, but his energy was . . . indulgent?

"I thought we agreed Slade's love life was none of our business."

"No, you lectured and I merely grunted noncommittally."

"Are you looking for a spanking?"

The sexual energy in the room spiked dramatically. Allie ambled over to Caleb with an exaggerated sway to her hips. "Could be. You've been distracted lately."

His mouth softened and his eyes narrowed. "Maybe we'll have to take care of that later."

"Maybe?" He hooked his hand behind her neck and pulled her in. Allie went with the pull, leaning against his chest, smiling up into his face. And that fast they were in their own world. "I've got to warn you, I've been feeling restless."

"Then definitely."

She laughed and pulled him down for a kiss. Jane had to look away. If she'd ever wondered if vampires truly felt love, she had her answer.

"Jane." She looked up as Caleb called her name. He tossed her the energy damper. She fumbled it twice before finally getting a grip on it. Why did everyone assume she had athletic ability?

Caleb waited until she set the device on the desk. "If you don't want Slade finding you, I suggest you put that on and get out of here."

"He's looking for me?"

"Yup." Caleb put his arm around Allie's shoulder and steered her out of the room. "And looking as cheerful as a thundercloud."

"Wonderful."

Allie leaned back over Caleb's arm. Her blue eyes were sparkling with humor. "If he gets too persnickety, Jane, you can always do what I do."

She was almost afraid to ask. "What's that?"

"Start unbuttoning buttons until his attitude changes."

The blush started at her toes. By the time it reached her cheeks, Caleb was laughing. "Allie girl?"

"Yes?"

"Hush."

❧ 18 ❧

JANE fondled the energy damper and watched the door shut behind Caleb and Allie. The solid thunk it made didn't give her that twinge of satisfaction she normally felt at the exclusion of the outside world. A lab had been her shelter for many years, fulfilled all her needs, but even before Slade's little Vamp Man icon had popped up on her computer screen, she'd been getting ready to leave. She could see that now. Reaching out to him had been her first step. As first steps went, it was a doozy, but she had been in the process of emerging from her cocoon when he'd contacted her. Accident or by higher design? Allie would no doubt say the latter.

Tapping the top of the vial of her blood, Jane pushed the chair back from the desk. Her sneakers made little sound as she crossed the tile floor. Keying in the combination, she reopened the door. Immediately, the aroma of chili, what the McClaren weres were having for dinner, surrounded her. More proof of the life she'd been missing. Her stomach rumbled. A whisper of sensation touched her mind.

Slade.

She looked over her shoulder. They'd met in this environment. It should feel right that they talk here. But it didn't. Punching the code in the panel, she closed and locked the lab before climbing the stairs and heading for fresh air.

Once outside, she started toward the corral. The night was clear, the stars hanging like party lights in the big sky. The moon was full. Her lips quirked in a smile. If a higher design was at work, they were bringing out the full cliché. Meeting a vampire to discuss their future under a full moon? Leaning against the top rail, she rested her chin on her hands, studying the horses as they lazed in the far side of corral. It did have its amusement factor.

She felt Slade before she saw him. The slide of his energy over hers was featherlight. Her breath caught. If he was downwind, he'd probably tell her he could smell the rise of her desire.

"I'm not, but I could be."

She did love the timbre of his voice. Just hearing it made her knees weak. With a smile, Jane turned. He stood a couple feet away. A tall, broad-shouldered silhouette in a Stetson, so quintessentially the cowboy, so completely sexy. "I can't imagine why you'd want to be."

He came up on her right side, lifting her hair off her neck, nuzzling his lips against that oh-so-sensitive spot just beneath her ear. "Because you smell very sweet."

She turned into his arms, resting her hands against his chest. Beneath her palms, his heart beat steadily, dependably. His fingers threaded through her hair. Beneath his smile she saw the tension he was keeping from her. The man was nervous. "Caleb told me you were looking for me."

His thumb stroked the side of her neck. "I thought you'd be in the lab."

"I've decided to expand my horizons."

"I see."

She could tell from the caution in his expression that he didn't. "What about you? Where have you been for the last twenty-four hours?"

"Gnawing at my bonds."

"Huh?"

"I'm sorry I lost my temper."

"Are you ready to tell me why?"

"Maybe."

She waited.

"You tied my hands early on in this relationship, sweetness. Necessary or not, I think we need to renegotiate."

Her stomach knotted. "How so?"

He rested his forehead against hers. "I want a future with you."

The knot began to unravel. "You said I was allergic to you."

"There's only a risk if I convert you."

"So what you really mean is you want a limited future with me."

"I'll take anything I can get."

She bit her lip and rocked back on her heels. His hand slid down to the hollow of her spine. This was the moment she'd been fearing. Looking into Slade's face now, though, feeling his energy wrap around her with the same strength of his arms, she couldn't think why. "What are you giving me in return?"

"What do you mean?"

"I'm giving up children, a man to grow old with me, sunlight. What are you giving me in exchange?"

"You know."

She rolled her eyes. You'd think she was asking him to tattoo a rose on his butt.

He smiled at the gesture. "You've been hanging around Allie too much."

"I like her."

"So do I."

"She sparkles."

Emotion darkened his eyes, scented his skin. Musky and masculine. She took another breath, holding it inside, shivering as it sank deep. Only Slade smelled this good, felt this good. The soft drag of his thumb across her sensitive lips brought every nerve ending to a tingling awareness. "While you burn with a seductive fire."

"And you like fire."

"Yes."

She could feel how much he did. He'd never been afraid of the fire, but walking into it was new to her. "Because the sex is good?"

"I can get sex anywhere."

"Lovely."

He shrugged. "It's the truth, but a woman who makes me smile just by being in the same vicinity? A woman who gives without losing herself? A woman who is smart, sexy, and has a wicked sense of humor? A man could spend eternity looking for that woman."

"So you got a bargain. You only spent a hundred and fifty years searching."

He didn't answer. She felt the touch of his mind on hers and then the immediate withdrawal. "What's wrong?"

"I'm trying not to influence you."

She started to unbutton his shirt. "Why? Do you think I'm so weak I can't resist your charms?"

He caught her hand. "Because everything inside me says to not give you a choice. To take what I want and to hell with the consequences."

An honorable man. In any place and time, deserving of respect. Her man. Jane slipped her hands free and started on the next button.

"So you intend to have a platonic relationship with me for the next twenty to thirty years?"

"Hell no."

She smiled to herself. "Then what are you offering?"

"Whatever we can manage without going too far."

Two more buttons fell to the wayside. "And what happens if we go too far?"

"You won't go alone."

She slipped her hands inside his shirt, savoring the contrast of his hair-roughened skin against her smooth palms. There was a time when she would have found his statement unbelievable, but she'd sat at Slade's side when he'd faced death. Felt the unimaginable pain of her soul being ripped apart. "I do believe that's the most heart-wrenching thing anyone has ever said to me."

"It's the truth."

She went back to unbuttoning his shirt. His stomach sucked in as her knuckles grazed his abdomen.

"I know, but I don't want you to die for me, Slade."

"What are you doing, Jane?"

"Unbuttoning your shirt."

"Why?"

She looked up. "Allie suggested it as a way to improve your mood."

The smallest of smiles touched his lips. "I think it's her shirt she unbuttons when Caleb starts yelling."

Spreading his shirt open, Jane ran her finger down the center of his pecs. Muscle jumped under her fingertips. She shivered remembering how he felt against her when he came over her. Closing her eyes, she projected the sensation to Slade. His response was a mental growl. She liked it when he growled. All their hottest moments started with a growl. "But I like *your* chest much better."

Leaning forward, she touched his right pectoral with her tongue. He tasted so good. Another growl rumbled in his chest. She smiled.

His grip tightened on her nape, pulling her up. With a slash of his nail, he cut her shirt open. "Come here."

She went, meeting him halfway, opening her mouth to his, her mind to his, letting his passion roll over her, feeling his delight beneath. He liked that she initiated this. He liked the feel of her skin, the touch of her tongue. He liked her.

She blinked and pulled back. "You really do like *me*."

Frowning down at her, he let her take a step back. "What the hell made you think I didn't?"

"I'm a stuffy scientist, and you're . . ." With a wave of her hand she indicated his washboard abdomen, his broad shoulders. His handsome chiseled face, the raw sexuality he exuded so effortlessly. "Good grief, look in the mirror." Could vampires see their reflection? "If you can that is."

"I'd rather just get my impressions from you. You make me sound downright irresistible."

"You are."

And it scared her. She was always in control, but with Slade there was no control. She had to trust him, and honorable man or not, she found trust hard.

His thumb smoothed the moisture from her lips. The heat in his eyes kept her blood simmering. "Why?"

She didn't pretend to misunderstand. "You were in my mind. You know why."

"The man in your past."

"Yes."

"Tell me about him."

She didn't want *him* anywhere near this relationship.

"You already know."

"I know what I saw."

"Then that's enough."

"No, it's not."

"I don't want to talk about it."

"We have to."

She stepped back, pulling her shirt around her, feeling exposed where before she'd been comfortable. "No."

He looked around. Following his gaze, she noticed faint movement in the distance. The guards and other members of the compound. Her night vision wasn't as good as his, but it was definitely better than she'd had a week ago.

"But maybe not here."

"Not anywhere."

"But we can talk about my being a vampire?" he asked.

"It's not the same thing."

"They're both standing between us."

"That's not true. I've never wanted what happened to come between us."

"That doesn't mean it's not between us. It's there in your mistrust, in your holding back, in your fear of commitment."

"I've never—"

Slade's expression hardened. His energy snapped out. "I know what he did to you, Jane. I know what you planned to do to him. What I don't know is how to get you to see me without the taint of him."

She'd had no idea he'd felt that hesitation in her, but she should have. She took another step back. His fingers slid down her arm. He caught her hand and stopped her retreat. She shook her head. "I didn't come here to talk about this."

"What did you come to talk about?"

"Forever."

Energy leapt from his hand to hers. She absorbed it, feeling his excitement, his panic, and ultimately his denial.

"No."

This time it was she who halted his retreat. "I've decided I'm interested in forever."

"I can't give it to you."

Panic flared inside, immediately soothed by the touch of Slade's energy.

Broderick walked by. He gave a curt nod in response to her hello. It was as close to a snub that a pack member could give another without coming to blows. She watched him walk away. "He's not very pleased with me."

"His pride's hurt. It's hard for a young wolf to accept any loss, but to a woman . . ." He shook his head "Well, it's probably safe to say he'll never live it down that a woman took mental control of him."

A woman? Sheesh. Her sympathy faded. "Holding on to chauvinistic views will do that to you."

Slade chuckled.

She licked her lips. The conversation was now back on the subject she wanted to broach. The one she was afraid to broach. What if Slade didn't really want forever? What if he just felt safe offering it because he thought it could never happen.

"I'm not that complicated, Jane."

"Damn it, stop reading my mind!"

"Then stop refusing to talk to me about the elephant in the room."

He wanted to talk about her stepfather Jerry. The man who'd made her childhood hell. "Maybe I don't want to talk about the elephant because it's ugly and I don't want it in our house!"

"Shit, Slade," Jared commented as he came up the path from the main house, rifle barrel resting on his shoulder. "Even I know you don't give a woman an elephant and expect a smile."

"Son of a bitch. Go shoot something, Jared."

Jared stopped. Dropping the rifle off his shoulder, he turned it sideways and held it out to Jane.

"You want to borrow this?" With a jerk of his chin he indicated Slade. "He's healed enough; anything less than a head shot won't kill him."

"Yes." She glared at Slade. "I mean no. But thank you."

Slade put his arm around her shoulder and drew her away from the gun. "Don't encourage him, Jane. He's recently decided he has a sense of humor."

All the Johnson brothers looked similar. The differences lay in their eyes and their personalities, and Jared came off as hard as granite. His cracking a joke was definitely out of character.

"Least I know not to try and tempt Raisa with a goddamned elephant. Allie's right. We've got to get you out of that lab."

"The hell you do."

"Though this"—Jared tipped his black hat, indicating their closeness—"is a good start. Nothing like soft moonlight and a pretty woman to get a man's mind off work."

Slade shot Jane a suspicious look. "Did you give Allie that idea?"

"Me? I'm in the lab as much as you."

Jared's chuckle drifted behind him. "We do occasionally figure things out for ourselves, you know."

Slade groaned. "There goes the peace and quiet of my lab."

"Would that be so bad?" Jane asked.

"It depends. Are you going to give me a reason to be elsewhere?"

"I'm trying, but you keep changing the subject."

"It's all the same subject, sweetness. Just different parts."

She moved back into his arms. She didn't even try to mask the satisfaction she felt at the connection. "I'd rather concentrate on this part."

His hazel eyes searched for hers. Stubbornness settled into his expression. She added a mental plea to the mix.

"Unfair, Jane."

"I don't care. I've spent twenty years making that part of my life not matter, and now you want to bring it into the one good thing I've got." She slapped his chest. "Yes, I'm going to fight you. I'm going to fight you with everything I have." She wanted to hit him again, harder. Hard enough to make him understand. "I have to, Slade."

"Shit." He caught her hand and brought it to his lips. The kiss was soft, gentle. Understanding.

"You'll let it go?"

"For now. But you should know I hit the send button on that sweet little revenge you had set up."

She tried to step back. "How could you?"

"It was either that or hunt him down and shred him to pieces."

"That was my revenge to take!"

"No, that was your test to fail."

She blinked. Her muscles were nothing against his as he pulled her against his chest. "Did you think I didn't unerstand?" He shook his head. "You wanted to prove you were better than him. You did."

"But you had to push the button."

"Yes. You can hate me for it if you want, but that son of a bitch wasn't getting off free and clear. And this way it's done."

A period on a part of her life she'd tried to forget. She didn't know how she felt about that. "Why are you telling me now?"

His thumb stroked down her cheek. "I told you. I don't want anything about that bastard coming between us."

Even the revenge he'd taken in her name, freeing her from the morass of guilt and hate and fear that had immobilized her every time she'd tried.

Cupping his cheek in her hand, she smiled shakily. "Thank you."

"Do I get a reward?"

Sliding her hands up his chest, she dropped her restraint. "Maybe you should take me back to your house and collect."

"Maybe I should just collect here."

The thought sent a thrill through her veins, quickly followed by horror.

Slade laughed. "Not as adventurous as you thought."

"No."

With a laugh, he scooped her up into his arms. "Good, because the only one I want seeing my woman going wild is me."

She linked her hands behind his neck. Resting her cheek on his chest, she relaxed, enjoying the sensation of being taken care of. "*Woman*, not *mate*. Are you trying to tell me something?"

"I was human once."

The biggest part of him still was. His boots thudded on the porch steps. Her smile spread. Each boot step meant they were closer to their bed. To their future. "And this is important why?"

He stopped at the door. Reaching down she opened it.

"If you can't be vampire, then I'll meet you halfway."

"I don't understand."

"It occurred to me that if the application of your research were moderated, a vampire could cheat immortality. Gradually. Over time."

She grabbed the doorjamb with both hands. "Hold on."

"What?"

"You're talking about killing yourself."

With a flex of muscle, he popped her grip free. "I'm talking about aging gracefully with the anticipated result at the end. The same as you."

"Killing yourself," she repeated. "Dear God, do you think I'd ask that of you?"

"No." He let her slide down his body. "That's why I took the decision out of your hands."

"Good God." She rubbed her hand over her forehead. "You do know how to kill the mood."

"I thought I was setting it."

"I'm beginning to wish I'd never started that research."

"But you did, and we can use it."

She took another step back. "No, we can't."

"Jane?"

She sat on the couch. The ramifications of the formula running through her head. And no matter what scenario she ran, the answer was always the same. Disaster.

Slade stood over her. "What is it?"

"You have to understand, when I made that formula, I had no idea vampires or werewolves existed. I certainly didn't know there was some supernatural war going on. I mean seriously, who knew anything like that existed outside of the movies?"

He knelt in front of her. "Jane."

She shook her head. "Don't say anything yet. Just hold me."

He pulled her into his arms. "All right."

She rested her head against his shoulder and breathed his scent, taking her strength from his. "One thing is for sure, Vamp Man. You sure know how to shake up a woman's world."

His big hand cupped her cheek. She loved when he did that. The touch of his hand curving around her face, the touch of his energy curving around her heart, it just completed some invisible circle she'd never known lacked closure. It gave her courage.

"I want you to make love to me, Slade."

"After you tell me what's wrong."

"No. Before."

"Why?"

She took his hat off his head and tossed it on the coffee table. "I'll tell you after."

"What makes you think I can perform under such duress?"

She tugged her shirt over her head and unhooked her bra. "I plan on providing incentive."

He shrugged out of his shirt. "That's some incentive."

She dropped her bra to the floor. "I've always thought rewards should be worth the sacrifice."

He came over her, using his weight to press her back into the couch cushions. She went down without a protest. Wiggling into a better position, she drew her leg up so his cock rested against her pussy. Even through two layers of clothing, the impact was stunning. She closed her eyes as every fiber in her being whispered, "Yes."

"Make that hell yes."

She opened her eyes to find Slade smiling down at her, his expression one of love and passion. "Hell yes."

He chuckled. And reached down. Harsh rips preceded the removal of her jeans. Tiny nips preceded his path down her body. A growl of satisfaction punctuated his arrival at his destination. He was going to kiss her there. She couldn't breathe, couldn't move, couldn't do anything but wait for that first touch of his tongue. And he made her wait, keeping her suspended on the high wire of anticipation, caressing her with his breath, his mind, smiling as the tension in her coiled tighter. Anticipation turned to tingles. Tingles turned to lust. Lust to demand. She grabbed his hair.

"Slade."

"Just savoring the moment."

"I'd rather you savor me."

"Duly noted."

It wasn't the first time a man had loved her with his mouth. She'd had her wild years and her misguided years, and for the last few years, her cautious years, but this was the first time a man had truly made love to her. With every touch of his lips, every luxurious pass of his tongue, Slade told her he loved her. Sweetly. Passionately. Tenderly. Drawing out every sensation until she wanted to scream with the pleasure. She started crying instead.

"Jane?"

She shook her head, wiping at her tears.

Slade kissed his way up her torso, wiping the tears from her cheek. "What's wrong?"

It just made her cry harder that he hadn't probed her mind for the answer.

Turning them so she lay across his chest, he cupped her head in his hands, wiping her tears with his thumbs while his beautiful eyes studied every nuance of her expression.

"You love me."

"I thought that was understood."

She shook her head. "Why didn't you say something?"

"Because you would have run."

She sniffed. "You make me sound so messed up."

"You've been hurt."

"So were you when you were younger."

"I've never been betrayed. It makes a difference."

"Damn it. Why do you have to be so honorable?"

"Excuse me?"

Wrapping her arms around his neck, she buried her face in his throat. His scent immediately surrounded her. Hot, male, with that light addictive undertone that was uniquely his. "I was going to trick you into converting me."

"Why?"

He didn't sound surprised. "If you tell me you knew all along, I'm going to stop feeling guilty."

His fingers threaded through her hair. "I knew all along."

"Damn it. You won't even let me feel guilt."

He pulled her head back, studying her face before shaking his head and kissing her softly. "We agreed however this goes, it goes our way. No guilt. No manipulation."

"Then you need to convert me."

"You don't want that."

"Well, I don't want you poisoning yourself."

"Then we'll work out something else."

The blood tests were her safety net. By not telling him, she could buy time just in case things with Slade didn't work out. All she had to do was keep her mouth shut. For once, hedging her bet wasn't appealing. "Something else might already be in the works."

His smile grew broader, took on a certain knowing air. There could be only one reason. Pushing up, she glared at him. "Oh my God, you checked my tests."

"I already told you, everything about you is my concern."

"Then you already know that somehow, someway, I'm already on my way to being vampire and that conversion isn't going to kill me."

"Yes."

Another thought hit her. "But you offered to grow old with me anyway."

"Just because I accidentally started you down a road you didn't want to go, doesn't mean you should be forced to continue."

"You really meant that?"

"Yes."

"Why?"

"I've lived over a hundred years without you. I don't have any interest in going backward."

The Johnsons might as well be wolf the way they love.

She hadn't understood what Creed meant at the time, but she did now. Slade loved her. Not for the moment. Not for convenience. Not for what she could bring him. He loved her the way she loved him. For who she was. With all his heart.

"You're going to make me cry again."

"I'll overlook the weakness if you tell me what I'm waiting to hear."

"For heaven's sake I risked my life to keep you alive. You've been in and out of my head more than the thought of chocolate. You have to know . . ."

He just kept staring at her. This close she couldn't miss the flicker in his energy. He wasn't as sure about her as he appeared. Reaching between them, she unzipped his pants and eased his cock free. Thick and hard, it filled her hand, pulsing with power and life.

"Jane?"

"I'm sorry. I always joke when I'm nervous." Leaning down, she aligned her mouth to his, edge to edge. Breath to breath. Raising her hips, she aligned her pussy to his cock, pressing lightly, maintaining the connection, holding him on the same edge of anticipation upon which he held her.

This time his "Jane" was more guttural. More urgent.

"I love you, Slade Johnson. More than my life, more than my next breath, and while I may not have waited as long as you have, I'm not willing to go backward, either." She slowly took him into her body, shivering at the pleasure. Groaning as his cock flexed within her. "I want you in my life, every day," she gasped. "In every way, no matter what comes."

"Hell yes." With a push of his hips, he took over, filling her so completely she had to pause to absorb the impact.

"Oh my God."

"Be sure, Jane," he gritted out. "Because I won't settle for less than all of you. Ever."

"Neither will I."

Unbelievably, he laughed.

"Good."

She didn't know who took whom. It didn't matter. All that mattered was that they were here, together. Her inner muscles rippled and stretched around his cock. Her nails dug into his chest. His hands tightened on her hips. Lifting her up until only the tip of his cock teased her pussy, he kept her there for a heady second before bringing her back down in a slow delicious thrust. Sweet, it was so sweet.

"Oooh."

"You like that?"

She nodded.

"So do I. Let's try it again."

They did. Again and again until sweet wasn't enough. She ground down on him. He pushed up into her. She couldn't get enough, give enough. She needed more. So much more. Pressure built in her head. Fire flared beneath her skin, energy whipped around them in a frantic storm.

"Slade!"

"Shit. Hold on."

She did, digging her nails into his chest until the scent of blood joined the scent of passion. Holding on as he fucked her harder, deeper, sending her spiraling higher. Looking down, she watched his cock piston in and out of her pussy, lowering the barriers in her mind, projecting to him the utter perfection of both the sight and sensation. Perfect. It was so perfect.

He growled in his throat as the tension in her coiled into a hot ball. Her pussy flared and pulsed. His thumb slid between her labia, sliding through her thick juices until it found her swollen clit.

She screamed and clawed at his chest as his thumb circled and pressed.

"Oh yes. I like you wild."

And he did. She could feel his pleasure, his lust, but under it all she felt his love. That incredible love. She needed to be closer. So much closer.

Pleasure blended with desire. Love with lust. And under it all the fire burned and spread, pushing her toward . . . something.

"Slade, I need . . ."

She didn't know what she needed, but Slade did. She knew he did.

"Please."

"Right here, baby."

"I need—"

His thumb rubbed harder. "Just let go."

She shook her head. Her hair flew about her face, blocking her vision. She couldn't.

"It's not enough. I need."

Her nails raked down his torso. *Blood.*

Gathering the energy around them, she thrust the image into his mind, his mouth at her neck. His cock in her pussy.

"Jane. Stop."

She wouldn't stop. Couldn't. She needed this. Needed him. She gathered more energy, projected harder, cried out as Slade hooked his hand behind her neck and pulled her down. His breath hit her skin in a hot promise.

Yes!

Hell yes! She felt the graze of his teeth as he thrust up hard. Her head tipped back, inviting his bite, his possession. There was a sharp pain, and then nothing but white hot ecstasy as her body convulsed around his, taking all he had to give, milking him of every last drop of pleasure as he bound them irrevocably. Forever.

"**I** ought to paddle your ass," Slade drawled fifteen minutes later, stroking his fingers up and down her arm as they lay together on the couch.

Jane cracked an eyelid and tried to work up to concern. "Could you wait until I recover my strength?"

Slade chuckled. "Want a running start?"

She shook her head and wiggled her butt, smiling slightly when he gave it a pat. "I just want to have enough energy to enjoy it."

He chuckled again and brushed his lips over her hair "That was a dangerous move."

"It wasn't planned."

"I know. I was right there with you, but I gave you an order."

She tilted her head back so she could see his face. "Seriously, you're going to complain about the fact that you get me so hot I totally lose control?"

"Well, when you put it that way . . ."

She kissed his chest. Beneath the lightness of his tone she could hear his worry. "I'm fine, Slade. But I do think you need to add a new entry into that notebook you're keeping in regard to conversion."

"Oh yeah?" He changed positions, coming over her, smiling down into her face. Her outlaw. "And what would that be?"

"It won't be denied."

"Not when you're the one being converted."

"Are you saying I'm aggressive?"

He laughed and deflected her half-hearted swat at his arm. "I'm saying you're perfect."

She huffed. "Perfect for you."

He traced the fading mark of his bite. "Absolutely."

Folding her hand around his, she bit her lip. As much as she hated to disturb the moment, there was something else they needed to talk about.

"I know."

"Stop reading my mind."

"It's not as easy as you would think."

"Well, try."

"Will do."

"We need to destroy the formula."

His smile vanished. "No."

"As long as it's written down anywhere, the chance that Sanctuary will discover it increases exponentially. And its potential for destruction is simply too great."

"Destroying records of it will make you the sole focus of their search."

"I'm a target anyway."

"But not like you'd be if you were the only method of getting the information."

"What else can we do? Erasing my memory isn't an option. Not only is that technology iffy, Joseph's condition isn't likely to remain stable."

"Shit." Slade sat up. "That's what you meant when you said you had a feeling we were running out of time, isn't it? It had nothing to do with Joseph."

A shiver snaked down her spine. "Yes."

"We need to talk to Caleb and the others."

She grabbed her clothes. "What are they going to do?" she asked, dragging her T-shirt over her head.

Slade shot her a look. "Prepare."

"**ARE** you sure you want to do this?" Caleb asked, her laptop and Slade's sitting on the edge of the big wood chipper. The kind that ground trees into dust. In a rusted barrel to the right, all the papers containing her notes were waiting to be torched.

"Are you? When they figure out my research is gone, they'll stop looking for it and come after me."

Caleb's expression was carved in stone. Beside him Allie stood, holding Joseph. Her expression just as serious. To the right stood Jace and Jared. To the left, Tobias. "Let them come."

"I appreciate your sacrifice, but you need to think—"

"Jane, you saved my brother's life twice and also my son's. Even if you weren't Slade's mate, that buys you a lot of alliances."

"But it doesn't hurt that we like you," Jace added.

In the background, a horse whinnied. She looked to Tobias. "What about you?"

His left brow cocked up. "I think you have promise."

"As what?"

"That I haven't figured out yet." He sounded annoyed. She kind of liked the idea of being the one piece in his puzzle he couldn't make fit. Reaching out, she took Slade's hand.

"What about you?"

"You already know what I want."

Her. Any way he could get her. Taking a breath, she nodded. "Then let's do this."

The chipper made mincemeat of the laptops. The fire consumed the notes. As she watched the smoke rise into the night, a chill raced over her skin. She stared into the night beyond the compound. The darkness pressed in on her.

They were out there. And sooner or later, they would come for her.